SPOILT

SPOILT

❦

GEORGINA HAMMICK

CHATTO & WINDUS
LONDON

Published in 1992 by
Chatto & Windus Ltd
20 Vauxhall Bridge Road
London SW1 2SA

Acknowledgments

'The American Dream' was first published
in *Winter's Tales* (New Series 5);
'Uncle Victor' appeared in *Critical
Quarterly* and was subsequently published
in *Best Short Stories 1991* (Heinemann);
'High Teas' first appeared in *The Listener*
and was subsequently published in
Best Short Stories 1988 (Heinemann) and
The Minerva Book of Short Stories 1990;
'Habits' was published in *New Writing*, a
British Council–Minerva anthology, 1991–2;
the lines from the poem by Gerald Bullett
quoted in 'The Wheelchair Tennis Match' are
reproduced by permission of the Peters, Fraser
& Dunlop Group.

A CIP catalogue record for
this book is available from
the British Library

ISBN 0 7011 4133 6

Printed and bound in Great Britain by
Mackays of Chatham PLC, Chatham, Kent

To A.V., without whom.

CONTENTS

CONTENTS

Maeve Goes
to Town

The invitation came from a successful art dealer Maeve knew. Not knew exactly, was acquainted with. Maeve's ex-husband Patrick had bought several paintings and prints from Clarissa Friedlander's gallery, and as a result they got asked to all the exhibition preview parties. They also, from time to time, got asked to dinner in Clarissa's Kensington house. After Maeve and Patrick split up, the invitations, addressed to Mr and Mrs Patrick Mansell, kept coming, and Maeve and her ex took it in turns to go, or neither of them went, depending on what else was happening in their lives. What was happening in Patrick's life was cellular telephone systems, personal communications networks (optical fibres! digital switches!) and cable television franchises. In addition to these was Lara: long-legged, big-bosomed and twenty-nine. What was happening in Maeve's life was teenagers and teenage moods, an up and down marriage to a washing machine, a not-too-secret affair with a Safeway shopping trolley.

Maeve was in two minds about accepting Clarissa's invitation. There were points for, and points against. The points against included Clarissa Friedlander herself, an alarming woman in her mid-thirties whose working clothes, which Maeve had witnessed on a daytime visit to the gallery, comprised skinny bright-white jeans, bulky designer knit with sleeves pushed up to the elbows, and black pumps like ballet shoes. There was a lot of chunky gold, or it might have been platinum, on her ears and wrists and fingers. Enterprise culture, her appearance seemed to say, arts-oriented executive, post-feminist together person. And it was true: Clarissa was highly motivated and go-getting. Private-sector support is where art's largely at these days, and Clarissa spent a lot of her time targeting the business community, researching potential sponsors, focusing on fundraising. She kept detailed files on the companies she approached, and never gave up on the ones who initially failed to show an interest. 'After all, love, you never know!' Another thing Clarissa believed in was taking art to the customer, which meant setting up exhibitions in banks and boardrooms. 'Basically, I see it as my role to establish imaginative links between Fine Art and commerce.' Maeve had read this in a colour-supplement interview, and had found it depressing.

'Why on earth should you find it depressing?' Patrick, in a hurry, on his office telephone, sounded exasperated. 'All Clarissa's trying to do is get work for her artists – to get people like me to buy their bloody pictures. What's wrong with that? It's happened throughout history. Or is it just that you resent people, women, being successful?'

Maeve said she wasn't sure why, and of course she didn't resent success, and she had nothing against Clarissa; it was merely that she'd always felt, for some reason, though it was probably stupid, that Art should, ideally anyway, be for Art's sake and –

'Fucking hell! Look Maeve, I can't discuss this now. I just need your confirmation that the children will be on the ten-fifteen train. And could you please see they've got something decent to wear – we've got friends coming in on Saturday night. Last time they came to us they looked like tramps.' Clunk.

We. We've got. She was never going to get used to this We that embraced Lara and excluded her. It was We this and We that, all of a sudden. It was Us and Ours. When she and Patrick were married it had very often been I and Me and Myself and Mine.

Another reason for refusing Clarissa's invitation was because it was for drinks, not dinner, at Clarissa's house. Drinks parties were bad enough when you had someone, a husband, say, to go with and to leave with. To dissect the event with in the car on the way home, or over supper. In bed. Braving a drinks party on your own, when you were unlikely to know anyone there, that had to be madness, didn't it? Masochism.

The points for accepting – what were they, what did they include? Well, Patrick being away, in New York with Lara (a business trip for both of them, he explained), for a start. Someone had to keep Clarissa's doors, and Maeve's options, open. Also, receiving very few Christmas party invitations this year – only three including this one – had made her feel even more than usually marginal and peripheral. Added to these was family pressure.

'You must go,' Maeve's sister Isobel insisted, disregarding Maeve's prevarications about who would feed the dog and who would stop the children smoking themselves to death or setting the house on fire. 'You can't shut yourself away or people will forget you. You've got to be seen around.'

'Around where? What for?' asked the defeated and negative Maeve.

'Because. Because you never know who you might meet. You never know. One minute there's no one in one's life, the next minute there is. That's how it happens, just' – and Isobel, contentedly married to the same country solicitor for twenty-five years, snapped her fingers to add zip to her argument – 'like that.' There weren't any unattached men in the country anyway, Isobel reminded her sister, spare men were like gold dust, the only ones to be had, the only fun ones, were in London. So if Maeve wanted one of those she had to go.

'You gotta go, natch.' Maeve's son Michael, stretched full length on the floor between the gas fire and the television set, his gold locks resting on a plate that had recently contained fried egg and ketchup, rattled his crisp bag and, finding no joy, exploded it. 'Could be Mr Deeds will be in town.' He jerked an elbow in the direction of the black and white hero on the screen. 'Could be Gary Cooper will be at your rave. Go for it.'

'I'll have you know that film you're watching was made before I was born! Also, Gary Cooper's dead.'

'So?'

Another of Maeve's children, Jessica, informed her that partying was a basic human right and good for people. That you couldn't expect to get anywhere in life unless you were prepared to socialise. Maeve's jaw dropped at this. Jessica never went to parties. She'd been refusing to go to anything that might loosely be termed a party for eight years now. At the age of eleven she had all the makings of a recluse.

The week of Clarissa Friedlander's party, Maeve drove to her nearest town, nearest town, that is, that was any use for clothes shopping, and bought herself an outfit. In a new and deserted shopping mall, in an empty-of-customers boutique called Funfare, in a pre-Christmas sale, she bought a silk jacket in jewel colours and a matching skirt. Maeve was small and short-legged, and the skirt that fitted her in the waist came down to her ankles. She was worried about this, but the assistant said, Why worry? Skirts could be worn any length this season and anyway longer equalled more elegant and made Maeve took taller. The assistant held out the promise of free air miles if Maeve decided to go ahead with this purchase, which she did. Afterwards, in a shoe shop similarly forsaken save for a mother with two weak-looking small boys who were expressing strong views on trainers, she bought a pair of patent leather high heels whose red more or less matched the red swirls in her dress and jacket. Then, cutting through the market on her way back to the car park, her eye was caught by a stall offering Genuine Paris Perfume's At Less Than Half The Recommended Retail Price!!! And she came away with a minuscule bottle of Poison, a scent she'd never tried because too expensive. 'Perhaps the worst thing about not being married any more,' Maeve had once confided to her daughter Maggie, 'is having to buy your own pong.' Maeve had meant this as a joke, the sort of wry remark people make to prove to others and themselves that they haven't gone under yet, that no matter what life throws at them, they're still hanging on in there. She didn't seriously think that no one to buy you scent was the worst thing about being divorced, even though there was, yes there was, something pitiful and poignant about a woman having to buy her own. Maggie hadn't been amused, however. How could her mother say anything quite so vulgar? When half the people in England were on the breadline, having their homes repossessed because they couldn't, through no fault of their own, but because of the interest rate and no job, keep up their mortgage payments? What would all those single-parent mothers struggling to feed handicapped children in bed-and-breakfast accommodation say if they could hear Maeve moaning on about no perfume or scent or whatever? Maggie shook her head, more in anger than in sorrow. (For it's children who are the moral guardians now; it's the younger generation who dictate what their elders should think and how they should behave.) 'I didn't mean it, it was a joke,' Maeve had defended herself wearily. 'I must be allowed to say something silly from time to time without having the social ills of the world thrown at me. And it isn't my fault if this country's in such a mess – I'd remind you I voted Labour last time round. And SDP the time before.' 'Champagne socialist,' Maggie had muttered, not quite under her breath.

Maeve felt no pleasure as she stacked her carrier bags in the boot of her car, she felt guilt. The money she'd spent on her own adornment was part of the money she'd put aside for the children's Christmas presents. And she dreaded what Maggie's reaction would be when she saw the new clothes. I'll burn the bags and tell her the stuff came from the OXFAM shop, Maeve decided. Or I'll say, 'New? What, these old things? Surely you remember these? I've had them for years!'

*

The drive to London from Maeve's house took two and three-quarter hours on good days and if you were lucky. On bad days, stormy or foggy or dark or rush-hour-traffic-ridden, it could take a lot longer. So Maeve had to be ready to leave for Clarissa's soon after three-thirty in the afternoon.

In her bedroom, before going down to make her goodbye speech to her children, Maeve concealed her new clothes and old jewellery under an antiquated camel coat, buttoning it to the neck in the hope that her extravagance would not be discovered. On her feet she wore her driving shoes, a pair of scuffed loafers, and she carried the new high heels in a Boots plastic bag. It was just her luck that on the way down the stairs she should meet her daughter Florence on the half-landing.

'Let's see, let's see what you're wearing.' A hand shot out and tweaked the hem of the camel coat. 'Silk. Ace one.' Florence was thirteen and the only one of Maeve's daughters to show what her mother considered to be a natural, and healthy, interest in clothes. She was also, probably (her parents were agreed about this), the kindest and nicest of Maeve's and Patrick's children. She peered into the Boots bag. 'I like your shoes – tart-y! Only problem is – ' Florence held her hands up, palms forward, and waved them from side to side, a gesture to indicate that the following remark was not to be taken too seriously, was in quotes you understand ' – power dressing is out. The Caring Nineties are in. Get real!'

Maeve's self-confidence, which a few minutes earlier had been given a little lift by an encounter with a glamorous and young-for-her-age-looking woman in the bathroom glass, drained away into her loafers.

'Oh dear, am I too dressy, d'you think? I don't know if I've got anything else that would possibly – '

'Of course you're not, you look ace! Some foxy guy'll take you out to dinner, I'm sure. And you smell ace. Didn't know you wore Poison,' said Florence who, scourge of the

local cosmetics counters and their testers, had a nose for
these things.

' . . . and Johnnie's to be in bed by half past nine at the
latest. The last upstairs must remember to let Silas out, and
lock up, and turn off the fire and the lights – though it
would be a kindness if you could leave the outside light on
for me. Please write down any telephone messages. The fish
pie's in the bottom oven. I trust you not to smoke . . . '

Anyway, what was the point? None of them was listening. They lay like collapsed dominoes, leaning into and
against each other, eyes and minds fixed on the square of
jittery light at the far end of the room. They were holed up
and dug in as though for a siege. The fruit bowl, the biscuit
tin, bags of nuts and low-fat crisps, mugs of tea, cans of
Diet Pepsi, had been placed about the floor for easy access.

'Did you hear what I said? I said this room's got to be
tidy before you leave it.'

A few arms waved, vaguely, in the air. And Michael,
half-turning, called as she reached the door, 'Chill out,
Mothereen. Enjoy, enjoy . . . '

Maeve liked being alone in her car. When she'd shut the
door and adjusted the seat – for Michael was five foot
eleven and learning to drive – when she'd settled herself
and her belongings and fastened her seat belt and driven
through the gate, she very often felt elated. She very often
felt light-hearted and free, even if her journey was only
to the supermarket or the cash dispenser. She liked the
knowledge that no one could exactly know what she was
up to or where she could be found; she relished the pos-
sibility that she might, if she suddenly felt inclined to, take
off somewhere – to the seaside for the day, to Wales or
Scotland or Paris for a night or nights. She had never made
these trips, but you never knew, she might. She liked the
silence within these walls that allowed her to listen to a
radio play, if there was one, or to cassette music of her
own choice.

The privacy of the car, the self-containment of it, admitted of other needs and other moods. It was in the car that Maeve went over and over her broken marriage. The form this often took was a letter to Patrick, spoken aloud, in which she expounded the grievances that eluded her when she had a pen in her hand; or else blamed herself alone for her plight and then begged him to come home. In the car she wept and howled, allowed the tears to stream down her face unchecked, rocked backwards and forwards in her seat, gave herself entirely over to grief. Or she would, thumping the steering wheel in rage, conduct fights with Patrick, playing both parts so credibly that afterwards she would be able to convince herself that he had really said those things, those wicked and hurtful things. On the occasions when she was able to banish Patrick altogether, she did so by imagining the man she hadn't met yet who would replace Patrick, and who was waiting for her somewhere – on a train, in the checkout queue, at a drinks party she hadn't planned to go to.

At Clarissa Friedlander's party?

No, looking forward to anything specific, having hopes about it, was dangerous; was enough to court serious disappointment, or worse. Dread was the only safe emotion to feel.

If I dread this party enough – thought Maeve as, ignoring the speed limit at Hammersmith, she obeyed the injunction in the word 'Flyover' – I might just enjoy it. This party is going to be hell, she told herself, braking just too late to abide by a red traffic light in Talgarth Road; it's going to be a complete bummer, it's going to be the worst party I've been to in my entire life.

Clarissa's Kensington house was an opened Advent calendar as Maeve parked her car, each window of its dark face enclosing an alliterative surprise: a candle; a Christmas tree; a cat; a couple under the mistletoe. A chandelier, radiating love and hope from the fanlight above the front door,

succeeded so well in its disguise that when the door opened
to admit her, Maeve was disappointed to discover not Mary
and Joseph, and the Babe lying in a manger, but a pair of
quarrelsome early leavers wrestling with their coats. At
once she wanted to leave with them, but instead allowed
herself to be propelled through the hall and up the stairs
to Clarissa's bedroom, a sullenly purple, and fringed and
bobbled, chamber of antique aspect and dusty palms. ('I
indulge my Gothic side in here,' Clarissa had confided,
throwing open the door, on Maeve's first visit. 'It makes
for an amusing contrast with the spare elegance of the rest
– don't you think?') In the centre of the room a sepulchral
fourposter had come into its own tonight as a repository
for the remains of wild and not so wild animals, of bear
and beaver, leopard and lynx, kid and calf, or for – more
probably – synthetic versions of the same. Maeve buried
her mangy camel among these. She wanted to check her
face for damage and her teeth for lipstick, but the lighting
– 30-watt bulbs veiled by grey toadstool hats – was unhelp-
ful, and in any case the several gloomily ornate looking-
glasses in the room were obscured by others of her sex
who'd had the same idea. 'Vanity, thy name is woman' –
Patrick, arms folded, amusedly watching Maeve's dressing-
table ritual from the doorway. Maeve had never forgotten
this, the injustice of this. Vanity? Frailty, more like. Insecur-
ity, more like. Lack of self-confidence, more like.

Downstairs, the first thing was to get a drink. It had been
Patrick's opinion that new arrivals at parties should not
have to brave crowds of established merrymakers without
the bolster of a full glass of something very good and very
strong, but there was no drinks table in Clarissa's sparely
elegant hall. In her sitting room ('My double cube,' as she'd
explained it to Maeve, 'equalled only in splendour by the
one at Wilton'), the merrymakers were all giants, and
famous. Laughter, in cannonades, in sudden sharp fusil-
lades, exploded here and there above an unspecific boom
as Maeve pursued the flash of white tablecloth that came
and went at the far end of the cube. Along the way she

apologised to shirt buttons and elbows and bespoke waist-
coats and little black crepe bosoms. 'Excuse me. Sorry. So
sorry. Excuse me. Excuse – ' And then, just as her goal was
almost within reach, she saw that immediately in front of
it, and barring her access to it, was an unmistakable backview, a long creamy neck, a sleek gold club-cut. She touched
this goddess on a black, ruched crepe shoulder and Clarissa
swung round, and peered, and looked blank, and looked –
after a second or two – triumphant.

'Darling, you made it! Wonderful! Maeve is one of my
favourite people,' Clarissa said to the famous man she'd
been talking to. 'She's come all the way up from the
COUNTRY – isn't that brave? I'm sure you know everyone,' she said to Maeve. 'Haven't you got a drink yet? The
white's the one to go for. Where's your lovely husband? I
do hope you've brought him along! Maeve's married to a
captain of industry – '

Maeve wanted to say No. No to the lovely husband; No
I haven't got a drink; No I don't know anyone at all,
introduce me, please – but her hostess had turned her back
and was talking to three other people, all men, all famous,
and all-attention to Clarissa.

'Red. Thank you.' Maeve recognised the barman. He
worked in Clarissa's gallery. He was the one who'd taken
Patrick's cheque the last time they'd bought a painting
together, a painting for the custody of which Maeve and
Patrick had recently fought – and Maeve had lost. She hated
the knowledge that Lara was looking at the painting now,
living with it. It had nothing to do with Lara.

The barman held up a glass to the light, as though he
were looking for something, and lowered it, and poured
wine into it. He had a waxy complexion and two ugly
moles on his left cheek. His hair, flattened with water or
grease and combed straight back from his forehead, had no
parting. He handed Maeve the glass.

'How's trade?' Maeve asked, after she'd bestowed on the
barman a winning, we-know-each-other-don't-we? smile.

'What?' The young man cupped his ear with a delicate

hand. 'Right, Sir Ian. Two whites, one red, coming up,' he said to the extremely famous Shakespearean actor at Maeve's elbow.

Maeve moved away from the table, keeping her glass at a distance for fear of spilling it down her front – but not too far out for fear of spilling it down someone else's. When she could, when a tiny pocket of space opened up in the crush, she inclined her head to the glass and took a sip. The wine, just a taste of it, triggered, as it always did, a craving for nicotine – but how do you get cigarettes out of a bag, and then light up, with a glass of wine in one hand? Maeve made her way back to the table. She put down her glass and her bag. The bag, which was not the one she'd intended bringing, which was not the carefree piece of non-sense on a string she'd meant to transfer the essential min-imum into before leaving home – no, that one was still on the kitchen table beside the tin of cat food she'd been bullied, at the very last minute, into opening – was loaded with the day-to-day clutter of Maeve's life: chequebook and paying-in book and Family Allowance Book; diary and wallet and purse and loose change that had escaped from the purse; car keys and house keys; two Pentel pens, one without its top; a stick of spearmint gum that the last hot summer had irrevocably welded to a sheaf of second-class stamps; a letter whose air mail envelope had doubled as a Christmas shopping list. Her cigarettes were sitting on top of these, but the lighter wasn't. She put her hand into the battered bran tub and let her fingers do the searching for something smooth and round. Ah-ha! But you cannot light a cigarette with a lipstick – a cracked lipstick, as fingers stained and sticky with Hot Cherries proved it to be.

I wish I was married, Maeve said to herself; if I was married I'd go and find my husband now, and creep up behind him and raid his coat pocket for a lighter, and then he'd turn and put his arm round my shoulder and say to whoever he was talking to, 'I don't believe you've met my wife. Maeve darling, this is . . . ' Maeve began removing items from her bag and placing them on the table. While she did this she talked to no one and no one talked to her so she went on talking to herself. I am very unhappy at this party, I am very unhappy indeed. This is a terrible party and I am hating every minute of it. This must be the worst party I've been to in my entire life.

All around her were people jostling to have their glasses filled. All around her people were laughing and shouting and shrieking and hailing each other.

'Is this a white-elephant stall?' It was a man's voice, a familiar voice. Maeve looked up. She saw a face she knew well. She knew the cleft in that chin, the bump on that nose, the quirk of those eyebrows. She knew that widow's peak and that Adam's apple. She did not know how she knew those things, and she could not remember his name.

'I lost my lighter,' Maeve explained, 'but I've found it now.' She held it up proudly, like a small child who expects congratulations. She smiled an enchanting smile. Then she turned to the table and swept the treasures she'd placed there into her bag. I've got someone to talk to, she told herself. I've got a man, a famous and attractive man. She hoisted the bag on to her shoulder. She repossessed herself of the wine glass. 'Do you . . . ?' she began.

To a vanishing backview. To no one.

You've got to get away from this table now, Maeve instructed herself, you've been here too long, you've got to circulate. She tried to make her circuit of the room appear purposeful, not desperate. She tried to make it seem as though she were looking for someone, on her way to speak to that someone. As though that someone were looking for her.

Looking purposeful or desperate, Maeve worked her way through the middle of the room to the door and back again. She made a tour, clockwise, of the room's perimeter, followed by an anti-clockwise one. She crossed the room diagonally, left to right, and when she had accomplished this, right to left. On the way she apologised to Garrick ties and Paul Smith shirts and Giorgio Armani belts and Chantal necklaces: 'Excuse me, I'm just trying to . . .' Every so often she stopped to sip her drink or to ignite a new cigarette, attaching herself, whenever possible, to a couple or a threesome or a larger knot of chatterers.

'Now that the bottom's fallen out of the Impressionist and the Contemporary Art markets,' a florid man in a navy pinstripe was saying to a pale, and younger, man in a leather blouson, 'and if Sotheby's and Christie's and Phillips, if the big boys, are catching colds, where does that leave the likes of Bonhams and Lawrence's?'

'Prints are still holding up,' Leather Blouson replied. 'Victorian water colours are still doing okay. Small is still beautiful.'

Maeve, several floors below them, inhaled deeply and coughed, and nodded sagely into her glass and smiled a knowing smile.

'Did you say something?' Navy Pinstripe peered down at her. Damp-looking curls, clinging to a bull neck, spilled out over his collar in a little choirboy ruff. 'Do you have a connexion with one of those outfits?'

Time for Maeve to affect a little maybe-I-do, maybe-I-don't shrug. Time for her to drift away. To look a touch superior, or bored.

I'm bored as hell, Maeve told herself as she battled her way to the drinks table for a refill. I'll have one more glass and then I'll go home. She downed her refill in a gulp, set down the empty glass and appropriated an abandoned full one – of white, but what did that matter? Then, having stubbed out her cigarette on a plate of broken cocktail sticks and olive stones and scorned cheesy biscuits, she lit up again, alarmed to discover there were only six cigarettes left in the packet. She picked up her wine glass.

You're driving, you're not supposed to be drinking, a voice in her head reminded her. You could kill yourself or someone else. You could go to prison or lose your licence for a year. You have children at home you love and who need you.

She left the table. Lights from the Christmas tree, a perfect triangle perfectly fitting the frame of a tall window, beckoned and mocked. Only yesterday, she'd looked on critically as her children raided the decorations box, fighting each other to be the first to loop the branches of their lopsided spruce with the battered tinfoil stars and crescent moons of their kindergarten pasts; and when, with whoops of excitement, they'd exhumed those old Blue Peter angels, fusions of yoghurt pots and paper and tinsel and the card-board insides of lavatory rolls, and Sellotaped them on, she'd said, 'Look, don't you think it's time we threw those out? They really are very bashed, and you're not babies any more. Couldn't we try for something a bit more grown-up and glamorous this – ?' Her words had been lopped by an amazed silence, by stares that contrived to register hurt and pity and reproof and disbelief.

On her way to the grown-up and glamorous tree in the window, Maeve caught sight of a woman she'd met at one of Clarissa's dinners. The woman had been introduced by Clarissa as 'my friend, the old-style feminist art historian'. 'I'm a feminist, of course,' Maeve remembered confiding to the art historian as they sat on the sofa after dinner, 'but I'm not quite sure how much of a feminist I am.' (Maeve had suddenly been aware that she was drunk; a second earlier she'd been okay, and now, without warning, and for no reason, she wasn't.) 'I'm never quite sure what I believe,' Maeve had continued, trying to jerk her head away from Clarissa's Collier Campbell cushions and to manoeuvre her-self into a sensible talking position. 'It varies. I'm never exactly sure what I feel or where I stand or what I want or who I am.'

'Then it's time you made up your mind, lovey, isn't it?' The art historian had risen from the sofa and conferred on Maeve the travesty of a smile. 'People who walk in the middle of the road tend to get run over.'

Maeve was in two minds now about accosting this person, whose name she was trying to remember. She had no desire to be run over by her again. On the other hand, any conversation, however brief and uncongenial, had to be better than none. So she hovered on the edge of Janet?

– no, Jackie! – of Jackie's circle, hemmed in on all sides, bracing herself to break in as soon as she caught the historian's eye. While she waited she sipped her wine, rehearsing in her head confident smiles, plus the sort of whacky and upfront greetings that might be likely to disarm.

'Yeah, sure, but wouldn't you agree he's kind of funky and counter-cultural in terms of visual style? I mean that whole visual-grammar bit – ' A man's voice, American, directly behind Maeve, isolated itself in the buzz.

'He's crap.' A new voice, male and English, cut in. 'It's a third-class mind. A colour-supplement mind. End of story.'

Maeve did a little half-turn on her heels so that she could hear, and see, more of this.

'Did you hear him on *Kaleidoscope* last week? I thought they'd at least wheel on some sort of heavyweight who could be expected to land a few punches, but no, it was reverence all the way. And Paul Vaughan treated him as though he was God, for God's sake.'

Maeve did not know who they were talking about, but this did not stop her smiling into her glass and giving a little corroborative snort. If the last speaker were to notice her now, he would turn his head and say, 'Ah. So you heard the programme too. And you agree.' And then Maeve would say, 'Yes. I think he's crap, total crap,' and then . . . But he did not notice Maeve.

I like being me, Maeve told herself as she made her way once more to the drinks table, I like being a country person. Country people are real. They're genuine, they have roots and integrity. Country people are . . . She stopped. A blush, a hot flush of shame, was spreading from her bosom to her neck to her cheeks. She shut her eyes tight, as though by the action she could black out the mental picture she had of herself, only yesterday, at a drinks party in the village. At this, a gathering of selected locals in the house of a retired schoolmaster and his wife, she had been trapped first by a deaf, although not dumb, octogenarian air vice marshal, and second, as soon as she'd managed to escape him, by his wife. She had had to be civil – it was the season of goodwill – to her farmer neighbour who the year before, and despite petitions and protest, had wangled planning permission to convert the stone barns on his side of the wall that separated them into twelve holiday cottages (with garaging for upwards of twenty-four cars). She'd had to dodge the vicar whose workplace she had not entered for six months except to clean it and to show off, to a visiting friend, the rose window and the poignant simplicity of the twelfth-century font. All this while trying to get some mulled wine, the only drink on offer, down, without at the same time ingesting a silt of lemon pips and peel and nutmeg and cinnamon and cloves. She had not been able to smoke at the party because, having asked Barbara, her hostess, if she minded, she'd then been bound by Barbara's reply: 'I most certainly do! Put those cigarettes away, you naughty girl!'

Frustrated and bored, she'd wandered away to the fireplace and was examining a painting of ducks flying in formation against a wintry sky, when she'd been joined by her host, doing the rounds with the punch bowl. 'Here, hold out thine goblet.' A ladleful of citrus pulp had made a cautious descent to her glass. 'Maeve, I don't believe you've met the new owner of Dormers . . . ' The new owner of Dormers had told Maeve about the hazards of moving house in December. He'd told her about the dud heating system and warped kitchen units he and his wife had inherited and what he planned to do about these. Then, perhaps realising he hadn't asked Maeve a question yet, he'd asked her, 'Which of the handsome fellows here is the lucky one who takes you home? Point me out your better half.' 'I'm afraid I haven't got one of those.' (Maeve had meant this to sound jokily defiant, but it hadn't come out that way.) The new owner of Dormers had said, whoops, sorry, he'd got it into his head, from something the Doc had told him, that Maeve was married and had hundreds of children. 'I was married. I do have hundreds of children.' He was sorry if he was being insensitive, the new owner of Dormers said, but she looked too young, and much too

glamorous, to be a widow, it was not something that had
occur – 'I am *not* a widow!' She'd almost screamed this.
The new owner of Dormers had reeled as though from a
heavy blow. 'Pardon me,' he'd mumbled, ''scuse I, better
get back to the wife, excuse . . . ' On Maeve's way to the
door, the vicar's wife, Lesley, had put out a detaining arm.
'Maeve! Just the person I wanted to see. Now about those
mince pies for the wassail. I'm not sure yet how many I'll
need you to make, but I'll give you a tinkle Saturday lunch
time – will you be in? If all the tickets are sold we might
require a few extra sausage rolls, and I've been thinking –
a cheese fondue would ring the changes and be a pleasant
and tasty addition . . . ' And Maeve, looking for her coat
in the hall, had thought, What does it matter? What do all
these dreary people matter? This time tomorrow I shall be
at a proper party, full of amusing people, my peers, where
I'll be appreciated and where no one will decide I've got
two heads just because I'm divorced.

Refilling her glass at the table – the barman had abandoned his post and was nowhere to be seen – Maeve pitied
the naive person of yesterday who had thought these things.
Who had believed them. And she tried to shut out Patrick's
lecturing voice, as she had heard it once after a similar do:
'Why are you always so critical of everyone, Maeve? Why
do you have to be so bloody superior? You like to think
you're shy – you're not shy, you're superior. You never give
out to people, you're too busy thinking about yourself and
your reactions. You never take part. You stand on the
sidelines, observing, criticising, sneering. Why? What have
you got to be superior about? Tell me that. Go on, tell me.'

This one is for the road, Maeve told herself. 'My children
think I'm wonderful, anyway,' she said aloud. 'Clarissa has
no children and she's jealous and that's why she has to try
and put me down. She has to convince herself that a single
life in the fast lane is all a woman needs, but underneath
she regrets not having had babies. She's envious, that's all.'

'Why are you telling this to me?' The man who asked
this was short, shorter than Maeve in her heels, and balding

with ginger tufts above his ears; and he wore a surprising, blue-black beard. It was impossible to tell what colour his eyes were because they were guarded by red and swollen eyelids. 'Got a snout to spare?' he asked, seeing her light up.

Maeve was delighted to give this unappealing person one of her cigarettes, even though it meant she now had only four left. Gratitude dictated that she light it for him.

'Are you a hackette?' He blew a funnel of smoke into her face. 'This bash is stuffed with them.'

'No. Are you?'

'Funny one,' Bluebeard said, 'funny one. I like it.'

'A painter then. You're a painter.'

Bluebeard passed a fat and freckled hand over his eyelids. He shuddered. 'Please. Do me a favour. No no no, I'm a poet.'

'A poet!' Maeve tried to give the exclamation an enthusiastic ring.

'A poet!' she said again. 'Why?'

'Why? I could just as well ask you why you've chosen to dress yourself up as a bad stained-glass window.'

'I didn't mean why,' Maeve said crossly, 'I meant what. I mean what sort of poems do you write?'

'What sort of question is that?' The poet raised his eyelids to the ceiling in an attitude of mock, or it might have been real, despair. 'Would you be any the wiser if I told you?'

'Well, perhaps . . . ' Maeve began, but did not finish. For the floor and walls of Clarissa's double cube were on the move. She put a hand on the table to steady herself. In the distance the Christmas tree was a kaleidoscope, its pattern shifting and breaking up as she tried to fix on it. Shifting and breaking up and re-forming. 'I think I need some fresh air or a drink of – '

The poet snatched up a bottle from the table and leant forward and spilled some wine into Maeve's glass. He sniffed at her neck, noisy excited sniffs, like a terrier. 'What's that poison you're wearing?' He sniffed again. He reeled. 'Jesus!'

*

Maeve was standing in front of the Christmas tree, examining it with great concentration, fingering a silver bauble.

'I think that I shall never see
A poet lovely as a Christmas tree,'

she sang to the tree, which responded by dissolving into a
blur of tears. Maeve's song had without permission transported her to her mother-in-law's bedroom. It was soon
after her mother-in-law's death, and Patrick and Maeve
were kneeling on the stained mushroom carpet, sorting
through old clothes and old letters and old bills and old
medicine bottles, stuffing them into boxes and dustbin
sacks. It was cold in the bedroom which in its owner's
lifetime had been a furnace, but the lack of heating today
had not been able to dispel that disturbing, stale but sweet-
ish smell that in Maeve's time the room had always had.
They were edgy and bad-tempered, not enjoying their job,
guilty at manhandling treasures Patrick's mother had never
allowed anyone to touch; rifling through drawers and cupboards they would until this afternoon never have dared
(and had had no desire) to open. And then, turning out yet
another drawer, this time of his mother's davenport, Patrick
came across a theatre programme for an ancient production
of *Twelfth Night*. Inside, there was an engraving of Shakespeare's head and large lace collar, and a photograph of
'Mr H. Beerbohm Tree as Malvolio'. 'Poems are made
by fools like thee' – Patrick pointed a serious finger at
Shakespeare – 'but only God could make Beerbohm Tree.'
After that they cheered up. A three-quarters-full bottle of
Famous Grouse, uncovered from a commode and drunk
out of a smelly bone beaker from the washstand bracket,
made conspirators of them. Alcohol speeded their task. It
caused letters to fly into the wastepaper basket unread. It
sent whole drawersful of support stockings and corsets and
hairnets and grey knee bandages and pink face powder into
the dustbin sacks. Later, when they'd done their best, or

worst, in this room, they went home and straight up the stairs to bed, and made love – the first time for months.

'How could we have let it happen?' Maeve asked the Christmas tree. 'How did we let all that shared experience, that shared life, just go? Patrick's mother was fond of me. I know she was. Lara never even met her. Lara never had to do her shopping or cook her lunch. Lara didn't give birth to Patrick's children, she didn't have to nurse them through measles and mumps and gastroenteritis and chickenpox. Lara hasn't weathered any storms. She hasn't been tested at all. What has Lara got that I haven't got?'

Well, youth for a start. A firm body. A big bosom. Long legs.

But Patrick, when they were married, always insisted he didn't like young women, even pretty ones. He had nothing to say to them, he said. He didn't fancy them. He found them empty and uninteresting. Patrick always swore that the only thing Maeve had to fear was if he should meet a fascinating and worldly older woman – of fifty, say. Fifty-five. If he did meet one, then, yes, Maeve might very well have something to worry about.

One thing, when they were married, Patrick always swore he did like, was Maeve's smallness, her tiny hands and feet, her narrow back, her little breasts. ('Breasts' was the word he used. 'Breasts', which in speech had a tendency to collect some extra s's, so that it came out 'breassstsss', was a word Maeve could not say and, whenever she came across it in print, skated over. It was the plural, it was 'breasts', not 'breast', she had a quarrel with. For whereas a single breast had the capacity to be erotic, or maternal, or metaphorical, or, in middle life, fatally medical, the addition of an 's' reduced the word to the sexual – the crudely and humour-lessly and unsexy sexual.) Patrick liked Maeve's little breasts, and he even liked her short legs. 'I really like your legs,' he used to tell her, 'you may not believe this, but I do. A doll with duck's disease is certain to please.'

'But it's such a cliché!' Maeve had screamed at Patrick in the final mud-slinging before he left. (She couldn't touch

him or reach him by this stage. Words which when he loved
her would have stung were powerless now that he did not,
now that he loved someone else.) 'How can you leave me,
how can you leave your children, for that baby?'

'Oh Maeve.' Patrick had been sorrowful and patient. 'If
only you knew. Lara may be only twenty-seven, but she's
far more mature than you are. She's not self-absorbed and
masochistic. She's a grown-up. You've never grown up.
You'll never be a grown-up if you live to be a hundred. I
need a real woman in my life. I need a partner. I need a
wife.'

'Everyone needs a wife,' Maeve told the Christmas tree, 'I
need a wife, all women need wives.' The tree was decorated,
symmetrically, in white and red and silver. A Milky Way
of tiny crystal lights, spangling the dark green, struck dia-
monds off red and silver and frosted-white glass globes
which hung, twisting and spinning, from the tip of every
branch. At the tip of every branch, a wreath of silver ribbon
blossomed into an unlit scarlet candle. It was a designer
tree, Maeve suddenly saw, a window display tree, the kind
they have in Harrods. It was free from vulgarity, and poign-
ancy and history; it was without magic.

'Are you going to join us at Nico's?' Maeve, swaying on
a little cushion of alcohol in front of the tree, thought for
a moment the invitation was aimed at her. 'Digby had the
nous to book a table for twenty before he left the office, so
ne soyez pas faible – venez!'

'I'm quite drunk,' Maeve told the designer tree, 'I'm quite
sad. I think I'll go home now.' But as soon as she said the
words she realised she was not fit to drive; that it was not
even open to her to sit in her parked car and wait until she
sobered up. A friend of hers had been caught that way. No
amount of explaining, to the policeman who'd stuck his
head through her window, that she did not intend actually
driving the car, had saved this friend from the breathalyser
and prosecution and the loss of her licence. A glass of water
was what Maeve needed now. Milk. Black coffee. A lie-
down in an upstairs room.

'Goodbye,' she said to the tree. 'Too bad nobody told you that power dressing is out. The Caring Nineties are in. Get real!'

Maeve didn't see her children until half past twelve the following day. They never got out of bed before noon in the school holidays. When they did finally get up they'd wander half-dressed into the kitchen and grind coffee beans and squeeze oranges and scatter cereal while she was trying to get lunch together. This morning (this afternoon) Maeve was short of sleep and her head hurt. She slammed a jar of Nescafé and a carton of orange juice in front of them and went straight into the attack.

'Very thoughtful of you, I'm sure, to leave the gas fire full on for me. I appreciated it no end, I can tell you.'

'Did you enjoy the party, Mum?'

'Not putting Silas out was a mistake, a mistake I'm not going to be responsible for. One of you can clear up the mess, the rest can club together and pay the cleaner's bill for the carpet which, I'd remind you, is Turkish and very – '

'Did you enjoy the – ?'

'There are no telephone messages on the pad. I realise you were probably much too busy last night working on your geography projects to write down any messages, but if by some small chance anyone did ring for me, perhaps you'd be good enough to give me the gist of – '

'Daddy rang. From New York.' It was Jessica who said this.

'Oh?' Maeve, about to clamp a saucepan lid on a saucepan, paused, and turned, and caught a row of closed, thoughtful faces and caught Florence's frown, directed at Jessica.

'It's all right, don't worry,' Florence said quickly and comfortingly, 'he didn't want you. He rang to talk to us.'

He didn't want you. He didn't want you. Imagine it. Imagine, only a few years ago, Patrick ringing from anywhere on the planet and not wanting her, and not wanting to talk to her, first and foremost, above all. Imagine it.

'Mum. Did you enjoy the par-ty?'

There were days when Maeve would have given in at this point, when she would have stopped banging cupboard doors and crashing saucepan lids for a while, and sat down, and confided in them: 'If you want to know, the party was hell, I hated every minute of it. Hardly anyone spoke to me at all.' On such a day, she would have embellished the misery of the evening, dubbing Clarissa's bedroom a mausoleum, going to town on the double cube and the Christmas tree and the media folk and the overheard conversations. On such a day she would have sent herself up, also, exaggerating her drunkenness. And there would have been rewards for this sort of confession: laughter, for a start, that embraced all their social failures and made nonsense of them. Comfort, as a follow-up: 'Don't worry about it, Mum. Don't think about it. Those sorts of parties, those sorts of people, are unreal. You're the greatest!' On such a day she could have made allies of her children.

'The party was fine, thank you,' Maeve said briskly, 'it was great fun. Heaps of interesting people — had a long talk with Terry Ross, you know, chat-show host' (she had suddenly remembered who the famous person who'd made the white-elephant-stall remark was), 'had a fascinating discuss — '

'Did you get lucky, Mum? Did some handsome hunk take you out to supper?'

Did some handsome hunk . . . ? Maeve had thrown a dustsheet over the later part of her evening. She couldn't recall much of it anyway. She did have a vague memory of being roused, at some point, from fur-smothered oblivion, by Clarissa's voice: 'Well well well! What have we here? Who's been sleeping in my bed?' She did have a fuzzy picture of herself, hours later probably, trying to turn a key in the frozen lock of her car, hunting for de-icer, hunting for gloves, having to rub frost off the windscreen with the sleeves of her coat . . .

'Ah. That would be telling.' She put on a mysterious face. 'That would be telling.'

'Tell us then. Don't be mean. Tell us about lover-boy.'

'Romance. Is it romance?'

'Wouldn't you like to know? Well, sorry, I'm not going to tell you. You have your secrets, I must be allowed mine. I must be allowed some privacy, some life of my – '

The telephone, drilling from the sitting room, was brilliantly on cue. 'That'll be for me. Don't anyone move. I'll get it.'

Maeve banged the kitchen door behind her and ran to the sitting room. Before picking up the receiver, she shut the sitting-room door, a double precaution, lest an eavesdropper should catch some libidinous chat with Lesley, the vicar's wife, about wassails and mince pies and sausage rolls and cheese fondue.

The American
Dream

They sing a lot, now they're in America. They sing the songs everyone is singing and whistling this year – 'Cruising Down the River' and 'Put Another Nickel In (Music! Music! Music!)' are two – and they sing the commercial jingles that interrupt wireless programmes over here. *Radio* programmes. They sing about jello and shampoo, soup and soap. One of the jingles they like best, that appeals to them most, because so far-fetched, is a duet. A male voice starts off:

> 'Here comes the Camay Bride –
> Oh! What a lucky groom
> To have a girl with a complexion
> Just like roses in bloom – '

and a female, a girlish, voice intercepts to explain:

> 'It's the Camay mild soap di-et,
> Give up careless care and try et –
> With your vurry vurry first cake of Camay
> Your skin grows softer, smoother, right away-ay.'

They're singing this today as they run down the stairs. They run out of the house and into the street with their ball, and begin kicking it about on the pavement (or on the sidewalk: the words they choose, the words they use, depend on their mood; depend on whether they feel, at a given moment, pro- or anti-America and Americans, loyal or disloyal to home). They are identically dressed in red and white striped T-shirts, cotton dungarees and sandals.

It's a hot day, and after a bit they get fed up with kicking the ball, and head towards Meakin's store for a popsicle. While the boy jogs and dribbles the ball, dodging the shoppers, his twin sister negotiates the tops of low brick walls. She careers like a tightropist, in jerky bursts and sudden stops and headlong dashes, her outstretched arms seesawing for balance. When the street runs out of wall, she jumps down and trots beside him.

A woman in a mauve poplin dress and with a little mauve hat tipped over one eye, and with her arms full of shopping, stops in front of them.

'Say, are you two twins?' this woman asks. 'Aren't you perfectly darling!'

The girl nods vigorously. The boy shakes his head.

'No, no relation at all,' he says.

The woman seems amused. She laughs. She shifts her shopping from one arm to the other. She shades her free eye with her free hand.

'You're British,' she says. 'Why, that's wonderful! I just love your accent. It's the cutest – '

'We're English. We haven't got an accent.' The boy frowns. He bounces his ball twice. 'You're the ones with the accent, not us.'

'Well well well,' the woman says. 'My my.' She does not stop smiling, but her smile now has a stuck-on look about it. If I tug at the corner of that smile, the boy decides, it will rip off in one go, like Elastoplast, and afterwards there'll be a black hole in her face.

The woman stares at them for a moment, still smiling; and then steps backwards and then sideways, and then walks on.

This is not the first time they've been stopped by a stranger. They've been accosted, in one way or another, ever since they arrived in Washington. It even happened on the *Queen Mary* coming over. They might be film stars, the amount of attention they're getting. They might be *movie* stars.

They walk on down the street. The street, Q Street, is empty of school-age children because it's a Tuesday afternoon in term time and school-age children are at school. They're not at school because when their mother went to the nearest suitable one to enrol them, she was told by the principal, yes, sure, it'd be a real pleasure to have Robert and Josephine in school while their father was in Washington; they were nine years old, did she say? – they'd go into the fourth grade. Their mother argued with the principal about this. She'd been round the classrooms, she'd cast an eye over the maps and nature posters on the wall, she'd glanced at the exercise books of people in the fourth grade. People in the fourth grade were just about learning to read and write, their mother deduced. Robert and Josephine had been reading and writing for years, she told the principal, they were extremely articulate, they had an unusually wide vocabulary, they'd been learning French for a whole year at least. Robert was due to start Latin in the autumn. They'd be wasting their time in the fourth grade. The principal, so their mother told them afterwards, shrugged and spread his hands at this, and said he was sorry, you couldn't skip grades. Not in his school. That was how the education system was geared to work in the United States of America, and it worked just fine.

'But we can't have you bimbling about all morning, getting under Carrie's feet,' their mother said. 'We can't have you getting in Celestine's hair.' And so, when there's time, she takes them on sightseeing tours and educational outings, and she sets them work to do at home.

They do this work, which their mother calls their assignments, in a little room at the top of the house that looks over the thin houses, and thin trees, opposite. At a table in the window they sit side by side and write essays on 'My Favourite Painting in the Mellon Gallery' (this, for both of them, is 'The Dead Toreador' by Edouard Manet), 'Our Day in Williamsburg', 'The Visit to Chesapeake Bay', 'A

Walk in Rock Creek Park'. They draw portraits and self-portraits, they paint imaginative compositions and still-lifes. They design posters and book jackets. They learn poems from *The Oxford Book of English Verse* by heart, and write them out in their best writing. When they know the poem, when they're both word perfect — Josephine invariably the first to reach this stage, Josephine 'the literary one, "the chiel amang us",' their mother tells visitors, 'we think, we hope, she's going to be a writer one day' — they take the book to their mother so that she can test them. Their mother will be in the kitchen, showing Celestine how to cook the lunch; or she'll be seated on her dressing-table stool, waving her hands up and down to dry the polish on her nails; or she'll be at her desk, writing letters home. (Or she'll be lying on the sofa with her eyes closed, listening to *The Story of Helen Trent* on the portable.) Wherever she is, whatever she's doing, she'll say, 'Well done, good children, but I haven't time now, I'll hear your poem later.' Their mother, like all mothers probably, leads a busy life. She doesn't always have time to hear their poem later.

No arithmetic, no 'math', is done in the room at the top of the house because their mother is no good at it. It doesn't matter. They're only in America for six months. They aren't missing anything they won't be able to catch up on when they get back to school.

The only thing they might be said to be missing is the company of children their own age, but they have each other. And there is America, new and shiny, loud and colourful, a land of plenty where sweets are not, where candy is not, rationed. It was the 'Land of the Dream', their father told them once, the place where if you bought the product, you got the girl; the country where even a bellhop could, in theory anyway, make it to President. It was the Land of the Free, a term they understood through their being allowed, for the first time in their lives, to roam the streets — of Georgetown — unaccompanied and at will. Not least, it was the land of advertising jingles and peanut butter.

At Meakin's store, they buy double popsicles and tubes of Lifesavers, rum butter and wild cherry. The store is empty except for Mr Meakin and a Negro. The Negro is sitting on an upturned orange box; he holds a bottle of Pepsi in one hand and a bag of salted peanuts in the other. Every so often he shakes a few nuts from the bag into the bottle, and then he tilts back his head and swigs, chewing the nuts and swallowing the Pepsi at one and the same time. How is this done? They drop their popsicle wrappers in the trash can, and stand in the doorway and watch. The Negro is wearing a wide straw hat, tipped back off his face. Sweat, like tears, streams down his cheek and his neck, trickles over a sharp and painful-looking Adam's apple. I will never forget this, Robert tells himself. I will always remember this Negro on this orange box, swallowing and chewing.

Robert discovered this remembering, storing trick two years ago, when he was seven. He was hiding under the grand piano in the Music Room at school, during the hobbies period they have there on wet Saturdays. He was homesick, or perhaps it would be more true to say, mothersick; and while all around him boys and girls (the girls included Josephine: their mother chose a co-educational school so the twins should not be separated) buzzed among the scratched yellow tables and swapped cigarette cards and stamps; or sat at the tables and impressed sheet after sheet of rough drawing paper with pencil Spitfires and Messerschmitts, and bullets and flames and smoke, he stayed under the piano, sniffing his knees and staring at the rain hosing the windows in squally bursts. A climbing rose had broken loose in the wind, and it flailed and whipped the window nearest him. Black rosehips, thrown at the glass one minute, were torn away the next, and the sound they made – a rattle, a sawing scrape, a relentless tapping, like someone desperate to get in – was the most desolate sound he'd heard. I shall remember this afternoon, he told himself then. I shall remember that sound, and the rain, and the way my knees smell. Now, in America, if he chooses to, he can recall every detail.

When the Negro has finished his Pepsi and the nuts, Robert and Josephine leave the store.

> 'Pepsi-Cola hits the spot!
> Two whole glasses, that's a lot!
> Twice more flavour, twice more pep –
> Why take less when Pepsi's best?'

It's Josephine who sings this. 'Shall we go to the drugstore?' she suggests. She's taken the popsicle from her mouth and is examining it. The tip is bleached now, drained of sweetness and of orange juice.

'No point. The new comics won't be in yet.'

And there is no point, for they go to the drugstore for the purpose of reading the comics. Occasionally they may sit at the counter and have a banana split before reading the comics, but mostly they don't bother. The comics are kept on a low rack on the left of the entrance. They'll go in and kneel on the lino tiles and read *Batman* and *Superman* front page to back, and then replace them in the rack. Mike, the drugstore manager, never objects. Perhaps because they're twins, perhaps because they're British, he never suggests they buy a comic.

On the way home Robert dribbles his football through the shoppers and the hurrying businessmen, and Josephine dances beside him, counting her steps in sevens. She starts with the right foot: 'One two three four five six seven,' then shifts to the left: 'One two three four five six seven,' then returns to the right. Everything she does has to be done in sevens. She has to climb stairs this way, she has to brush her teeth twenty-one times – seven goes on the right side of her jaw, seven on the left, etcetera. Robert cannot stop her, although he, and everyone in her orbit, has tried. Josephine has had rituals before. Until the age of three she was a head-banger, unable to get to sleep without first thumping her head against the pillow, at the same time emitting a monotonous moaning hum. She could keep this up for hours. After the head-banging, there was a period of touching things – railings, or lamp posts, or pillar boxes – on walks, of having to go back and touch any she'd left out. And when that blew over, or lost its power? Something to do with neatness, and shoes, and joins in the carpet. Josephine never chooses to explain, or perhaps cannot, what her rituals are about; she won't disclose the terrible consequences she's certain will result from a failure to carry out her 'orders'.

Eight doors from home, the toe of Robert's sandal lifts the ball over a low wall and into a front yard. A fat girl in a frilled cotton dress is staring from the yard. She picks up the ball and holds it against her chest.

'You lost your ball?' She hugs it to her. She looks about the same age as they are, except that she has bosoms already; they can see them wobble through the thin cotton. She has mousey hair, parted in the middle and held at the side with pink plastic bows. The hair is quite short and it sticks straight out from her face, perhaps because the ends are frizzed.

'It's dumb to play ball on the street,' the fat girl says. 'Dumb and dangerous. I'm not permitted to play ball on the street.'

Without consulting each other, they jump on to the wall at the same moment, and jump off it again into the fat girl's yard.

'I saw you two before today. You're twins,' she informs them.

'You don't say,' Josephine says.

'You talk real strange. You foreign or something?'

'Yep yep yep.'

'Why aren't you in school?' Without warning, the fat girl throws the ball at Robert, a dud throw that manages to be both short and wide. He retrieves the ball; then he asks her why she isn't at school anyway? For example?

'I'm sick,' the girl says. 'I've had a fever. I've been sick four days now.'

They stare at her with interest. She doesn't look sick, particularly, merely fat and pale.

'My name's Yvonne,' the sick girl says. 'It's French. My second name's Claybeau. That's French too. My ancestors were French on my daddy's side. My daddy's an admiral. What does your daddy do?'

Their father is a diplomat, and English. Robert tells Yvonne this.

'Uh-huh.' She doesn't seem impressed. 'Uh-huh.' She turns to Josephine. 'What's your name?'

'Josephine,' Josephine says. 'It's a French name, I believe, although I myself am not French.'

There's a silence after this. Robert bounces his ball twice in the admiral's flowerless yard. He turns to go, and so does Josephine.

'Hey! Do you two twins have skates? Come back Saturday. Come lunch time Saturday and meet my mommy and my best friend Bobby Jane. If I'm not sick by then we'll skate the block. Come a quarter after twelve.'

Yvonne Claybeau is a blancmange. It's impossible to envisage her on skates. It's impossible to imagine her wearing anything other than a pink frilly dress.

'Be tactful,' their mother says as they lace their skates on Saturday morning. 'Come home straight away if you're not expected,' says their mother, who like most mothers, probably, does not believe in the validity of invitations issued by nine-year-olds, especially when the parents of the parties concerned are not acquainted.

The Claybeaus are expecting them, however. Admiral and Mrs Claybeau are very old, more like grandparents than parents. Mrs Claybeau's hair is blue-white, and she wears it in a fancy roll down the back of her head. Her large corseted body is draped in a clinging lilac dress. There's a lot of lilac about this year, and mauve. Their mother wears it, and it suits her, but it does not suit Mrs Claybeau, Robert decides. It makes her skin look grey.

The admiral is large also, and unfit-looking, and he has a snub nose. He is a tall, old, masculine version of his daughter Yvonne.

Then there is Bobby Jane.

'This is my vurry best friend Roberta Jane Dyson,' says Yvonne, who is wearing Bermudas today, pink ones, so tight across her bottom the line of her underpants shows through.

'Hi,' Roberta Jane says. She shakes hands. She is skinny and tall, taller than Robert, he is displeased to see, skinnier than Josephine, who is not skinny. (Josephine is not fat, either. Not fat. 'Well-covered,' visitors to the house sometimes remark. 'Bonny. What a bonny girl Josephine has become!')

Bobby Jane has an interesting face. She has dark-blue eyes that have a darker ring round the iris. She has dark, straight eyebrows and corn-coloured hair. She is pretty, she may even be beautiful. Josephine's plaits are short pigtails, the texture of horsehair, always escaping their ribbons, but Bobby Jane's plaits hang down her neck in two neat silken cords. She has on old blue pedal pushers that don't fit, they're too big for her, a faded red T-shirt, white gym shoes. White *sneakers*. There's something about her, an air, a look, that isn't young, that's not like a child. She's ten and two months, they'll learn later that day, but she could be twenty. She is the Camay Bride, it comes to Robert. 'Oh what a lucky groom.'

Lunch is peanut butter and jelly and lettuce and mayonnaise sandwiches, and strawberry milk shakes. They eat it in awkward silence in the kitchen, standing up, leaning against the margarine-coloured worktops. When they're finished, Yvonne Claybeau dabs at her mouth with a pink paper napkin.

'You guys wanna come see my boudoir now?' It's more of a command than an invitation, but they're curious, and they follow her through the thick-carpeted hall, up thick-carpeted stairs, along a thick-carpeted landing. Yvonne chooses a door and holds it open.

'No, not you,' she bars Robert, who's waited till last. 'You wait here. Boys can't go into little girls' boudoirs.'

He's seen it, though. Pink walls. A pink, silky bed, smothered with cushions and dolls. Above the bed, a crucifix, its crossbar strangely looped with a string of beads. A downcast plaster Virgin on the windowsill. A picture of Jesus wearing a nightdress and a crown of thorns – wearing an enormous, spiked halo.

'Halo everybody, Halo!
Halo is the shampoo
That glorifies your hair, so
Halo everybody, Halo!'

Robert sings this on the landing, kneeling outside Yvonne Claybeau's closed boudoir door.

From now on they meet Bobby Jane and Yvonne after school on weekdays, and in any spare time they have at weekends. The meeting place is always the Claybeaus' house, and arrangements are made by a telephone call to Yvonne. They imagine she must sit by the telephone all day: it's always she who answers it. 'Admiral Claybeau's resi*dence*,' she always says, 'spea*king*?'

At the Claybeaus' house they sit at the kitchen table and test each other on general knowledge, and they swap travellers' tales. The Americans have the advantage when it comes to knowing the population of Arkansas, and they can argue between them about exactly how long it takes to get to Baltimore on the Pullman; but neither of them has the faintest as to what Big Ben might be, and neither of them has been abroad. Neither of them has seen an ocean-going liner. When Robert and Josephine, in order to give some idea of the size of the *Queen Mary*, describe her staterooms and shops, her swimming pools and ballrooms and dining rooms; stopping here to elaborate on the amazing Cabin Class menus and on the decorated menu cards –

a different design for each meal of the five-day crossing; when they enthuse about the mechanical horses they rode every day in the Cabin Class gymnasium, the Americans have nothing to counter with except silence. Silence and raised eyebrows.

At the Claybeaus' house they play Kick the Can in the back yard; they watch *The Lone Ranger* and *The Howdy Doody Show* on TV. Occasionally Mrs Claybeau will take them to the cinema. On these expeditions she chauffeurs the admiral's Lincoln convertible, and they ride in the back on stiffly upholstered, sickly green seats which smell horrible (but she won't allow them to have the window open). Once in the ticket queue, she'll turn suddenly and extend a fat gloved palm, as if offering sugar lumps to a horse, and this is the signal for them to produce their money. The first time this happened, they hadn't any money on them. (It was their mother's fault; they'd asked her for some, and she'd said, 'Mrs Claybeau won't expect you to pay, sillies, you're her guests!' Their mother had laughed at the very idea.) Mrs Claybeau tapped her handbag as they went through their pockets. Josephine eventually came up with a nickel. 'Bring it round tomorrow,' Mrs Claybeau said. 'You two twins had better shape up.'

The Camay Bride never comes on the cinema outings, a blow to Robert because he has fallen in love with her, and thinks about her all the time, and hopes, and fears, to sit next to her in the dark. When the cinema visits are planned she always seems to have something else to do. '*Red River* was wizard,' he told her, 'you really missed something there.' It was the best film he'd seen, he told her, 'better than *Yellow Sky*.' But she hadn't seen that one, either. She listened politely as he recounted the plot. 'Movies are no big deal, I guess,' she said.

'They don't like boys,' is Josephine's explanation when he complains about the huddles the girls get into and the conversations he's excluded from, after tea, in Yvonne's pink boudoir. 'They haven't got brothers,' she reminds him. 'The boys at their school are mean. They call Yvonne a fat pig and they swing on Bobby Jane's plaits. They have no reason to like boys. They put up with you because you're my brother.'

Nevertheless, Josephine's facts do not square with Yvonne's continual boasts: 'We'll be dating boys soon, Bobby Jane and me. We'll be dating boys when we're eleven. I'll be permitted to wear make-up next year, and then I'm gonna date Irving Wentworth. He's the best-looking boy in our class.'

Robert wants Bobby Jane to deny these promises, made on her behalf by Yvonne, but she never does, although she won't confirm them either. When Yvonne goes on and on about boys and dating, she stares down at her hands, spread out on the kitchen table (her nails are oval and clean, and have little white half-moons at the base). Like a sheepdog separating a ewe from the flock, he tries sometimes to nudge her away from the others and get her on her own, but she will not be nudged. His efforts at conversation she blocks, politely evades, slides round.

'Do you like reading?' he asked her once – for despite their mother's lack of faith in the American educational system, it's clear that the two fourth-graders they know can read, and better than haltingly. They were standing in the Claybeaus' kitchen, drinking banana milk shakes that tasted of Kolynos.

'Sure I like to read.' Bobby Jane removed the flattened straw from her tumbler, pinched it to make it cylindrical, blew through it. 'Everybody does, I guess.'

The offhand put-down was a lie – everybody did not like reading – but he plugged on: 'What books then? What d'you like best? Adventure? Murder? Ghost stories?'

'Oh, all kinds.' She smiled, but she didn't look at him. She tipped her glass; with her mouth she guided her straw into the remaining bubbles, where it stuttered like a motor-bike. She turned her face and her attention away from him to Josephine.

'I like your plaits,' he said another time, the words

coming out in a rush of breath as he caught up with her in Pennsylvania Avenue. 'Your plaits are . . . swell.'

She stared at him. She rolled upright, in perfect control, back and forth on her skates. Back and forth. He pointed. He didn't dare touch her plaits.

'Oh. My *braids*. Oh. Thanks.' She flipped one over her shoulder, then locked her hands behind her back and swooped off, neatly zigzagging.

What Robert knows about Bobby Jane he learns from his sister, information imparted voluntarily without his having to probe, but released only slowly, in short bursts – when they are doing their assignments, when they are cleaning their teeth, when Josephine feels like it. When she feels generous. Or is it mischievous?

'Her father's dead, you know,' Josephine remarks as they sit over their Quaker Oats ('Delicious! nutritious! makes you feel ambitious! The giant of the cereals is Quaker Oats!') at supper time, waiting for *The Shadow* to frighten them out of their wits. 'Perhaps I told you? He was a bomber pilot, stationed in Suffolk. He died at the very end of the war. Bobby Jane doesn't remember him, hardly. Hey, it's time.' Josephine stretches a hand to their mother's portable, and fiddles with the knob. 'Who knows what evil lurks in the hearts of men?' Orson Welles enquires menacingly. 'The Shadow knows.'

'Her mother's a cripple,' Josephine announces casually, 'she caught polio when Bobby Jane was six. That's my rubber you've got there, I need it,' Josephine says. (They are not enjoying their assignment which is: 'Give a brief history and, where applicable, explain the functions of the following: a) The White House; b) The Capitol; c) The Lincoln Memorial; d) The Pentagon; e) The Washington Monument. Illustrate in pencil: if you can, from memory.'

'She's a writer,' Josephine says, 'she writes poetry. She's a famous poet, Bobby Jane says. *Quis?*'

'*Ego* decent.'

But it's not decent; it's only Josephine's postcard view of 'The Capitol under snow', which she wants to swap for

Robert's 'The White House in cherry-blossom time'. They got the postcards from the drugstore. They were hoping for an aerial-view shot of the Pentagon – how could you make sense of its five sides otherwise? – but the postcard stand hadn't held any view of the Pentagon at all. 'Well well well,' Mike said when they told him why they needed it, 'that's a kinda serious request. Let's see now what we can do for our friends the twins.' He went through a drawer first, and then a cardboard box of old, black and white, bargain-price postcards, but no luck. He seemed as disappointed as they were, and perhaps because of this wouldn't let them pay for the cards they did find.

'Bobby Jane is a sort of housekeeper,' Josephine confides. They're in the drugstore again, squatting on the lino floor in their dungarees, reading *Batman* and *Superman*, cover to cover. 'She does the shopping and the cooking, and the washing. They haven't got a maid or anything.'

What must it be like not to have a maid or anything? There was always someone in London. In Washington there are two: Celestine, an eighteen-year-old Jamaican who lives in and whom their mother is teaching to cook – 'but it's hopeless,' their mother sighs, 'quite hopeless. She's incapable of retaining the simplest instruction' – and Carrie Hawkins, an American, a Negress, a grandmother, who comes in daily to do the laundry.

Celestine is sad and giggly by turn. She wears a large-brimmed black hat, indoors and out, 'to keep the devils away'. For work she wears a cyclamen-pink cotton dress with white buttons and white collar and cuffs their mother bought her. When not in the kitchen, trying to make sense of their mother's instructions, she shambles about the house with a feather duster. She stares out of windows a lot. They worry about her. They ask her, 'Are you homesick, Celestine?' (They are homesick themselves sometimes, for England, for English newsreaders on the wireless.) She giggles or weeps, but she won't say.

Celestine's bedroom is downstairs, in the basement, and next to it is a shower room – Celestine's own. Once, creeping down the basement stairs, they saw Celestine in the shower. She hadn't bothered to pull the shower curtain round. They sat on the stairs and watched amazed as Celestine's blue-black body – long strong legs, firm stomach, big breasts – dazzling and shiny with water, revolved under the jet like a doll on a musical box.

The basement is where Carrie Hawkins does the laundry. It has a concrete floor, perfect for roller skates, and while Carrie transforms the jumble in the laundry basket into uniform flat parcels on the ironing board, they skate round her. Carrie doesn't mind this. 'You go right ahead, honey,' she says, 'you don't bother me one bit.' While Carrie irons she sings, old sad Negro songs about cabins and cornmeal and cotton fields and deep rivers. About Lindy Lou.

'Lindy, did you hear that mockin' bird singin' las' night?' Carrie will sing, pressing both hands and all her birdlike weight on the iron to remove a stubborn crease, lifting the iron to her cheek as though she's listening to it. 'Honey, it was singin' so sweet in the moonlight.' Every so often she'll place a finger on her tongue and then touch the flat of the iron to test its heat. This produces a hiss and a little puff of steam. It shows off the softness and pinkness of Carrie's tongue in contrast with the dark cracked leather of her lips. 'Lindy, I'd lay me right down and die, and die, if I could sing as that bird sang to you-oo, my little Lindy Lou-oo.'

Robert feels sorry for Bobby Jane that there's no one like Carrie Hawkins at her place. He knows where her place is – a depressing apartment block, a few doors down from Meakin's store. A couple of times after school he's skated there on his own and loitered, but she's never appeared and asked him in. And there've been no invitations to tea there, not even for Josephine.

'She doesn't ask us because of that supper, I bet,' Josephine says. 'I know I wouldn't if I was her.'

By 'that supper' Josephine means the one they invited Bobby Jane and Yvonne Claybeau to, at their house. They asked if they could eat in the kitchen, the way the Claybeaus do; if they could cook it themselves, if they could have a proper American menu.

'You know, Ma, hamburgers, hot dogs, fries, ketchup; ice cream 'n' chocolate sauce. Coke. You know, things they're used to, things they like.'

Their mother was writing letters when they petitioned her. They stood either side of her desk, right up close, as close as they dared, and watched her blue fountain pen etch the blue air mail paper. She wrote in firm bursts, the pen hovering above the page when not pressed to it, her beautiful mouth folded into a concentrating line, the line twitching a little at the corners.

'Okay, Ma?' Robert picked up a heavy glass dome and turned it over and studied the green baize on its bottom.

'Don't say "okay", and don't call me "Ma".' She didn't look up. 'Don't fiddle, there's a good child.'

He put the paperweight down.

'Can we though? Is it all right, Mother darling?'

'Don't be cheeky.'

The pen reached the end of the page. Their mother read through what she'd written, and blotted it, and plucked a new sheet from the tooled-leather paper-holder. He made a face at Josephine. She was sometimes able to succeed where he failed. If he had the advantage of being a boy and the first born – by twenty minutes – she had the bonus of being a girl and the 'baby'.

Josephine shunted sideways to within an inch of their mother's elbow.

'May we, Mummy, please? Please.'

Their mother removed the hornrims she wears for close work and laid them on the empty sheet of paper. She leant back in her chair. Then she picked up the hornrims and put them on again. Then she picked up her pen and continued with her letter.

'We'll see,' she murmured, folding her lips together. The pen gathered speed. 'If you're good children. We'll see.'

On the night they didn't have supper in the kitchen – of course not, it was impossible, they never did – they had it

in the hall, which in Washington has to double as dining
room. To its formality was added Celestine's gloom as she
shambled in and out in her hat with plates and dishes. They
sat in silence while she made her sad entrances and exits,
just the four of them at the too-large dining table. (The
moment their visitors had arrived their parents had gone
out, dressed to the nines, to some do at the French
Embassy.)

'Hey, what kinda soup is this?' Yvonne peered into her
bowl and sniffed.

Robert looked at Josephine; Josephine looked at Robert.
They recognised the brew, they knew what it was – their
worst, their mother's favourite – a boiling-up of chicken
carcass and insides, plus onions and celery and pearl barley,
the concoction masked by parsley and a shiny, wrinkling
skin of fat. Blistering fat. 'Yum yum chicky broth,' their
mother always greets this abomination, taking no notice at
all when they gag and moan and slide off their chairs and
hide their heads under the tablecloth, 'full of nourishing
goodness.'

How could she have done it to them this evening? How
could she? How?

'It's chicken,' Josephine said. 'More palatable with a ton
of salt, in my experience.'

'You call this chicken?'

Impossible to blame Yvonne, for once. Nothing less like
Campbell's Cream of Chicken could be imagined; could
have been devised.

They picked up their spoons.

Immediately, at the first sip – in their anxiety they'd failed
to warn the Americans to blow on their soup – Bobby Jane
burnt her mouth. She cried 'Ow!', she spluttered, her face
went red. Robert looked away, to the portrait of their
mother in an emerald evening dress above the doorway;
but Josephine jumped up and ran to the sideboard and
grabbed the water jug (where was the Coke they'd ordered?)
and filled Bobby Jane's glass.

'It's okay. I'm okay now.' Bobby Jane put out a fending-off hand. 'No, really, Josephine.' Josephine slunk back to her chair.

They picked up their spoons again in silence. They lifted and sifted the contents of their bowls.

'Uh-oh. Uh-oh.' In Yvonne's spoon, held out for them across the table, lay a grey something with little holes in it, a rubbery something with whiskers sprouting out of it. Yum yum chicky skin. Yum yum yum. *Uh-oh*.

'I can't eat this stuff,' Yvonne said.

'Neither can I, I guess. I'm sorry,' Bobby Jane said.

They put down their spoons.

Hardboiled eggs in cheese sauce, with bullet rice and spinach-in-a-pool, came next – and left again, rearranged on the plates but otherwise untouched, minutes after. The twins had been brought up – 'There's a war on, remember' – to eat everything that was put in front of them no matter how unappetising; even when the war was over there were the 'starving Russians' to 'think of'. To feel guilty about. Robert felt guilty now. Not so much about the Russians, who hadn't been invoked recently, but about Celestine's hurt feelings over her rejected, wasted, cooking. If the visitors weren't prepared to eat it, though, if they weren't even prepared to try it, how could he and Josephine?

When Celestine had taken away the plates, shaking her head sadly as she did so, she set about clearing the rest of the table. She did it very very slowly. Egg dish, rice dish, spinach dish; saltcellar, pepper grinder, serving spoons. Four punishing journeys, made without a tray. She refused to let them help her. Meanwhile nobody spoke. Bobby Jane crumbled a piece of bread and examined the ceiling. Yvonne giggled behind her hand. By this time the twins were in despair at their failure, and their guests ravenous.

'Ice cream, please Celestine! Ice cream! Ice cream! Ice cream!'

Celestine turned at the door. She looked perplexed. She looked bruised.

'Yo mother say nothin' 'bout no ice cream. Dere'm no ice cream.' And she brought them the fruit bowl. In it

were five bright red, tough-skinned, sleepy apples. The one
Robert had rejected at elevenses still had his teethmarks in
it, upper and lower jaw, not a bad print, the flesh dark
brown now where the skin was broken.

It's not surprising there've been no invitations from Bobby
Jane. But if she doesn't ask them soon, it will be too late:
they sail for England, for football and netball and new
brown walking shoes and new grey knee-socks, in three
weeks' time.

She asks them one day when they're taking off their
skates in the doorway of the Claybeaus' kitchen. (Mrs
Claybeau does not permit skates in her kitchen. They make
black marks on the linoleum, she says.)

'You guys wanna come round my place Wednesday?'
Bobby Jane's head is bent over her laces, her face hidden
by her braids. 'It's okay with my mother if you do.'

The question comes as such a surprise, is so out of the
blue, no one answers.

'We can watch *The Howdy Doody Show* and *The Last
of the Mohicans*.' Bobby Jane sounds casual. She doesn't
care one way or the other. 'Let me know Monday. I have
to go now. I have to fetch the groceries from the store.'

'It's too bad I can't go to Bobby Jane's place,' Yvonne
Claybeau says sweetly when Bobby Jane's gone. It's clear
she's longing to be asked why not, and eventually, reluctantly, they allow curiosity to get the better of them.

'Why can't you go?'

'Well. We-ell.' Yvonne stops and puts a small fat finger
to her lips. 'My mommy doesn't like me to.' She simpers
and stops again, then says in a fake whisper, 'Bobby Jane
and her mother aren't Catholics.'

'But we're not Catholics!' Robert is incensed. 'And you
came to our house, I seem to remember.'

'I know, I know' – Yvonne's tone is sweet and pitying –
'but you do go to the Episcopalian church Sundays. You
and your folks are kind of friends of Jesus, I guess.'

Friends of Jesus? Is that what they are? It does not describe their yawning Sunday mornings in the Episcopalian church. The dull sermon, the dreary hymns, their formal, uncomfortable clothes. The only service they've enjoyed in America is the one Carrie Hawkins took them to, at her church. They were the only white people in the congregation. On arrival they were handed cardboard fans, shaped and decorated like palm leaves, and during the sermon and the singing of cheerful and catchy hymns they swayed and fanned themselves as everyone else did. The preacher struck his chest from time to time and cried, 'We're all sinners, Lord!' and from all parts of the church men and women, and even one boy not much older than themselves, leapt up to agree: 'So right! Yes Lord!' Having to give up their fans when it was over was a disappointment, but afterwards they went back with Carrie Hawkins to her place for Sunday dinner: fried chicken and sweetcorn and fried potatoes; apple pie and toffee-nut-crunch ice cream.

'Bobby Jane's mother isn't able to go to church,' Josephine reminds Yvonne. 'She can't walk. She's paralysed. So how could she get to church?'

'She could go in a wheelchair. Or the priest could visit her maybe. If she wanted. The problem is' – Yvonne whispers this – 'Roberta's mother doesn't believe in Jesus. She's taught Roberta that Our Lady was just an ordinary woman, and Our Lord was just an ordinary man. She's raised her that way. Isn't that terrible? Anyways, that's not all. The Dysons aren't our class. They're poor. Real poor. Their home is just a two-room apartment. They have to share a bathroom with three other families across the hall. The bath tub isn't clean, either.' She shudders. 'I saw it once. There's a green stain all over the bottom of the tub. The faucets have gotten mould on them. The living room's real shabby too. They don't have a machine to wash the clothes, they don't have a maid to do the laundry – '

'Seeing is believing!' Robert says. 'See an Oxydol wash! See how Oxydol washes whiter than any other soap product!'

'Bobby Jane's always very clean,' Josephine says, 'and her hair shines. She's much cleaner and tidier than me. She's got white teeth,' Josephine continues, 'as white as Celestine's. And her breath never pongs, except of peppermints.'

'Pep pep Pepsodent toothpaste,' Robert sings,

> 'Beats film on teeth and cleans breath too!
> Pep pep Pepsodent toothpaste
> Beats film on teeth – the old schedule!'

Yvonne Claybeau ignores these interruptions. 'Bobby Jane does the laundry in the sink,' she tells them, 'the same sink where she washes the dishes. They don't have a kitchen, it's just a railed-off corner of the living room. The living room smells bad. It smells of fries and beans. Ugh. It's awful.' She leans back in her chair and puts her hand over her mouth and speaks through her fingers: 'Awful.'

'Gee whizz. Golly gee. Jeepers creepers. Holy smoke.' (But irony is always lost on Yvonne.) 'I thought Bobby Jane was supposed to be your best friend. Your very best friend, you're always telling us.'

'She is too, she is so, Robert Partridge. She can come round my place any time. My mommy's always pleased to see Bobby Jane. It's not Bobby Jane's fault if she doesn't believe in Jesus, my mommy says. It's just that I'm not permitted to visit with her anymore. That's all. But it's okay, I'm never gonna tell her why I can't go to her place. I always think up reasons, so she won't ever know.'

On the way home Josephine has to circle every seventh lamp post seven times, difficult to do on skates. She makes three tours clockwise, three tours anti-clockwise, one tour clockwise.

' "The drapes in the living room aren't clean," ' Josephine lisps. (She's having a breather, between lamp posts.) ' "The whatsits have gotten mould on them. And you should see the tub – ugh" ' – she wrinkles her nose – ' "it's awful, awful dirty." '

'You haven't quite got it, if you don't mind my saying. You don't sound sweet enough. Listen. "Admiral *Clay*beau's resi-*dence*. Spea-*king*?" '

'Anyhow, I can't wait till Wednesday,' Josephine says in her own, nettled, English voice.

But on Tuesday Josephine caught a feverish summer cold, and on Wednesday she's kept in bed, where she wheezes and streams and coughs and blows.

'Poor me, I'm so disappointed.' Little moans from Josephine into a wet handkerchief. 'Poor me, poor Bobby Jane.'

Robert wants to go to Bobby Jane's place. He does not want Josephine's cold. He stands in the doorway, leaning back, trying not to breathe.

'I could go by myself, I suppose,' he says in a bored way, pinching his nose.

'She won't want you without me.' Josephine is authoritative about this.

'She'll have made cookies and cakes though. Someone ought to go. Someone has to eat them.'

'No. Yvonne told me they only had cinnamon toast when she went there. It tasted real bad, she said. But you could go down there and tell her why I can't come.'

Josephine buries her nose in the wet handkerchief. She's having to blow seven times with the right nostril, seven with the left, etcetera. It's very tiring, she tells Robert, and it makes her nose and lip sorer than ever, but what can you do?

On the way to Bobby Jane's place, Robert sees his father's old black Chevrolet parked on the opposite side of the street. The windows are down, and there is his father in the driving seat, one shirtsleeved arm hooked out of the window, fingers tapping the car roof. He's listening to the baseball game, a substitute for the cricket he misses, and something he often does if he comes home early. He chooses the car radio, he tells them, so he can listen in peace without fear of children. (It's true he does fear children and avoids them as much as possible.) Once though, when he saw Robert in the street messing around with his football, he called him over and invited him to listen to the game. Robert enjoyed this occasion – the being singled out for attention, the smell of his father's cigarette smoke, the humbugs his father produced from the glove compartment, his comments on the commentator of the game – but he doesn't want to catch his father's eye today. He puts his head down, and skates on.

Outside Meakin's store he brakes, and goes through his pockets and counts the change he finds there.

'A jar of sourballs please.'

Mr Meakin has his back turned. He's replenishing a shelf with large tins, with large cans, of cling peaches, with smaller ones of fruit cocktail.

'Libby's fruit cocktail, a great selection,
Look to Libby's for perfection!
When you go to the store, look in Libby's direction
Look to Libby's for perfection!'

'You're a crazy boy.' Mr Meakin shakes his head. He has a thin face, all lines and wrinkles, and his grey hair, closely shaved at the sides, grows like a brush on the top of his head. A bristly brush. The brush Celestine uses for the stairs. Mr Meakin wraps the sourballs in striped paper. The skin of his hands is shiny and loose; it resembles the rubber gloves he stocks, Large, Extra Large and Ladies, in a cardboard box on the counter.

'Hot day,' Mr Meakin says. 'How's your mother?' he asks. 'Your mother's a real English lady.' Mr Meakin always says this, or something like it. 'Where's your prettier half?' he says. 'I don't believe I ever saw you two folks apart.'

His mother is well, Robert tells Mr Meakin. She's gone to Garfinkel's for a new dress, or it might be a hat. His sister Josephine's in bed with a cold. 'How much are those, Mr Meakin?' He points to some bunches of red roses gasping in a bucket by the door.

'They're past their best this time of day, I guess. They should be a quarter a bunch, but I could let you have one for fifteen cents. Aw, go on. A dime.'

Outside on the sidewalk, Robert sniffs the roses. They're scentless. A few are still in bud, but the buds look too heavy for their stems and are turning black. It's obvious they will never open. This is the first time he's bought flowers for anyone and he feels foolish, holding them out in front of him as he skates along, while simultaneously trying to keep the sourball jar wedged under his other arm.

'Where are they?' Bobby Jane peers round him. She holds the street door half-open, or half-shut. She's wearing an embroidered blouse with ribbons on the sleeves. She's wearing the blue skirt with red appliqué cherries on the pockets that she often wears and that he particularly admires. He wants to flee. He speaks very fast to get his explanations and embarrassment, her disappointment, over with. When he's finished, Bobby Jane says, 'Oh. I see.' But he can tell she doesn't believe a word of his story about Josephine.

'Even if she had been allowed out of bed, we didn't think you'd want the germs.'

'No,' Bobby Jane says flatly, 'Mother mustn't catch cold. She gets real sick if she catches cold. She had pleurisy and pneumonia once, that way.'

'Josephine sent her love.'

Silence. She's waiting for something. What's she waiting for?

'Oh, and I have a message from Yvonne. She rang just before I left. She said to tell you they've got visitors, so she's got to stay in.'

'Uh-huh. Strange. She was in school today. We talked in recess. How come she never told me then?'

Silence.

'The visitors must have arrived unexpectedly.' But it sounds lame, even to him.

Silence.

'I can go home now, if you like.' Then he remembers the flowers. 'These are for your mother.' He shoves them at her. He pulls the jar of sourballs from under his other arm. 'These are for you.'

Bobby Jane says, 'Thanks.' She says she guesses he'd better come in, her mother is expecting them all. She says her mother hasn't been too well lately, that she doesn't have too many visitors right now.

He takes off his skates. He follows her through a dingy hallway. Behind them, the heavy street door clangs to, shutting out the sweltering afternoon, and locks itself.

The Dysons' living room is shabby and untidy, at first impression much as Yvonne Claybeau described it. Yet within seconds he feels at home in it, and this feeling of recognition and belonging is new: he's never felt really 'at home' at home. (He's wanted to, he's expected to, but each beginning of the school holidays when they've returned to South Kensington, and run from room to room to re-establish themselves, he's met with disappointment, solid as a wall. The ordered flat, the glassy furniture, arouse no response in him except disappointment and a vague unease.) Now, standing in Bobby Jane's living room, taking in the frayed comfort, and the books, he perceives that there will be places he can belong to and feel at ease in, and that this might be achieved without Josephine.

Yvonne Claybeau made no mention of books. They're everywhere: on shelves and tables and chairs, on the floor, on the windowsill, on the divan at the far end of the room where Bobby Jane's mother lies, propped against cushions, under a tartan rug, her back to the wall.

'That's too bad,' Mrs Dyson says when Bobby Jane has explained why Robert is on his own. 'Never mind, honey, we'll get along fine without those girls. Won't we, Robert?'

He nods. Bobby Jane says, 'Mother, Robert brought these flowers for you.' She holds out the roses. They look crushed and sad. They look almost quite dead, he decides.

'Why, aren't I the lucky one! I haven't been bunched by

a young man in years.' She touches the leaves with thin fingers, she sniffs the black buds of his scentless roses. 'Wonderful! You'd best put them in water, honey.'

And he's alone with Bobby Jane's mother.

'Pull up a chair,' she says, 'any old chair. Shove the books on the floor.'

He chooses a chair, he removes the books. Mrs Dyson reaches for a pack of Philip Morris on the table beside her. She shakes a cigarette from the pack. Her hands tremble, the matches rattle in their box, she lights up.

'Camels are milder,' he says by way of conversation. It's what the Camel advertisements are telling everyone this year.

'Which may be why they're no use to me.' Mrs Dyson inhales and then coughs. She stares intently at him. 'Tell me what it's like to be a twin,' she says. 'Tell me the good and bad, all of it. How does it feel to have someone around who looks like you and talks like you, and maybe even thinks like you? I haven't met Josephine, of course, but Roberta tells me you're very alike. I imagine you must get compared all the time. Are you able to have any kind of separate life and identity?'

No one has asked these questions before. The questions he and Josephine do get asked are usually no more than social and incurious and jokey enquiries: 'Are you the Heavenly Twins?' or 'Which twin has the Toni?' – requiring no more than a frown in reply. Mrs Dyson's questions, he senses, are real ones, but he hasn't any answers. Being a twin is just a fact of his life. He's known nothing else, so how can he say? He takes refuge in the medical dictionary he and Josephine looked up once, when they were meant to be doing their assignment.

'We're not identical twins, we're not the same sex. We came from separate eggs. We're fraternal twins. It's only by chance, by coincidence, we look alike.'

'Okay, okay, so you're not identical. But you did spend nine months together, just the two of you, in a confined space before you were born. That must count for something.'

He's thinking about this when Bobby Jane comes back into the room. She walks slowly to the window, bearing his roses in a green glass vase. She places the vase on the windowsill. The neck of the vase is too wide for so few roses, the stems will not stay down in the water, they float to the surface. The dark red flowerheads and the black buds lean almost horizontally over the rim of the vase; they look desperate to get away. They look mean. Why hadn't he bought two bunches?

'Thanks, honey,' Mrs Dyson says, 'that's pretty. How are you doing out there?'

'I'm doing okay.' Bobby Jane crosses the room without looking in Robert's direction, and goes out through the curtain.

'I have the impression you're not too happy to discuss the twin question,' Mrs Dyson says, 'so maybe we should talk about something else. I'd be interested to know,' she says, removing a cigarette from the pack, laying it on the tartan rug, 'what you plan to do or be when you're through college. When you're grown.'

Another poser. He doesn't know; he hasn't thought about it. The future, the very idea of looking forward, frightens him. 'This time last week' is something he says quite often. 'This time next week' is not a phrase he uses often; if he does use it, or something like it, it's with his fingers crossed: 'This time next week the exams will be over.' 'This time tomorrow where shall I be? Not in this academy.' But an answer is expected, and he searches the room for clues, and his eye lights on the terrifying wheelchair – why hasn't he noticed it before? – in the corner, on its canvas and leather straps and chrome. No, not a doctor. What else is there in the room? Books.

'I'm going to be a reader.'

'A reader? An academic, you mean? A publisher's reader? A proofreader?'

'I meant a writer.'

'Oh! Like your sister Josephine! Roberta told me. Two writers in the family – that's really something. Roberta doesn't plan to be a writer, I've put her off, I think. She can't abide poetry. As you know, as she'll have told you, she's figuring on being a gymnast, to teach gymnastics.'

He nods. But she hasn't told him, and Josephine hasn't told him, and he doesn't know.

You get to meet people as a teacher, Mrs Dyson continues, but it's a lonely life being a writer. Did he know that? Also, you have to have something to write about. Ideas, experiences. Does he keep a diary?

He doesn't. Josephine does. He shakes his head.

But he can make himself remember things, he suddenly tells her; and he's reasonably observant and imaginative, his mother has said.

Mrs Dyson blows a long funnel of smoke at the ceiling. He should keep a diary even so, she tells him, it's good discipline. Memory, she'd like to remind him, is only fiction. We invent our own version of the past, of history, to suit ourselves, we improve on it as time goes by. Isn't that true? Doesn't he agree?

No. No, he doesn't, no – and he's about to say so when Mrs Dyson starts off again. She's being unfair on him, she says, he hasn't lived long enough to find out. 'Why don't you go give Roberta a hand,' she says, 'she's baked a cake and some cookies. There are only three of us, so we can have a feast.'

On the other side of the curtain, in the tiny railed-off kitchen, Bobby Jane is putting plates and knives on a trolley.

'Tea's all fixed,' she says, 'I baked a cake.'

'Swansdown cake flour! More women use Swansdown cake flou-err than any other package cake flou-err in Ameri-caarr,' he informs her.

'It's Betty Crocker,' Bobby Jane says flatly.

'Just add water, mix and bake
Betty Crocker angel cake!'

'Oh sure. I made devil though. The devil mix tastes better.'

'We haven't got adverts on the wireless at home.' Something in her tone makes him think it wise to explain this.

'Wireless. Adverts. You slay me. Anyway, I know you don't. Josephine already told me, ages back.' Bobby Jane takes two glasses from a shelf and puts them on the trolley. She smiles at him suddenly. 'Milk okay with you?'

Tea is over, *The Howdy Doody Show* is over, episode six of *The Last of the Mohicans* is over. He and Bobby Jane are sitting side by side, tailor-fashion, in front of the television set. Their elbows are almost touching. They're so close he can smell Bobby Jane. It's a fresh, sweet smell, of Halo shampoo perhaps, of the Camay mild soap diet, of pep pep Pepsodent toothpaste. Bobby Jane springs up suddenly and switches off the set.

'I'd better go home now,' he says reluctantly, 'I'd better get back to Josephine.'

'Okay. You can help me do the dishes first.'

They guide the trolley between them, over the bumps and ruckles of the carpet, through the curtain. He does not tell her, of course, that he's never washed or dried a plate in his life; that at home in England, that even in America, he's not welcome in the kitchen and goes there only briefly: to get himself a drink of water, to steal a jam tart, to take a message from his mother to the cook. It would not be tactful to tell Bobby Jane any of this. But the silence now is not the comfortable one they shared minutes ago in front of the television set, sitting cross-legged with only inches between them, cramming their mouths with popcorn, passing the paper bag until it was empty. He must say something.

'I like your place. I like your mother. I'm sorry she can't walk. Perhaps she will one day.'

'No,' Bobby Jane says, 'Mother's paralysed from the waist. She won't ever walk. But you don't have to worry about it. I look after her, and the nurse visits Tuesdays and Fridays.'

Nurse? The matron at his school is called Nurse, it's the name they have to call her by. Nurse wears a flowing white headdress like a nun's, she has a chalky creased face, she wears glinty-rimmed spectacles and she blinks all the time, probably because her eyelids are encrusted with warts. After breakfast Nurse waits outside the bogs with a notebook and a two-leaded pencil, her eyes blinking and watering. You are not allowed to pull the chain until after she's inspected what you have, or haven't, done. A red tick beside your name if you've 'been', a blue cross if you've 'failed to go'. Two consecutive crosses, and she comes at you with the castor oil. All the time they've been in America he hasn't given Nurse a thought, Nurse has ceased to exist. Next time he comes out of the bog and finds her hovering and blinking, he will, he is certain, remember today. He will see Bobby Jane's arms in the sink, the dark water splashes on her skirt, this sunlight on this windowsill. He will see himself standing here beside Bobby Jane, drying blue plates, imagining Nurse.

'Why don't you like boys?' It isn't the question he meant, he has no idea why he asked it. He knows at once that it's dangerous.

'I never said I don't like boys. I don't know too many boys, not that well. Those dishes don't go there, dum dum, they go there.'

'Why do you like Josephine better than me then?'

'What kind of question is that?' Bobby Jane is drying her hands on the roller towel. She examines the palms, then she turns her hands over and inspects the backs. 'How should I know? Maybe Josephine is more my kind of person than you are. Is there a law that says I have to like you both the same? Just because you're *twins*?'

But she says this in a light way, a teasing way, that succeeds in taking some of the unkindness out of the words themselves.

*

'Come again real soon. I enjoyed your visit.'

The cigarette packet on the table beside Mrs Dyson is empty now, the ashtray full. She sounds tired. She's no longer propped up, she's lying flat with one cushion under her head. He looked away while Bobby Jane manoeuvred her mother into this position. Their intimacy was disconcerting; he could not envisage touching his own mother, taking charge of her, in the ways Bobby Jane did and was used to doing.

'I like to meet Roberta's friends,' Mrs Dyson says to the ceiling. 'Did she ever tell you her father's name was Robert? It's a good name. Come back another day, Robert, and bring your sister with you.' (Has she forgotten they sail for England on Monday?) She turns her head towards him and he sees, for the first time, the purple semi-circles, like bruises, under her eyes. She lifts a hand from the tartan rug. The fingers hang limply; he's afraid to take her hand.

'Thank you very much for having me.'

'Thank you for the tea,' he says to Bobby Jane in the hall. 'Thank you for the chocolate cake and *The Howdy Doody Show* and *The Last of the Mohicans*.'

'You're welcome.' Bobby Jane unlocks the street door and holds it open. The evening sunshine, still hot and smelling of pavement, rushes in.

'We had fun, I guess, Robert, even without your sister and Yvonne.'

He's thinking about this accolade, he's down the steps and in the street and putting on his skates, when she says something else, something he can't catch.

'What?'

'I said I can't make Yvonne out. She always accepts Mother's invitations, she always says she'll be glad to come to my place, and then she doesn't show. I don't get it.'

Bobby Jane confiding in him! How extraordinary! How amazing!

'It isn't Yvonne's fault.' For although he can't bear Yvonne, although he and Josephine have never been able to understand how Bobby Jane can be best friends with her, it isn't, strictly, her fault. 'She isn't allowed to go to your place.'

'How come?' She frowns. She seems altogether nonplussed by this.

He hasn't planned to tell her anything. He doesn't think he has. Now, having embarked, he sees that here is a way of getting back at Yvonne. But he's not sure. He wants Bobby Jane to know, and he does not want her to know. He wants both.

'*Well?*'

It's the 'well', the demanding way she says it, the impatient way she puts her hands on her hips, that decides him, that makes him explain how Yvonne isn't allowed to go to her house because they're not Catholics, and because they're poor, and because they're not the same class as the Claybeaus, whatever that might mean. He says he knows all this because Yvonne told him. She told him and Josephine. 'So it isn't Yvonne's fault, exactly.'

After this there's a silence, during which he understands that he's made a devastating and irreparable mistake.

Bobby Jane stands there for a minute, staring at him. Then she tucks her skirt underneath her and sits down on the step. She rests her head on her knees. With the index finger of her right hand she begins drawing slow circles on the step. Big circles and bigger circles, smaller circles, figures of eight.

'You shouldn't have told me that. I didn't want to know that. I never wanted to know any of that.' She doesn't look at him. She's looking at her finger, the one that's making loops and circles on the step. He keeps his eye on the finger.

'What you just told me hurts. I never did anything to hurt you, Robert Partridge.' The finger slows, then stops. 'Yvonne would never tell me what you just did. Josephine would never tell me those things. Josephine may be crazy in some ways, she may be some kind of nut with all that counting stuff, but she'd never say anything to hurt me.'

He keeps his eye on Bobby Jane's finger. The finger's important. It's important to keep his eye on it. It's drawing zigzags now, or mountain ranges. The Alps, the Rockies, the Pennine Chain. Zigzag. Zigzag. Zigzagzig.

'How would you like it if I told you the roses you brought my mother were just dead old roses, ready for the garbage? How would you like it if I told you I don't eat hard candy? You wouldn't. But I wouldn't say those things.'

But she just has. She's just said them.

'It's an odd feeling,' Bobby Jane says slowly. 'Yvonne is my best friend, and I can't see her anymore. Mother'll want to know why I don't go round the Claybeaus' place and I won't be able to tell her. I'll have to fib. I'll have to *lie*.' She pauses. 'I've been friends with Yvonne since we started grade school. We're in the same class. There's no one else in our class lives on this block. There's no one else my age, even. There's no one else at all.'

She gets up from the step. He's aware that she's staring at him – or is it through him? She says, she shouts, 'I want to forget those things you said just now!'

He shakes his head, he can't say anything. What can he say? All of a sudden he wants his twin, he wants Josephine. If Josephine were here . . .

Josephine? Josephine's in bed, sneezing and blowing. Waiting. Waiting for the moment he'll come round the door, so she can pat the bedclothes and say, 'Go on, tell me. Tell me all about it, every single detail.'

'I have to go now,' Bobby Jane says. She takes the street-door key from her pocket. 'I have to get back to Mother. Mother'll need to go to the bathroom.'

And she's gone. She's gone inside without saying goodbye, without saying another word.

They're on the boat going home. The SS *Parthia* is a let-down after the *Queen Mary*, a slow small tub that takes seven days to make the crossing, whose menus and menu cards and gymnasium leave a lot to be desired. On the boat, Robert invents a new ending for his visit to Bobby Jane's place.

In this new ending, Bobby Jane doesn't confide in him
about Yvonne. Yvonne isn't mentioned, she simply doesn't
come up. He and Bobby Jane say goodbye, in a friendly,
reluctant way, on the step. She smiles and thanks him for
the sourballs – her favourite candy, she says. At the last
minute he bends down (bends down? No, he can't do that,
she's taller than he is), he leans forward and kisses her
cheek.

Later on, hunched under the grand piano in the Music
Room during the hobbies period they have at that school
on wet Saturdays, he'll remove the kiss as being unlikely,
as being not something he'd have the courage to do. (As
being not something Bobby Jane would accept. She would
probably have ducked, he'll realise, or pushed him off:
'Hey, what's with all this kissing stuff?' She would have
giggled. Or slapped his face.) The kiss is too much at odds
with what actually happened, so far from the truth it only
manages to point the truth up. So he'll get rid of it. Eventually, for the same reason, he'll reject the bit about sourballs being Bobby Jane's favourite candy.

But the new story won't stick, it refuses to stay down, in
the way that a badly gummed label on a used envelope
refuses, curling back instead to reveal an earlier, and more
authentic, life.

Years later, considering these events, Robert will decide
that when Mrs Dyson suggested that people reinvent the
past to suit themselves, she must have meant the process,
largely unconscious, whereby subtle, gradual shifts and
repositionings and blurrings occur deep in the mind. Shifts
of perspective, repositionings of events, blurrings of motive,
that will be transmuted, in the course of time, into real
distortions. That will emerge, eventually, as full-blown
fictions. As downright lies. As the truth. Mrs Dyson must
have been talking about self-deception.

She could not have meant that facts can be altered at will
(or by an act of will), and the mind, the cosmic centre, the
conscience, accept them.

Robert's invented version, polished and improved on,

will not be the one that returns to him in dreams. It will remain, at most, an alternative, somewhere alongside, but never supplanting, the truth.

The truth? In middle age, when the twins are reminiscing ('Remember *The Dead Toreador*? Remember the blood on his shirt? Remember when we lay on the floor of the gallery and imagined ourselves dead?') about that time in Washington DC ('Murder capital of the US now!'), Josephine will say that that business at the end with Bobby Jane 'happened, in fact, if you want to know, Rob' to her. That it was he who was stuck in bed with a cold. That he never set foot in the Dysons' flat the whole time they were in Washington. He only remembers it, he only thinks he remembers it, Josephine will say – pacing up and down, stubbing out her umpteenth cigarette, lighting another – because she confessed it at the time. It's her story, Josephine will insist. Her nightmare. It was never his.

Uncle Victor

We were avid readers of fairy tales when we were small. In fairy tales, the youngest son is the favoured son. Favoured by life, and also by the narrator. Youngest equals beautiful, good, brave, intelligent, true. It is the youngest, when his elder brothers have failed – through stupidity or laziness – their tasks, who will succeed; who will slay the three-headed monster, who will win the princess's hand, who will rule the peaceable kingdom, who will live happily ever after.

Of our Uncle Victor, youngest son of our paternal grandparents and the black sheep of the family, Father once said, 'Should a stranger stop you in the street and say, "I'm your uncle, lend me half a crown" – never fear, he will be.'

We were children at the time, Althea, Amarantha, Lucasta, Chloris, and I, Dianeme (our names allotted to us, as we came along, from Father's passion for the Cavalier Poets whose study he was making his life's work). Gratiana was a baby still, or perhaps not even born.

Years later, when we were all, excluding Gratiana, grown-up, I reminded Father of his stranger-in-the-street remark. I expected him to say, 'Too true,' or to smile a wry smile. He didn't. He said, 'You know, Dianeme, I think I've been a bit rough on Victor. He's not a bad man. He has, after all, had a change of heart.'

A change of heart? Uncle Victor? Maybe Father was joking, his style of humour was so flat and dry it caught us out often. I looked at him. He was propped against the pillows, staring out of the window in an absent, abstracted way. I remember being worried by this, and then almost immediately consoling myself with the thought: Father's not himself because he has a fever; he's light-headed.

Father was feverish, if cold sweats can be called fever. A lassitude, a vague melancholy, which had overtaken him at the end of November, had turned into a cough, which had turned into – what? Somewhere around that point, the point of the question mark, he'd taken to his bed. He certainly didn't look well, but the truth is, he never did. He was one of the those tall, spare, pale men who, essentially robust, never give the impression of health. We were concerned about him, of course, but not really anxious. We were expecting him to be on his feet, and feeling fine, by Christmas Day.

The reason why I reminded Father of his long ago summing-up of our uncle was because of the flowers that had arrived that morning. They'd been sent by Victor. The night before, he'd telephoned, demanding to speak to Father. 'You can't,' Mother had told him, 'he's not well. He's in bed. Out of the question, Victor. Goodbye.' And she'd replaced the receiver before he could argue.

Uncle Victor's flowers stood in a jug on Father's bedside table. Blood-red roses and gladioli, white arum lilies. Crude, stiff, and, apart from the lilies, scentless blooms.

'He must have been to the cemetery and pinched them off a grave' – Mother's conclusion as she stripped the leaves and did her best to tweak some life into the arrangement.

Father, too, would surely have something sharp to say about this dubious tribute, and the message that accompanied it: 'Sorry to hear you're under the weather – chin up, old cove – Victor.' He hadn't. He fingered the roses; he read the message on the card. Then he laid the card gently on the counterpane and held it there, between a graceful finger and thumb.

Uncle Victor, given the name because he was born in 1918, and on Armistice Day, was a petty crook and a con man. We knew this, my five sisters and I, when we were old enough to know it; when we were, in turn, aware enough to be curious about the words 'embezzlement, fraud, counterfeit, bail, bailiff, Old Bailey, Wormwood Scrubs' — words that stood out, as though underlined or ringed round, from half-heard, half-understood conversations, and from behind half-closed doors.

Then there were the discussions that took place at breakfast and which were conducted over the tops of our heads. These had to do with certain letters Father received, written on what appeared to be lavatory paper, and contained in serious envelopes.

'To Althea, from prison.' Father dropped a lavatory paper letter on to my eldest sister's plate. 'Pass it along to your mother.'

Mother put on her spectacles to read the letter, and when she had done so she whipped them off again. She was furious.

'It's your mother's fault,' she told Father. 'She never stood up to him, she never said no to him. She always let him have his own way.'

'Too true,' Father said — and he stroked his nose, a habit of his — 'too true.'

'It's your father's fault,' Mother told Father (this was on another, not dissimilar, occasion). 'If he hadn't run off with all those trollops, if he hadn't abandoned the three of you when Victor was only a baby, Victor might have turned out, well, differently. What he needed, what he lacked, was a firm, father's hand.'

Father, who from the age of eight had not had a father's hand himself, but who had turned out very differently from Uncle Victor, said nothing. He spread his own hands on the table and examined them, as if for clues.

Father's hands were beautiful: long-fingered, oval-nailed, sensitive — yet masculine. Exceptional hands. We could see this for ourselves without Mother's telling us, though she did tell us, often.

'Hands are a giveaway,' Mother used to tell us, 'you can't disguise them. You can tell a lot from hands.'

'I couldn't marry your father for his money,' Mother told us, *ad nauseam*, 'because he hadn't any. I married him for his hands.'

Which surprised us. We'd imagined Mother had married Father for his interesting mind, or blue eyes, or handsome face; or simply because she was dying of love for him.

Our paternal grandfather, begetter of Father and Uncle Victor (and also of Tobias, the second son, who died in infancy when Father was three), was a rake. Not a black sheep. The difference, we were given to understand, being that, although he was a womaniser, a gambler and a profligate, Grandfather's activities were not, in the eyes of the law at any rate, criminal. Added to which, he had charm, Father said.

Didn't Uncle Victor have charm?

Not so you'd notice, according to Father.

What did he have then? We needed to know. He was the one uncle we had, Mother being an only child, and he haunted our home life: a ghost in the machinery of solicitors' letters and unpaid bills and reverse-charge telephone calls; yet we never met him. He did come to what Mother scornfully referred to as 'our sardine tin in Divinity Road' occasionally, but at night time, when we were in bed, or during the day in term time, when we were at school. After his visits, so she told us, Mother would check up on the silver and her two pieces of jewellery and Father's first editions. Having reassured herself on that score, she would run from room to room and throw open all the windows wide. She did this to let the devil out, she said.

The devil? Could it be that Mother, who in our experience feared no one, was in some way afraid of Uncle Victor? Did he, perhaps, have horns and a tail?

There were only old photographs in old albums to go on. In these, so far as we could tell from the bleached sepia, he was dark-haired and curly-haired, white-smocked and frilled, and he had fat knees. Old family snapshots and studio portraits are fascinating, of course, and we were fascinated; but they were no real help in the quest for our diabolical uncle. We consulted Father.

Victor's looks were undistinguished; no, he would rephrase that, they were ordinary, Father told us.

Ordinary?

'Yes, ordinary.' Father sounded bored, not to say irritated. We'd caught him in the boxroom that doubled as his study, trying to work. (Now that I think about it, it's a wonder that anything of an intellectual nature was achieved in that crammed cubbyhole. On the occasions when Father forgot to lock the door, we were in there in a flash, climbing over cots and pram wheels and golf bags and chipped picture frames to rummage through suitcases of old letters; or, in a sudden burst of nostalgia, to seek for some long-discarded plaything we'd decided we couldn't, after all, live without.) Our uncle was, Father said, 'nondescript. If you must have a description, well then, on the small side, on the stout side. Balding.'

How extraordinary. Father six foot five and very thin. With thick, white, straight hair – fine hair, that fell over his eyes when he was working, so that he had continually to push it back with his hand. Uncle Victor short and fat. And hairless.

But perhaps Father was having us on.

We tried again: Uncle Victor must have the family eyes, at least, mustn't he?

The family eyes were blue, a bright electric blue. Our grandfather, The Rake, had had them. We'd all inherited them. Even Mother had blue eyes of a sort. Father's were the bluest and most dazzling of all. 'A sailor's eyes,' Mother insisted, though there'd been no seafarers on Father's side of the family, so far as anyone knew.

'Victor's eyes are brown,' Father said, 'boot-polish brown, if you like. Almost black. Goodbye, and shut the door behind you.'

*

'Once upon a time, in the land beyond the mountains, there lived a merchant who had three sons . . . '

While we were curled in our corners, devouring our fairy tales, the youngest son of our grandparents was busy as usual. He broke into the coinboxes of gas meters and public telephones. He rode on underground trains without benefit of ticket. He forged cheques and insurance claims. He opened, but neglected to settle, accounts in high-class London shops, demands for whose payment would eventually find their way to our own front-door mat. And he 'borrowed' from anyone who was fool enough to 'lend' – women mostly: vulnerable widows; barmaids whose brassy exteriors concealed hearts of gold; a succession of dubious, live-in, lady friends. When these and other sources failed, he petitioned Father: 'Dear Hal, Find myself a bit strapped for readies at present and wonder if you could see your way . . . ' The excuses he gave were that he'd fallen on hard times and was behind with the rent; that he'd fallen downstairs and broken his leg; that he'd lost, through no fault of his own, of course, his job; that he'd lost his wallet. Naturally Father was never taken in by any of these. Our uncle had seldom been in honest employ for more than a fortnight without being sacked for 'misappropriation of funds' (fingers in the till, was Father's translation of this); and the one job, as a packer in a firework factory, he'd managed to keep for three months had had explosive consequences. Father, as I say, was never taken in, and his comments were sardonic. Nevertheless, he would get out his chequebook.

Which made Mother furious. 'He'll bleed you dry, Hal. You should let him stew. He'll bleed us all dry.'

We sympathised with Mother. She had come from Nowhere, she was fond of telling us, and was determined to get Somewhere. She had her sights on smart North Oxford, on the leafy filling of the Woodstock and Banbury Roads sandwich, and in anticipation of this move up in the world we were forced to attend Matins at St Margaret's every Sunday. Uncle Victor was to blame, entirely to blame, for the delay in achieving her heart's desire. As for us children, we needed new shoes and winter coats; we wanted bikes. Father had no illusions about Uncle Victor – so why bail him out?

It was more complex than we understood at the time. Father bailed out Uncle Victor and paid his debts in order to protect Grandmother, throughout our childhoods bed-ridden with arthritis in an Abingdon nursing home (the fees, of course, were paid by Father). Uncle Victor's begging letters amounted to blackmail. If Father didn't cough up, Victor would go straight to Grandmother and wheedle out of her what pathetic savings she had left.

Grandmother was deaf to any word against Uncle Victor. Whatever had gone wrong in his life, it was no fault of his. He was her own dear sweet boy, her blue-eyed boy, the generous son who sent her flowers.

'Look, darlings, at the beautiful roses kind Uncle Victor has sent your poor old granny!'

We looked. Grandmother's room was indeed a bower. We looked at Father, who'd brought us on the bus. (Mother never accompanied us on these visits; her blood pressure couldn't stand it, she said.) Father stroked his nose and raised his blue eyes to the ceiling. The roses must have fallen off the back of a florist's van, was his conclusion on the journey home.

'Victor started out on his blackmailing career very early, you know.' Father confided this, matter-of-factly and between mouthfuls of toast and Cooper's Oxford, apropos of a letter from our uncle that had just been delivered. 'From the age of about five he'd corner me and threaten: "If you don't hand over that sixpence" – or penknife, or whatever – "this minute, I'm going to kick Mother." I called his bluff the first time and he did kick your grandmother.'

Althea, Amarantha and Lucasta were approaching their teens when we learned this, and old enough to be shocked. They were shocked. Poor Father! What a terrible story! It

was the worst, quite the worst, thing they'd heard about
Uncle Victor to date.

The following day they put the volumes of Grimm,
Andersen, Lang, Perrault, Dulac, etcetera, into their satch-
els, and lugged them down to the school library.

The librarian, so they informed us afterwards, seemed
pleased, if surprised. She checked through the books, she
examined the flyleaves and the title pages, she lifted
the tissue veils guarding coloured plates, she pored and
lingered. 'These are very nice, Althea. Some of them, I'd
say, are valuable. Are you quite sure it's all right to make
this donation?' Althea nodded: she was quite sure. She did
not explain that the sacrifice – though it has to be said,
our three elder sisters had moved on to ghost stories by
then – was for Father, and for all hard-done-by eldest
sons, everywhere.

When Father was told of these events he was surprised,
and not pleased. His daughters had no business to rob their
unborn children, his grandchildren, of their inheritance.
The Dulac had been a christening present to Lucasta from
the Master of Balliol, he reminded them. The Violet and
the Green Fairy Books were first editions, the Perrault a
collector's piece. Were they cretins, or what?

Later, he relented a little. They hadn't burned the books,
which was something. They hadn't made a fast buck out
of them. Their criminal careers were not yet assured.

Keeping Uncle Victor out of prison while our grandmother
was alive was Father's aim, but as I've indicated, he didn't
always succeed. He didn't succeed when our uncle was
apprehended in the vicinity of an unattended newspaper
stand, his coat and trouser pockets weighted with pennies
and halfpennies and farthings and threepenny bits. ('How
low can you go?' Mother was beside herself. 'How low can
you go?') Then there was the Encyclopaedia Affair.

As usual, we heard about it over breakfast.

'My enterprising brother Victor has been selling encyclopaedias door to door,' Father began.

Mother had one eye on the clock; she was trying to get us off to school: Amarantha and Lucasta had A-levels looming. All right, so it wasn't an occupation for gentlemen, she said, but Victor wasn't a gentleman, and at least they were encyclopaedias, not brushes.

Father ran an exceptional finger down the length of his nose. That was not the problem, he told Mother. The problem was, there were no encyclopaedias. Victor had merely had order forms and a pamphlet printed, and gone round the houses with those. At the top of the pamphlet was a list of luminaries who unreservedly recommended the encyclopaedia. The luminaries included scholars and academics, one of whom was Father.

Father was wrong, we decided. Uncle Victor must have charm. How else had he persuaded all those housewives to draw out their National Savings, and pay cash in advance – entitling them to a discount of ten per cent – for a thirty-six-volume encyclopaedia that didn't exist?

Father did get up for Christmas Day, but he wasn't better. He was weaker than any kitten. On Boxing Day he went back to bed.

'Rest, and a light, nourishing diet,' the doctor said. 'Aspirin four-hourly; plenty of fluids.' He didn't seem to know exactly what was wrong with Father, what Father had got.

'There are so many bugs flying around this time of year, it's hard to say,' said the doctor, a man prone to hedge his bets.

What was wrong with Father? And why didn't he fight? Did the knowledge that his *œuvre* on the Cavalier Poets was at last completed, and with the printers, give him no satisfaction at all? Why wouldn't he eat?

'I'm not hungry, I'm tired,' Father said, 'thank you all the same.'

Uncle Victor, meanwhile, was telephoning every day, often twice; and eventually Mother took the receiver off its cradle. She couldn't stop the bouquets coming, though, nor the crates of Dom Perignon, nor the Special Christmas Hamper of *foie gras* and beluga caviar and potted shrimps and Parma ham. (The bills for these, from Moyses Stevens of Bruton Street, from Berry Brothers of St James's and Jacksons of Piccadilly, arrived early in January, but by that time Father was dead.)

It would be a partridge in a pear tree next, Mother didn't doubt.

Father was staring out of the window, and seemed miles away. 'How kind of Victor, how extraordinarily kind,' he murmured, lying back on his pillows, sniffing a blood-red, scentless rose.

There was no way of preventing Uncle Victor from attending Father's funeral. He was bound to see the notice in *The Times* or the *Daily Telegraph*.

He was immediately recognisable. On the short side, on the stout side, bald. The one brown coat amongst all the black and grey ones. Fur collar. Fur gloves. Cigarette hanging from his mouth. As we helped Mother from the car, he let the butt drop at his feet, and then ground it slowly with one desert-sand suede toe.

'One good thing, I suppose' – Lucasta turned to me in the porch – 'if our uncle's here, he can hardly be at home, pinching the silver.' There'd been a spate of what the media called 'bereavement thefts' in the Oxford area in recent weeks.

Mother had decided on family and close friends only for the funeral – a memorial service was to be held later in Christ Church cathedral. These old friends of hers and Father's were invited to the wake afterwards, at Divinity Road. We didn't see how we could stop Uncle Victor joining them. (But we did manage to stop him climbing into the hired car with Mother. There hadn't been room enough in it for all of us as it was: Althea, Amarantha, Lucasta and Gratiana had driven to the church with Mother; Chloris and I had followed in Mother's old Ford.)

'Uncle Victor, you had better come with Dianeme and me,' Chloris ordered him with a smile cold as the grave.

I drove; Chloris sat beside me. Uncle Victor, reeking of whisky and never-emptied ashtrays, took up the back seat. Chloris and I were silent; not unnaturally, neither of us felt like talking.

Uncle Victor talked all the way back to Divinity Road.

'This is a sad business,' Uncle Victor said, trumpeting into a red silk handkerchief, 'a sad, sad business . . . '

'Your father was a wonderful brother to me,' Uncle Victor said, and he wound down the window and tossed an empty cigarette packet into a passing hedge, 'I remember when . . . '

'I still recall the day . . . ' Uncle Victor droned on.

We tried not to listen to him. And I tried not to catch his eye — boot-polish brown, as Father said — in the driving mirror, but it was impossible: there were so many roundabouts and crossroads and junctions between St Margaret's and home.

'Constance — your dear mother — will have needs now . . . She will be in need of comfort and support,' Uncle Victor said, pulling off his horrible gloves, fumbling in his pockets for more fags, and for matches. 'You may rest assured I shall do all in my power . . . either of you young ladies care for a smoke?'

Uncle Victor lit up as I changed down for the corner. It was then, in the glass and for the space of a heartbeat, I saw them: Father's hands — his beautiful, his *exceptional* hands! — shielding the flame.

Habits

What is it keeps some married couples together long after their Best Before date – you know, when they're no longer compatible, when they don't even like each other any more, and when divorce has lost its stigma and is relatively painless to achieve? You can never guess, can you, which of your married friends will break up and which will stick it out; in fact haven't you noticed that very often it's the most unlikely ones, the obviously miserable ones, who stay the course, whereas the marriages that always seemed to you to have been made in heaven blow apart? And why should that be?

It was a stranger at a party who asked these questions of Nessa (they'd both had a fair amount to drink at the time). He didn't wait for her reply. Instead, he told her his theory, which was that unhappiness is a stronger bond than happiness. That would account, wouldn't it, for all those henpecked husbands and battered wives you read about, who find it impossible to break away?

The stranger leaned towards Nessa and smiled at her with the intimacy only a stranger can afford. He tapped her empty glass and asked her, how would it be if he were to go and get them both a refill?

This encounter took place a few days ago. At the time, Nessa had felt got at. The stranger couldn't have known anything about her marriage – he and Nessa hadn't been introduced and hadn't even bothered to swap names – nevertheless she felt he'd somehow, perhaps with the special, specious intuition of the inebriated, decided she was a battered wife, or Otto a henpecked husband. It was only afterwards that she considered the questions themselves, in particular the first one, the one about what it is keeps people together long after their Best Before date, as the stranger had put it. What was it kept her and Otto together then? Could it be they were bonded by unhappiness merely? What a terrible thought! What a throat-cutting idea!

'Was he right? Is that all we've got going for us?' Nessa asked her best friend Lindsey, via the telephone. (It was Lindsey's call, a Christmas call, ten days early because she and Duncan were off to Spain for the holiday, the first time ever they'd done such a thing.) Nessa and Lindsey talk a lot on the telephone. There was a time when they wrote letters to each other, long ones at regular intervals, but they haven't for years – no one Nessa knows writes letters any more. They do send each other postcards and they talk on the telephone, once every ten days or so, taking it in turns to foot the bill – for their husbands to foot the bill. In these calls they discuss Lindsey's children, the books they're reading, the films they've been to see or want to see, the television programmes they've watched or missed, people they both know. Sometimes, in a frivolous mood, whole conversations will be conducted in French, in school-text-book French:

'Eh bien, mon brave, qu'est-ce tu as fait ce matin?'

'Alors, je suis allée au marché acheter des légumes. J'ai envie de préparer une bonne soupe pour mon mari.'

'De bons légumes? Pour faire cette bonne soupe?'

'Mais bien sûr, de bons légumes!'

'Quelles sortes de légumes as tu achetées, dis donc?'

'J'ai acheté un kilo de carottes, et puis . . . '

'De bonnes carottes?'

'Assurément, de bonnes carottes!'

'You and Lindsey were made for each other. I can't think why you didn't get married' – Otto, jokey but sharp, coming in on the end of one of these exchanges.

Nessa and Lindsey talk seriously about serious things; they discuss their worries and their fears. Cancer, for example. They are both in their forties now, the age when breasts and wombs and cervixes become vulnerable, the time when X-rays and smear tests are advisable. Lindsey believes in preventative medicine and regular check-ups, but Nessa has a theory about cancer which is that if it hasn't been diagnosed it doesn't exist. Should you discover a small hard lump in your armpit, say (Nessa's theory goes), do nothing and it'll turn out the lump was only a boil. See your doctor, spill the beans, and before you know it you'll be under the scanner or being force-fed barium meal. And after that? Operations, radiotherapy, chemotherapy and downhill all the way. – Which was superstitious nonsense, in Lindsey's view. Dangerous nonsense. 'Jonnie would have been dead years ago if my mother'd gone along with your theory.' (Lindsey's younger brother Jonnie developed cancer of the femur when he was twelve. They'd had to amputate the leg, but Jonnie'd been okay. He was still okay, alive and kicking his umpteenth artificial limb, at thirty-four.)

'D'you think unhappiness really is our only bond?' Nessa asked Lindsey, in the course of Lindsey's Christmas call.

Lindsey said no, no she didn't think it was as dire as that. Marriage was complicated. Just as you couldn't tell, from the outside, what kept seemingly incompatible people together, so you probably couldn't tell from the inside, either. Also, habit came into it. It was often habit kept people together when they shouldn't be. Habits were hard to break. 'I mean, look at you and Otto, you've neither of you given up smoking for all your talk. You refer to your "cancer tubes", you make jokes about iron lungs and respirators, but you don't give it up.'

Nessa said she thought that was quite a neat analogy, though not comforting. And she did not tell Lindsey that Otto had cut down recently, from two packets to less than one a day.

Lindsey said that, strangely enough, it was habit, habits rather, she'd missed most when she and Mike split up. (Mike was Lindsey's first husband, and the father of her two children, Angus and Elaine.) She'd never thought about the habits, she'd never imagined she'd miss them, but then when they split up she did.

'What sort of habits?' Nessa wanted to know.

'Well, I can't remember them all now. But I do remember missing Mike saying things like, "I don't believe you've met my wife," to office colleagues and so on, and I missed my being able to say, "I think you'd better consult my husband on that one!" That habit – the habit of belonging, I suppose you could call it.'

Nessa stared at the stoneware jug on the table beside her that Otto's first wife had made and considered this habit, one she was familiar with. She thought: Do I enjoy it? At some level or other? Would I miss it? And decided that yes, she would. Unfortunately, she would. Yes.

Another thing she'd missed, Lindsey remembered, was being a unit, a hyphenated-sounding unit, Mike-and-Lindsey on Christmas cards and invitations, 'a sound and shape our friends all knew, that they recognised as being us'. She'd imagined, she told Nessa, that being just Lindsey again after she and Mike parted would feel like freedom, would restore her premarital sense of identity, but it hadn't. Rather the reverse. And wasn't that odd? Wasn't that an odd thing for a good feminist to feel?

That was the snare of being a woman, Nessa suggested, a woman of their age and class. (Nessa and Lindsey liked to imagine that they, or at least their roots, were working class. Which was crap, according to Otto. No street-corner tobacconist – Nessa's father – and no railway clerk – Lindsey's – was ever working class. Anyway, what about their grammar school education? Lower middle was their roots, middle was what they had become. Sorry, lassies.) 'Working class women of our age were brought up to believe that marriage is the be all and end all.'

'How's your best friend Marion, lovey?' Lindsey asked. 'Seen anything of her lately?'

This question, which anyone listening in would have been likely to consider innocent and genuine, for that is how Lindsey made it sound, was nothing of the sort. It was a tease. The truth was, Nessa did not like Marion, who was a neighbour of hers, and had never considered her a friend, merely as another – irritating and younger – woman, down the road. One thing Nessa didn't like about Marion was the habit she had of calling Nessa 'lovey', and of prefacing remarks with 'If you don't mind my saying'. Nessa usually did mind. 'If you don't mind my saying, lovey, blue is not your colour' – Marion, having watched Nessa lug the dustbin down the steps and on to the pavement, had sidled up and tapped her on the shoulder of her ultramarine sweater, first new garment in months.

'Funny you should ask,' Nessa said, 'I've been seeing a lot of her lately. We've really got a lot going for each other. I'm currently, at this moment in time, into a book she lent me. It's called *Uncoupling*, it's about wanting out and letting go, and it really engages with the issues, believe you me.'

It was true that Marion had lent Nessa a book called *Uncoupling*. Nessa hadn't asked to read it. Marion had got the book out of the library, and told Nessa it was an instructive, in many ways corroborative, read. Nessa ought to read it, Marion said. 'If you don't mind my saying so, lovey, it would concentrate your mind.' (Not long before this, she'd told Nessa that it was high time Nessa stopped playing a walk-on role to Otto's starring one. Nessa should leave Otto, Marion said, so that she could find herself and get to know herself and get to like herself, and use her talents and regain her self-respect and start living. Marion, who often looked careworn; who had mortgage problems and problems with her children – Barney was bedwetting, Natalie had been caught telling lies at school – was not a good advertisement for the manless life she advocated.)

'Is this your call or mine, by the bye?' Lindsey said. 'Ye gods, it's mine! Duncan will murder me. He's threatening to make me pay the whole of the last bill. "You made the calls, you pick up the tab" was how he charmingly put it.'

There was another habit, one that women shared (Nessa thought after Lindsey had rung off) which was to mention

their husbands in what sounded like a derogatory way, a
putting-down way, when all they were really doing was
expressing pride in owning, and being owned by, a man.

Most evenings after supper, if they were alone, Otto and
Nessa sat in the sitting room and listened to music – to
classical orchestral, Mozart opera, jazz. They listened in
silence. Nessa sipped a glass of red wine and stitched away
– she'd been making a patchwork quilt for three years
now; the 'bitbags' beside her chair had become permanent
fixtures. Her eyesight had got weaker since she started out,
her magnifiers stronger; even so her fingers were pin-
cushions, and she had to work right under the lamp, peering
and blinking, crick in the neck, ache in the back, pain in
the heart. And Otto?

Otto would lie back in his armchair, black leather and
steel, his eyes closed, his hands stuck to the frosted whisky
glass in his lap. Every so often he would push himself up
and transport his empty glass to the bookcase where the
whisky bottle and the water jug and the ice bucket were.
Every so often, when an uncompanionable silence fell, he
would spur himself to change the tape or the record. When
they were first married, and for several years afterwards,
Otto's travels within a room had been achieved by little
sprints and leaps and pirouettes, the floor beneath him
elastic as a trampoline; but for some time now his con-
trolled exuberance had for the most part been replaced by
a meandering stumble, a preoccupied shamble. Not that age
and whisky must have been wholly to blame. In congenial
company, Otto could still perform in his old manner, no
matter how much whisky he'd sunk; and in his studio –
where Nessa was rarely welcome – he would still bound
from canvas to paintpot. Once, arriving at his studio with
an urgent message, Nessa had surprised Otto conducting
the overture to *Figaro*, playing on the tape deck. From the
doorway she watched as he brought the violins in and
then banished them, nodded his furious head, pointed an

accusing finger at the woodwind, flung both arms wide, embraced himself.

Television bored Otto. Any programme Nessa wanted to see she watched by herself in the kitchen, bolt upright on a hard chair, her face within inches of the Sony portable's small face. Come and see this, Otto! It would really interest you! – For years, Nessa, who believed she wanted to share everything, whatever it was, with her husband, had run to the living room with her enthusiasms and offered them up like presents, although for an equal number of years since, she had not.

It's evening, a Tuesday, ten days before Christmas. Otto and Nessa are in the living room of their Hammersmith house. John Coltrane is playing on the Bang & Olufsen. Nessa is seated at a table in the window, writing Christmas cards. On the table is a pile of cards and another one of envelopes, plus the address book Nessa is working from. Working through.

Nessa's writing her cards, getting on with it, but her mind is elsewhere. This morning something momentous and terrible happened. This morning she learned something about Otto that she must tackle him with. She doesn't want to, but she must. She doesn't want to think about any of it. She can't stop thinking about it.

From time to time Nessa looks across to Otto, asleep in his armchair. (No, not asleep; although his eyes are closed, he can't be: his right hand is still gripping the whisky glass in his lap.) She gives him quick, surreptitious glances and long hard stares. In her head she's asking him: Is it true? and Who are you, Otto? WHO ARE YOU?

Out loud she asks him, 'Do you want me to send a card to the Donaldsons?' She feels she has to ask this because eighteen months or so ago Otto and Jim Donaldson fell out, a serious falling-out that hasn't been repaired. Nessa still doesn't know what it was about because Otto's stone-walled her each time she's asked. The Donaldsons are, or were, old friends, perhaps their best 'married couple' friends. Otto and Nessa used to go on holiday with the Donaldsons. Christmases were spent with them, at the weekend cottage they own in Suffolk. Nessa regrets the loss of this friendship, the discussions and arguments and jokes, the horseplay which could sometimes go too far, the freezing walks along Minsmere Cliffs. She regrets the loss of the Donaldsons' two boys, Danny and Sam, in particular Sam, the youngest, with whom she'd always had a rapport. She misses the evenings of Rummy and Oh Hell, and the steady wine-drinking that had accompanied these. Most, she misses Maura, Jim's wife, her accomplice in holiday kitchens and on holiday shopping expeditions, her ally in the ongoing war against the menfolk (this was the term, enclosed by invisible inverted commas, they used for Otto and Jim and Danny and Sam). 'What's up with the menfolk, then?' 'Can it be the menfolk have gone dahn the boozer?' 'Well, that's the menfolk for you!' A lot of giggling accompanied the menfolk talk. A lot of fooling around went on while they were preparing the menfolk's breakfasts and lunches and teas. A lot of drinking was done while they concocted the menfolk's suppers. Oddly, and hurtfully – for it wasn't their quarrel – Maura hasn't been in touch since Otto and Jim's bust-up, although Nessa has written two postcards to her. Sending the Donaldsons a Christmas card this year might (Nessa thought this at breakfast this morning; now she thinks: What does it matter? What the hell does any of this matter?) go some way to healing the rift.

'You can send the Donaldsons anything you like.' Otto takes a swig of whisky that nearly empties the glass. 'So long as you don't put my name to it.'

This Christmas will be the first nobody has asked them over for, not the Donaldsons, of course, not Otto's three married sisters in the home counties, not Nessa's weirdo Cousin Alec, not her mother and younger brother in Arbroath. For the first time in twenty years of marriage, Otto and Nessa will, barring a last-minute reprieve, be spending Christmas in London. Alone.

Neither of them has ever rated Christmas, mind you. Every October, when tinsel and coloured lights take over her local stationers and supermarket, Nessa says she'd abolish Christmas if she could, that Christmas is a farce. She won't be sending cards this year, she says, or presents. Perhaps she doesn't mean this: she always does. She buys presents for her relations and for Otto's, she chooses them for Otto's godchildren as well as her own. When the presents are wrapped, Otto writes his name on the label. He writes 'Otto', or 'Uncle Otto', or 'Your Favourite Brother-in-Law' in the space Nessa points to on the tag. She always tells him what the parcel contains so that he knows, so that he has no excuse for not knowing, so that he won't be caught out. What a waste of time! Otto never remembers, or pretends not to, and he's usually plastered by noon on Christmas Day. When a nephew runs at him with a novelty pen or a radio-controlled police Land Rover and cries, 'Thank you, Uncle Otto, it's just what I wanted!' Otto looks amazed. 'Did I give you that? Don't thank me! Thank your Aunt Nessa – she chose it, she bought it, she wrapped it up – all I did was pay for it!' Why does Otto do this? What makes him want to show himself in such an unendearing light always?

'I am me,' Otto says grandly, 'I am how I am. If you don't like it, too bad.'

Some people don't like it. Too bad for them. Once – this was years ago – at a supper party at friends, Otto (who'd had three double whiskies before leaving home) announced over the vichyssoise: 'What a bourgeois collection! What witless conversation! What dull pointless lives!' In the silence that followed, while shocked eyebrows were being raised and wounded looks exchanged, Otto picked up his spoon and carried on with his soup. The following day Nessa asked him, shouldn't he write to Harry and Joanie and apologise? For all those things he'd said? Why should he, replied Otto, when he hadn't said them? He had no memory of saying them, therefore he hadn't said them, therefore Nessa was making it up. When Nessa told him, exactly, precisely, what he had said, he was very amused. Or he pretended to be. He said he wished he was guilty because the remarks were true. Weren't they, weren't they? Come on now, didn't she agree?

Not surprisingly, Harry and Joanie did not forgive him. Not really. They weren't asked there to supper again. Nessa still saw Joanie – they'd known each other since before they were married – occasionally; she'd call in for a moment on the way to collect her girls from school, but there was a constraint between them, an edgy politeness they neither of them knew what to do with, although Joanie did try, because they were old friends and because Nessa was god-mother to her youngest, Marianne, to make it easier. To find excuses and explanations. Otto, she supposed, was what you might call a larger-than-life character. She sup-posed all artists were. There was a price to be paid for that, she supposed.

Well yes, there was, Nessa thought, though she did not say so.

But Nessa had a problem, not revealed to Joanie then or later. A part of her could admire Otto for his refusal to compromise, and even for his rudeness which seemed to her an aspect, merely, of his energy and masculinity. Otto was his own man, he didn't curry favour, he didn't care what people thought. When she was not being embarrassed or hurt by his behaviour, when she was not cut to the heart by it, she could, in a way, admire it.

'Stop staring at me!' Otto erupts from the depths of his gloom and his armchair. 'Leave an old man in peace!'

Nessa was not staring at him, as it happens, not this time. She doesn't think she was. She'd merely looked up for a minute and there he was, blocking her view of life, getting in the way of it, no chance of avoiding him.

And what was this nonsense about Otto being an old man? Otto wasn't old, he was young, he'd be fifty-two in

March. He looked forty. He had drive, he was someone who, when not drunk, could get a lot done. He got a lot done in his studio – not unusual for him to complete four large canvases in a fortnight – and he got a lot done at home. The bathroom in their first, rented, flat was plumbed by Otto; the tongue-and-groove panelling of their present kitchen had been sawn and planed and fitted by him. Even now, when they could afford to have someone, a team of professionals, in to do the repairs and improvements that need doing in houses from time to time, Otto was not above putting in a new set of bookshelves or reinventing a cupboard.

Otto was not old, and he did not look old, yet reaching fifty affected him badly. It really got to him. Nessa couldn't understand it. Why should he care? In her view, most men didn't begin to be attractive until they were forty at least. It was the most unfair difference between men and women, that just as a woman was losing her looks and having to work harder and harder with exercise bikes and nourishing night cream to keep a semblance of them, a man was finding his. Without any effort at all. Yet for months before his fiftieth birthday, and for months afterwards, Otto complained about his age. He peered into the shaving mirror, he made faces at himself, he pulled his eyelids down, he tugged the corners of his mouth this way and that, looking for trouble. His eyebrows were going grey – see that, Nessa? – He had old man's whiskers in his nose! In his ears! There was more hair in his hairbrush than on his head!

All nonsense. Otto still had a lot of hair on his head, much of it dark. He had more hair, and shinier hair, than many women of his age. Unfairly, given his drinking and his smoking and his preference for high-fat, high-cholesterol foods – Nessa once tried making her man a Flora man to no avail: the tubs of polyunsaturate in the fridge grew green fur coats unless she ate the stuff herself – Otto seemed in pretty good, trim shape. On the outside, anyway. Who could say what minute changes might be taking place in arteries and organs and blood cells? Changes which one day, perhaps tomorrow, might become significant and serious?

Otto's preoccupation with age and ageing was not just tactless. It was cruel. Reaching forty had far more implication for Nessa than reaching fifty had for him. On her fortieth birthday, after fifteen years of trying, after almost as many years of humiliating tests and consultations, Nessa finally gave up hope of ever having a baby.

'Goodbye, baby' – Nessa, in the dank back garden of the Hammersmith house, said this aloud. 'Goodbye, darling one' – rocking backwards and forwards in a crusty iron chair – 'Goodbye, my sweetheart.' (She'd had a lot to drink by this time, in celebration of her own birth, in recognition of her child's refusal – she saw it as that, a positive decision – to be conceived and born.) It was nine in the evening. Otto, who had forgotten it was her birthday, was late home from his studio. When he did get back, he was sorry for his neglect and took her out to the Tandoori round the corner. She didn't tell him it was the baby that had caused her to drink and then weep. The non-baby. The death of hope.

Nessa's best friend Lindsey, the only person from school Nessa kept up with, once wrote to her apropos of her own indecisive boyfriend Alan, who at that time kept moving in and out of her flat: 'There's always hope – unfortunately.' (This must have been twenty years ago or more; Lindsey's been married twice since then, and neither time to Alan.) Nessa understood this assessment of hope as a destructive force, a poison, a monster. 'Goodbye, baby,' repeated over and over in her dank back garden, killed the monster off. Almost.

There was no biological reason why Nessa and Otto had not managed to have children. No blocked Fallopian tubes, no uterine or ovarian, no penile or testicular, malfunction; no premature ejaculation, no poor sperm count.

'You and your husband are perfectly normal and fertile. Relax. Take a weekend break. Lie in the sun. Get drunk.'

Stress and anxiety were the enemies of conception, the experts agreed.

How many times had she had to listen to that? How many unrelaxed, scorching or sodden, increasingly sexless weekend breaks had they had to take?

Nessa knew Otto long before she married him. Before he married her. They first met when Nessa was at art school and Otto one of the tutors. Being taught by practising painters and sculptors, some of whom, not much older than the students, were beginning to make a name for themselves and to show their work in London galleries, was exciting to Nessa. London was exciting. She'd never been south of Edinburgh until then.

In her second week at the school, during a life class (this was 1965, before the Seventies ban, and when life drawing was still considered a relevant subject of study for art students), Otto came up and stood beside her easel. Nessa had spotted him earlier, talking to a student on the top floor, outside the litho room. She'd thought: What an attractive man! And then, almost immediately: How odd, he's not my type. (As most people seem to, Nessa had made up her mind early about what her type was and thereafter was reluctant to alter her decision, no matter how often events, and men, proved it fallible.) Nessa would have said that her type was thin and tall and fair. Blue- or, at a pinch, green-eyed. Pale and interesting. Haggard and poetic. Whereas Otto was on the small side, five foot six or seven, not much taller than herself. A dark man. His skin was dark, his hair was dark and cut short into a soft, curly brush; he had brown, dark eyes, black eyebrows that met in the middle – 'Murderer's eyebrows,' Nessa's mother said when Nessa told her she was thinking of marrying Otto – thick, dark, curly eyelashes, the sort that are often described as 'sooty'. His chin was dark, but that was because in those days he was economising on razor blades. And he was not thin at all, he was chunky and muscular.

Otto came and stood beside Nessa's easel, hands behind his back, pencil between his teeth. He was wearing a dirty-green corduroy jacket, black corduroys, a black polo neck (a sort of uniform then, anyone in the Arts, anyone who considered himself an intellectual, trying to look like Harold Pinter).

Nessa waited for him to say something rude. She'd heard about his rudeness, had been warned by the second years how rude he could be. She was not sure whether she should carry on with her drawing, or step back out of his way.

'Budge over a minute.' The pencil was still in Otto's mouth. He regarded her drawing, and then the model, and then her drawing. Then he leant forward and scribbled on a corner of her paper.

'See that' – the marks Otto had made were very pale. 'Use a hard pencil like this one. Any old rubbish looks effective if you use charcoal or a 6B.' And that was all.

'Yeah, he's attractive,' Sandra Davis said. They were hanging around the female students' washroom, wasting time before a litho class. 'But you want to watch out. Hard pencil. I'll say. He screws anything that moves. Once. Screw and dump, that's what he does.'

'I thought he was married.' Nessa was shocked by all of this. Shocked and disillusioned. Sorry for Otto's wife and for all betrayed wives. Scandalised. Excited.

Sandra Davis gave her a pitying look. She chased a splinter of black-grooved soap around the basin. She pulled the roller towel out and down, searching for a clean patch; there wasn't one. She shook her hands in the air to dry them, and then wiped them on her jeans. She left the cloakroom.

Nessa was a virgin when this conversation took place. Not a wise thing to be at art school she discovered, where the students' talk, when it was not about work, was about sex. She'd had several near-misses – or were they near-successes? – with boys her own age back home, and thought of her virginity as a technical rather than an actual thing. Now it seemed to her actual, and a problem. The other students knew about it. Not from anything she let slip, but from what she did not; from all the gaps, the omissions, the silences her end of the table in the coffee bars they frequented – the Black Toenail and the Kandinsky. Conversations in these seemed aimed at her, at finding her out.

'Size is important, don' you think, Scottie dog?' Angeline turned to Nessa on a thin grey elbow. 'One fellar I went with had a dick no bigger'n this.' She held up her little finger and jiggled it unpleasantly. 'Honest, no kiddin'. Couldn' feel a *thing*.' And she upturned a bowl of sugar and demonstrated, with a matchstick in the spilt demerara, on the red-mottled formica table top, what dimensions a dick had to have to be of any use to anyone.

Watching this, Nessa's curiosity was mixed with some other, not quite identifiable, emotion. According to Sandra Davis, Angeline had been to bed with Otto. What's more, Sandra Davis said, Otto had broken his once-only rule for Angeline. He'd had her twice.

Angeline's dirt-ingrained hands – it was not just the paint stains they all had – her black-polished yet bitten nails, her waist-length hair (backcombed on top and all the colours of the paintbox), her chalk lips and kohl-rimmed eyes, Nessa would see clearly when other images of art school life had smudged and faded. Angeline personified every resentful taxpayer's understanding of the words 'art' and 'student'. Nessa said as much to Otto in 1989 when they were lamenting the school's proposed closure, but Otto said he had no memory of Angeline at all.

Angeline was a grotesque, an attenuated clown. She reeked of rush-hour tube trains and midnight ashtrays. Why did all the boys fancy her?

Because she was dirty. Because dirt was sexy. Sandra Walters – there were three Sandras in Nessa's year – told her this over coffee in the students' commonroom.

Still, even though she had a bath whenever the hot water in her bed-sit allowed, and rolled Odorono over her armpits before setting off in the mornings, several of the boys at the school found Nessa sufficiently fanciable to try to get her into bed. Or on to the back seats of borrowed cars. Or, on one occasion, on to the sculpture department floor. (This was Roy, who had green teeth.) But Nessa, who wanted to do it, or at least to get it done and over with, couldn't. Confronted by a slobbering mouth, a trespassing finger, an excited trouser front, she froze. (Once to her horror, she laughed out loud.) The boy, whoever it was, would roll off her and sit up. He would say she was a cock-tease, a ball-breaker. Frigid. A lesbian.

'I hear you're a lesbian,' Angeline announced in the Black Toenail. 'What do lesbians do? D'ya fancy me?' She unbuttoned her shirt and revealed her bosom which was small and grey. She wriggled her shoulders provocatively. She put her arms round Roy's neck, leaning into him, and from this vantage point blew Nessa a pouting, noisy kiss.

The following term, her second, Nessa went to bed with Otto.

He had begun to flirt with her when he criticised her work. Not obvious flirting. A light touch on her shoulder, a comment, usually satirical, on her clothes or her red hair or her accent. He would mimic this, as she discovered English people often did, although in his case perhaps 'mimic' was not the right word. 'Adopt' probably came nearer to describing the way he picked up her rhythms and cadences, and then handed them back, recognisable but altered. He would peer at her work, moving in close, then stand back with crossed arms, eventually turning to give her a furrowed, quizzical look. He said little. 'Huh.' 'Uh-huh.' 'Getting there.' 'So-so.' 'So far as it goes.' 'Dishonest.' 'Crap.' 'Work work work, fame fame fame.' (This last chanted in a sort of sing-song.) He would take her pencil or paintbrush from her in such a way that she could feel a slight, only just detectible pressure from his hand.

His hand; his hands: broad palms, small narrow fingers, a ring on the wedding finger. The backs – and his wrists – were hairy. The merest glimpse of his hands, of the black

hair on the pale brown skin, triggered a dissolving weakness
in her stomach, low down. Another unsettling aspect of
him was his smell. No, not smell. Not scent or odour either.
This emanation had more to do with temperature than any
olfactory sense. It had to do with heat.

One morning he said to her, 'If you're not busy in the
lunch break, come and have a jar.'

It was not unheard of for a student to have a drink with
a tutor in the lunch hour, but it was not that usual either.
Not for a first year. Nessa imagined they'd go to the pub
the tutors habitually patronised, the Unicorn it was called.
It didn't occur to her they'd be going anywhere in Otto's
car. But Otto had to collect some notes and slides from
home, 'and then afterwards we'll have a wee bevvy, hen.'
Was this true? Or a seducer's fiction? It might be true, it
could be: Otto taught art history to the second years.

Otto's car turned out to be a souped-up Morris Traveller.
He drove it as though it were a racing car. He pushed it
through the gears and through the traffic. Once, when they
were stuck behind a delivery van delivering in the Old
Brompton Road, he pulled out left on to the kerb, and then
drove a few yards along the pavement to overtake the van
on the inside. Nessa wasn't frightened – Otto's driving was
too confident and authoritative to induce fear – but there
were other worries. The glove pocket on the passenger side
held a spiral-bound notebook with a shopping list on it in
writing that was not Otto's. It held an emery board and a
bottle of nail-polish remover. Otto's wife sits in this seat,
these objects reminded Nessa, the seat you're sitting on is
hers. How do you feel about this? How would Otto's wife
feel about your sitting here, in her seat?

In Otto's flat, in the living room, Otto stood behind
Nessa and laid his head on her shoulder. He lifted the collar
of her jacket and blew softly on the back of her neck. Then
he kissed her neck.

'No,' Nessa said, wanting to move; not moving.

'Yes,' Otto said. 'Yes.'

'No.' This second 'no' must have carried more conviction, for he released her.

'Let's have a drink. Wotcha fancy?'

'I don't need a drink.'

'I think you do. I know I do.'

While Otto was getting the drinks, Nessa examined the room, sitting room she supposed it to be. The room where Otto and Janet sat in the evenings and discussed the happenings of their day. Where they had tea, no, supper, on trays in front of the television. Where they made love on that settee. (It was grey wide-ribbed corduroy and large enough, if it did not look comfortable.) Examining the room, making a conscientious study of its colours and furniture and objects, was a way of dealing with a mix of feelings – with lust and resentment, nervousness and guilt. Nessa saw sludge-coloured walls, a curtainless bay window, a square of rust carpet on black painted floorboards. There were only four pictures in the room and these, a series of drawings of a standing female nude, backview, and recognisably Otto's work, were grouped together on the fireplace wall. The mantelpiece, the windowsill, the bookshelves, were supporters of stones or stone-like sculptures, stone-coloured jugs and bowls, and vases with wide bases and thin necks and runny glazes. An earthenware pot, large enough to house forty thieves, stood in the fireplace and contained ornamental grasses, feathery and grey. Otto's wife was a potter. Nessa remembered Sandra Davis telling her this. Not just a wife, not just a mother – as Nessa's own mother had been, as all the women in her childhood were and were expected to be: cooks and floor-scrubbers, fanatical table-polishers and chairback-starchers, nest-builders. These pots and jugs, on the face of it domestic items, described an independence unheard of in the marriages she knew. Their presence on ledges and shelves seemed to Nessa evidence of marital equality, and a real, punchy competitiveness.

The drink Otto brought her was gin and tonic, ice and lemon, only the second time she'd tasted this.

'Sit down, sweetie,' Otto said, 'take your coat off; I'm just going to make a phone call.'

It was hot in the room, but Nessa kept her jacket on. She perched on the corduroy sofa, stiffly upright, her knees together, her hands round the freezing tumbler, while Otto made his call.

'Halloo there,' an unfamiliar Otto cooed into the receiver, 'hallooo, it's me. No, I'm at home. Can't remember whether you wanted me to do anything else about supper? Yeah, I've got the booze, and the salad stuff. I've made the ice. Yes. Yes, okay. Mischa's going to be very late.' Otto swung round in his chair, and while he was listening to what his wife had to say about this news, he gave Nessa a severe, investigative stare. With his free hand he groped behind him on the architect's desk for his cigarettes, shook a cigarette from the packet, lit up and threw first the packet and then the lighter to Nessa.

'Fine. Okay. No, no one. No, I just came home for some art history slides. Did you say you'd be back about four? Yus. Yus I will. Yus. Promise. Love you.'

How could Otto do this? How was he able to? What shocked Nessa was not so much that he should lie to his wife, by omission, in that cooing, intimate voice, but that he should do it in front of her. How could he bear to show himself up in such a way to someone he hardly knew, to one of his students? What sort of person did he think she was?

'Would your wife mind if she knew I was here?' Nessa pulled hard on her cigarette. Her question was not a real one, because she had no doubts that Janet would mind. She had asked it deliberately, to disconcert Otto.

Otto was not disconcerted. Of course his wife wouldn't mind, he assured Nessa. Of course not! Why should she? Theirs was not that sort of relationship, the sort that cared about such things. They were both creators, creative people had needs, they both understood those needs. Seeing separate friends separately was one. They had no secrets from each other, as it happened, if Nessa really wanted to know.

So she needn't worry about that one! What was worrying him was that Nessa hadn't had anything to eat. He was going to go and concoct a sandwich now. Could she eat cheese and something? Cucumber?

Nessa hadn't remembered Otto taking his shoes off, but in the kitchen he wasn't wearing any. He sprung about the room in thick socks, from fridge to breadbin to table, where he buttered and chopped and sliced and sprinkled. Deft and efficient; lithe – like a cat, or a ballet dancer. He reminded Nessa of all the photographs she'd ever seen of Nijinsky.

'Who are Ben and Dom?' The mugs they were drinking their coffee out of had these names painted on them. Ben on Nessa's mug, Dom on Otto's.

Ben and Dom were his step-children, Otto said, Janet's sons from her first marriage. Janet was eight years older than him, he explained, leaving this information to hang in the air above their heads, where it gathered weight and significance.

Did he like them, Ben and Dom? Nessa wanted to know, did he get on with them?

Well yes of course he did! Why wouldn't he? They were good lads, they were very nice kids.

('Of course'? Why 'of course'? Nessa felt she might have believed him if he hadn't said 'of course'.) She asked him if he wanted children of his own, and Otto said, no, no he didn't, he'd never wanted children, and Janet didn't want any more, so that was all right.

'I do,' Nessa said, 'I want a lot of children. Four or five, mebbe.'

Otto said he'd got it into his head that she wanted to paint.

'I do. I want to paint and have babies.' (Why should this surprise him, when he was married to Janet?) 'I want both. Is there a toilet anywhere round here?'

The toilet was on a little half-landing between the basement and the hall. When she came out, Otto was sitting at the foot of the stairs, his head on one side, his thumb in his mouth. Little boy lost. Wouldn't she like to do a little tour of the house before they left? Little Boy Otto asked engagingly. Wouldn't she like to admire the fruits of his amazing, innovative, masterly, do-it-yourself labours?

No no no no no! But Nessa did not say this, and afterwards she blamed her failure on the gin. Instead she allowed Otto to take her hand and lead her up the stairs, which he did on tiptoe, as if there might be children sleeping on the floor above whom they must be careful not to wake.

Nessa lost her virginity in Ben's room, after she'd inspected shelves and cupboards about the house that Otto said he'd made. He'd even carpentered Ben's bed, he'd cut it down from an old worm-eaten fourposter that came originally from his grandmother's house in Galway.

Nessa hadn't wanted to go into Ben's room. Pinned to the door was a notice in red felt pen: BEN'S ROOM. ADMITENCE TO TICKET HOLDERS ONLY.

'We cannae go in there. We've no got tickets.'

But Otto said not to worry, he had a season ticket, he'd paid over the odds for it, it allowed him entrance any time night or day, she mustn't worry about it at all. He was standing behind her as he said this, and now he put his arms round her in a protective, consoling way, as to one who had suffered a bereavement; and blew on her neck, and murmured into her ear.

'A little lie-down is what we need after that climb,' Otto's voice said inside her ear, 'a little little lie-down. My sleepy Agnes.' His hands, sleepy-seeming themselves yet inexorable, travelled from her waist to her breasts as he spoke, robbing her of protest. (What Otto's hands were doing to her breasts, her nipples, was affecting another part of her body altogether. This was new. No one else's hands had achieved this.)

'You smell delicious.' Otto inched her, slow but very sure, nearer Ben's narrow bed. The bed that he had made.

But the worry over the lack of tickets remained. It inhabited a part of Nessa's mind all the time Otto was undressing her, and while he was undressing himself, and while he lowered himself on to her – the narrowness of the bed did not allow for two adult humans to lie side by side – and while he explored her person, and while he, methodically and devastatingly, occupied her person. The lack of tickets for Ben's room, plus the fact of doing it in Ben's bed, would haunt her with guilt and shame whenever she thought of that first time with Otto, the iniquity of her crime intensifying through the years so that in her forties Nessa would tell Lindsey that she believed, she really believed, it accounted for her failure to conceive a child. Not having babies was a punishment, she told Lindsey. (Lindsey said she'd never heard such nonsense, such dangerous nonsense.)

Afterwards they didn't light cigarettes, or lie still with their arms around each other. On the contrary, things speeded up. Otto looked at his watch and leapt into his clothes and threw Nessa hers. Dazed and sleepy from the gin, Nessa followed the speeding, speeded-up Otto. Down the stairs. To the living room, where he removed the ashtrays and the glasses. To the kitchen, where he washed these and the lunch things up, and dried them and put them away. Back to – taking the stairs three at a time – Ben's room, where he shunted the bed back to the position it had travelled from; and punched the pillows, and sniffed and smoothed the bedclothes, and withdrew the towel he'd thought it wise to fetch when Nessa – rather late in the proceedings – had mentioned it was the first time she'd done this.

The towel went into the twin tub in the kitchen, along with some socks and shirts and a bri-nylon babydoll nightdress Otto extracted from the bathroom on his flight down the stairs.

'Work work work, fame fame fame,' Otto encouraged himself cheerfully as he put on his shoes.

'What about the art history notes?' Nessa felt she had to remind him of these. It seemed strange he should forget them, when he'd remembered everything else.

In the car going back to the college, Otto took his hand from the gear lever and placed it on Nessa's thigh. He ran his forefinger the length of her thigh, pressing down firmly, drawing it along, cutting a groove. A knife through butter. (She would be able to feel that pressure on her thigh for always.)

'Bonnie wee Nessa,' he said, 'bonnie wee Agnes. You were lovely. You are lovely. We must do this again. Soonest.'

They didn't do it again. Not for years. (Not until Janet had left Otto, not until Nessa met him, by chance, one January morning, at the Tate.) Having screwed Nessa, Otto dumped her.

Why did none of the dumped students betray Otto? Why didn't she betray him? Nessa asked herself this then and later. An anonymous telephone call to his wife, or an anonymous letter, would have done it. Or she could have – any of them could have – reported him to the principal. No one reported Otto. At the time, Nessa asked Sandra Davis why not.

'You could have said no, mate,' Sandra Davis said. 'We can all say no, y'know. Anyway, Otto's good at it, and he's useful – if he likes your work. Andrea Watkins was a student of his.' Andrea Watkins was having her first one-man show at the Ariel Gallery just then. Her work had received a lot of critical attention. Nessa had been to see Andrea's show and had decided it was okay, nothing special, but okay.

'Anyway,' Sandra Davis said, 'look on the bright side. No one calls you a lesbian any more, so that's something.'

When men, in the Middle Life Crisis much written about these days, lose interest in their wives, it's invariably to do with sex, with unsatisfactory or boring sex. That's what the women's magazines say, that's what the health pages of national newspapers suggest. Nessa read a great many of these articles, the ones that tell you how to be inventive in bed, the ones with jokey headings like How to Keep Your Man's End Up Through Forty Years of Marriage.

What the message of these usually boils down to is this: that men being men (polygamous; natural philanderers), it is up to women (monogamous; natural homemakers) to keep the sexual interest – and thereby the marriage – going. 'Day after day there are girls at the office, and men will always be men; if you send him off with your hair still in curlers, you may not see him again.' That line of singing and thinking, thrown out in the feminist Seventies, shelved in the Eighties, seems to be being dusted down and polished up for the Nineties. Perhaps AIDS has something to do with it. Nessa thought so. AIDS, spelt out, or euphemised, came into the articles she read more and more.

Nessa and Otto's sex life wasn't satisfactory – well, it couldn't be, it hardly existed. It only ever existed if Otto initiated it, and nowadays he seldom did. Not that Nessa had ever been much of a leader, although for a time she was a keen follower. During those years she followed Otto anywhere his fantasies led him. Take underwear. She wore the black underwear Otto used to insist on when he wanted her to be naughty, and the white underwear he insisted on when he wanted her to be nice – that is, virginal; a school-girl. He would not allow her to wear a coloured bra and pants ever. No flower patterns or psychedelic swirls or day-glo spots – a turn-off, he said. This was a problem in the Seventies, when brilliant flower-power hipster briefs were all you could buy. In those days Nessa bought her white pants in the girls' school outfitters' departments of large stores: knicker linings they were called. In the mid-Eighties, when plain underwear came back in fashion, Nessa didn't have to make a trip to Debenhams, she could buy all the white pants she wanted in her local Marks & Spencer. But Otto didn't mention her nether garments any more. If he had a preference for lacy, strapless bras, if he had sudden and urgent desires to see her in cami-knicks or open-crotch panties, he never said so. Nessa knew this was her fault, that it was she who was to blame for Those Old Bedroom Blues (the expression used in one article she read to describe ordinary, uninventive, infrequent, marital sex) she and Otto

were suffering from. Otto was suffering from. For the truth
was, once she'd convinced herself there would be no baby,
she lost all interest in sex. What could be done about it?
None of the pieces she read made the connexion between
sex and babies. Sex for pleasure was what they were concerned with. Sex for warmth, sex for comfort, sex for
health. Sex as cement for crumbling relationships. Nessa
wasn't against any of these, she could see the value of them.
If asked, she would have said that most of them had been
contained, to some extent, within her and Otto's love-
making. Desirable in themselves, they had been part of
desire, and of its aftermath, of sweat cooling on exhausted
bodies, of a shared glass of whisky or of wine.

It was a shock, then, to discover at forty that none of
these aspects of sex counted. That all that energy and lust
and concentration had had for her one purpose only.

'Have an affair with him if you must, but don't, for God's
sake, marry him,' Lindsey said when Nessa was talking
about moving in with Otto. 'He'll no be faithful to you for
more than five minutes, and he does *not* want children.'

But Otto wasn't interested in screwing around any more,
he was only interested in Nessa. He loved her. He needed
her, and probably always had (he saw this now). His open
marriage to Janet had been – a hard thing to have to admit,
but true – a disaster. Commitment was what he was ready
for. Also, he'd changed his mind about having children.

'Having babies with you would be delicious,' Otto murmured into Nessa's ear as they were making love.

Nessa was teaching art full-time in a boys' grammar school
when she married Otto, a job she saw as a stop-gap, not a
career. She was going to be a painter, she was going to be
a mother. These were certainties. Teaching had not left her
much time or energy to paint, and the school holidays were
somehow taken up with other things, with visits home to

her mother, with visits to Lindsey, newly married and with a baby on the way; but now Otto's drive and ambition was going to rub off on her. Otto told her it was so, and she believed it. And he took practical steps to encourage her: he whitewashed the back bedroom of their Putney flat, he set her up with lighting and materials. He would do everything he could to help her, he had the contacts, there wouldn't be a problem when it came to showing her work – when she'd done the work. But she'd never get anywhere if she taught full-time.

So Nessa gave up the grammar school and got herself a two-day-a-week job at a comprehensive. Then she waited for inspiration and for babies to arrive.

Throughout Nessa's life with Otto there were mornings when she'd wake and think: Today is the day. Today it will happen. These were the mornings when she believed, from the first moment of consciousness, that she held the key to an enduring energy, a graspable vision, an attainable truth; that as soon as breakfast was over and Otto out of the house, she would climb the stairs to her studio – the room that Otto had whitewashed for that purpose – and paint the paintings, beautiful and true, beautiful because true, it had always been her destiny to paint.

Pie in the sky. Some demon in Nessa had other ideas. This demon kept her busy in the kitchen, washing up, drying up, putting away; wiping surfaces over and over, scrubbing the floor. He sent her into the utility room to wash a bundle of dirt- and polish-clogged dusters by hand, for God's sake (there was a perfectly adequate washing machine under the worktop). He decided it was the ideal day for airing the kelims on the garden line, and once they were there, for mugging them with a broom. (She would have to wash her hair afterwards.) He insisted that the lavatory seats were overdue for disinfecting, and the fridge for defrosting. He pointed out that there were mouse – or were they rat? – droppings in the larder, and water rings on the living room furniture. And how come she hadn't noticed until today how filthy, how stomach-turningly sticky and fluffy, the stair treads and the skirting boards were?

Only when she was exhausted would the demon let her go; only when she was quite safe from any obligation and responsibility to her vision. After that she was free.

There was one consolation Nessa hung on to. The bare walls of her studio, the near-empty sketchbooks and blank canvases that littered its floor, contained, didn't they, a paradox: somewhere in all this vacuity the truth remained intact. White hot. Inviolable.

Whereas Otto. Whereas, who was to say that Otto, in his quest for fame fame fame, on a journey that had taken him from vapid Fifties Figurative, through Kitchen Sink Realism, some Constructivist stuff ('motorway cones' one phase Nessa remembers), a fling with the Minimal and the Conceptual, to the paint-laden Abstract Expressionism of his latest work, had come any nearer to the truth than she had? Who had done nothing? Mightn't he even, with his mania for reinventing and making it new, have profaned the truth, or lost sight of it altogether?

There were times when Nessa could console herself with this hypothesis; moments when she knew her apathy and lack of achievement not her fault. In one household there can't be room, can there, for two burning ambitions, two artistic temperaments, two super egos?

(What about Otto's encouragement of her, though? She wasn't going to deny that, was she? – It was Lindsey who asked this. He'd always encouraged her, hadn't he?

No. Not really. Not unless you called years of head-patting patronisation encouragement. Not unless you did.)

Other times Nessa told herself that Otto was a gifted, courageous man. That looking after the needs of such a man, or indeed of any man, was a valid mission, and what she was for. What all women were for. That doing it well implied a talent not to be despised.

*

This morning after breakfast, Nessa went round to Marion, next-door neighbour but one, to return the book, *Uncoupling*, that Marion had lent her. Nessa hadn't read it all. *Uncoupling* hadn't concentrated her mind as Marion had predicted, only depressed it. Also, she'd noticed the book was three weeks overdue at the library, a fact which made her feel a criminal. Then there was the embarrassment of having something with so unambiguous a title on the table by her bed, and of reading it in bed while lying alongside Otto. Not that Otto often noticed what she read any more. It was years since they'd discussed the books they were reading, swapped them, read passages out to each other, laughed over or at them. Even so, she'd felt awkward reading *Uncoupling* within an inch of Otto's nose. And he had noticed it. He'd stopped her side of the bed on his way to the bathroom one morning, and picked up the book from her table and scrutinised its jacket.

'Uncoupling presupposes coupling – you have to couple first,' Otto said slowly. 'Or is this a book about trains? What a dark iron horse you are, Nessa, to be sure.'

Marion was doing her washing when Nessa called in with the book. She offered Nessa a cup of coffee. Marion used to be married to a university lecturer, an archaeologist, but divorced him three years ago. She has two children: Natalie who's eleven, Barney who's five. In her kitchen was evidence of this fruitfulness: messily pasted paperchains looped the ceiling; a red-felt-pen message on the pinboard reminded that Natalie's ballet class is on Fridays at six now, not Wednesdays at six-thirty; a magnetic Mickey Mouse clung to the fridge door. And the kitchen itself was an art gallery, a part-retrospective two-man show of Natalie and Barney's work. Most of Nessa's friends' kitchens had looked like this at one time or another. Maura Donaldson's had. Lindsey's had, for years. Alienating years, Nessa had found them.

'Well, apart from anything else, Otto couldn't manage without me,' Nessa said, on the defensive, in Marion's chaotic kitchen. Marion had just quizzed her on *Uncoupling*; she'd just asked if it hadn't helped Nessa make up her mind to leave Otto, once and for all. Nessa had often considered leaving Otto. She was constantly wondering how it was she'd wasted her life on Mr Wrong all these years, but in the same way that she could become a loonie Leftie when in a room full of Fascists, and Hitler when in a room full of loonie Lefties, so she felt a need, in the face of Marion's impertinent certainties, to defend Otto, and herself, and their sad marriage.

'Otto would go to pieces if I left him. His work would suffer. I know.'

Which was balls, according to Marion. Behind her, the washing machine, up to that moment a moaning depressive, turned suddenly manic: screamed hysterically, worked itself up into a complete spin, and went off its rocker.

'No, not balls!' Nessa had to shout above the din.

It was, Marion insisted. Nessa deceived herself; it was a form of conceit to imagine one's spouse couldn't manage without one. Otto had been married before Nessa came along, hadn't he? He'd found himself a new wife then, well, he'd do so again. Anyway, it wasn't Otto she was concerned with, it was Nessa. By turning the argument round to Otto and his needs, Nessa was refusing to engage with the real issue.

'Otto is a difficult man, okay,' Nessa said, 'but he's wrapped up in his work, he's not interested in women any more, not in that way. He can't be bothered. I doubt any woman would take him on. Also' – Nessa added a little, plausible lie – 'he depends on me for critical judgement. There are enough sycophants in his life – '

Marion snorted at his, and wrinkled her nose in an unpleasant way. On her otherwise pale cheeks two round spots of high colour glowed. The cheeks reminded Nessa of a Dutch doll she'd been given one Christmas when she was five, and never liked.

'No man welcomes criticism,' said Marion, whose fund of wise saws was perhaps surprising in one of only thirty-three, 'not from a woman. What men want from women is

to have them sitting at their feet, praising them, bringing
them sherbert.' She paused here to let a probable literary
allusion sink in. 'Otto is no exception.' Marion was silent
again while she spooned instant coffee into two mugs, the
insides of which were stained a dark rusty brown. 'What
beats me is why you've stayed with Otto so long, when
there was nothing – no children – to keep you.'

Nessa took the mug Marion handed her. She said it was
quite likely that it was not having any children that had
kept her and Otto together. That if they had had them,
they might well have landed up in the divorce courts years
ago.

She was not sure why she said this, but she saw at once
that it was true – it was contrary enough to be true.

Marion cleared a space in the leftover breakfast things
for her own mug, and sat down opposite Nessa at the table.
Then, leaning towards Nessa with a concerned and caring
expression on her face, one that somehow managed to
involve her eyes and her eyebrows and her mouth and the
attitude of her little sharp chin, she said, 'Nessa lovey, if
you don't mind my asking, what gives you the idea – what
proof have you got – that Otto isn't interested in women
any more?'

What an intolerable question! Nessa wasn't going to
answer it. She shouldn't have, but she did.

'Well, I'd know, wouldn't I? I don't need proof. I live
with the man. I know.'

'I wasn't going to tell you this, lovey. I'd hoped you were
going to take some sort of initiative yourself, but now I
think you should be warned – ' Marion made breaking off
to sip her coffee, and then stretching an arm for the sugar
bowl, an excuse for a significant pause. She was wearing a
white and dirty crocheted jumper with sleeves pushed up
to the elbows. Her forearms displayed the black moles and
wiry black hairs that are characteristic of a certain type of
white skin, the type that never tans in sunshine, only red-
dens and burns. Otto had told Nessa more than once that

he disliked that combination very much indeed, and that he found Marion physically repulsive.

' When you went home to see your mother last Easter – remember? – Otto came round here, and tried to get me into bed, tried to get into my bed. He came round twice, he tried twice.' Marion paused again, presumably to allow time for her words to have effect, then she said, 'I had to turn him out because he was drunk. And also because he didn't want me – though he wanted my body, of course. What he really wanted was a confessional, a convenient ear for his troubles. Otto may not be interested in women, lovey, as you say, but he's interested in *a woman*. He's been in love with a woman, a married woman, for years. They have a child. Her husband thinks it's his, but it isn't, it's Otto's.'

Not a quick screw and dump then, or a series of these, but a long-standing affair. A commitment, a loving commitment. With a child.

It wasn't true. Marion was a liar, anyone could see that, she always had been, the truth was not in her.

It was true.

What an extraordinary thing, Nessa thought from a long cold distance, from the uninhabited planet she'd just landed on, that it should be Marion to impart this news. To rain these blows. Blow after blow after blow. What an extraordinary thing.

' . . . Otto told me he's felt for a long time that you aren't really interested in him,' said Marion, who had yet more blows up her sleeve, 'and that you don't really like men. If you don't mind my telling you this, he's convinced you prefer women. "In every way" was how he put it.'

A picture presented itself in Nessa's head, a picture of herself and Maura Donaldson in Maura's cottage kitchen. They were concocting supper for the menfolk. They were giggling; they were adding, between swigs from a bottle of wine on the worktop, increasingly bizarre ingredients to what they'd feared was a dullish stew. And then, somehow – crossing the room? – rummaging for *crème de menthe* or peanut butter or caraway seeds? – they'd collided, collapsed into each other's arms, and stayed there. Hung in, hung on, and stayed there. Relaxed against each other and breathed in the scent of the other's neck, and stayed there. Stayed there too long. 'Well, this won't buy the menfolk a new pair of hiking boots,' Maura had said eventually, releasing herself.

That was all. After that, they'd got on with the supper, as though nothing had happened. Well, nothing had happened. And Otto couldn't know about it because of course Nessa had never told him. No one knew. Lindsey didn't know. No one.

But afterwards, when Nessa was at home in Hammersmith and thought about it, she'd come to the conclusion: 'If Maura and I had been alone in the cottage, and if there'd been a bed in the kitchen, we'd have landed up in it.' She knew this with certainty. What she could never be certain about was whether she was glad or sorry they had not been alone, and that there'd been no convenient bed for them to fall into.

' . . . Otto stays with you because he thinks you're helpless without him, he says he can't leave you . . . ' Marion's parting shots followed Nessa from the kitchen table and out of the house, chased her down the steps. 'He's convinced you aren't capable of earning your own bread. He says . . . '

On Nessa's desk, the pile of dealt-with Christmas cards is taller now than the untouched pile. She's got as far as the Ts in her address book. She's written cards to the Trevillions and Ira Tredgett and Bill Thorpe and the Templetons, and next she's going to do one for the Tuckwells.

Nessa is on her own in the living room. Half an hour or so ago, John Coltrane stopped playing his sax, and when he did Otto put his empty whisky glass on the floor and lay back in his chair and fell asleep.

Is it true? Is it *true*? Nessa, in her head, asked the

unconscious Otto. Is any of it true? When he wakes I'll confront him, she told herself. But when, some minutes later, he did wake, abruptly and noisily as he always did, groping his way to the door (like a blind man, or a sleep-walker, or a *drunk*) as he always did, she said nothing.

'Happy Christmas to John and Suzy,' Nessa writes inside her card to the Tuckwells, 'Love from Otto and Nessa.' John Tuckwell is a sculptor, an old friend, an old sparring partner, of Otto's. Suzy is his second wife. (The Tuckwells used to be John and Alannah, but back in the Seventies Alannah left John and their three children and went off into the sunset with a male model, a boy of twenty.) John and Suzy are in Canada this winter because Suzy, an art historian, has a lectureship in Montreal.

'No news from the frozen North, you so-and-sos,' Nessa writes to the Tuckwells in her version of the italic script she and Lindsey learned at high school in Arbroath. 'How goes it? Otto's retrospective is end of Feb – any chance you'll be back in England by then?'

Lying Doggo

✦❧

I sleep with her. That is to say, I sleep on our bed, above the duvet, under the eiderdown. Only on the coldest nights do I accept her invitation to come in. Usually, a need to preserve a modicum of independence sends me to the end of the bed, where I'll lie crossways on, though sometimes I'll curl into the triangle her bent knees provide (she sleeps in the foetal position as a rule). I have been known to lie with my head resting on her lower legs, and when I do, it is not for reasons of devotion but because of the warmth this posture affords.

She sleeps badly. Very often my dreams will be interrupted by the sudden curtailment of her own, by the bedside light snapping on, by a book thundering to the floor, by plashy gulpings from the bedside tumbler, by pillows being punished and rearranged. Selfish, she will want to make me accessory to her insomnia and her fears. Are you awake? she'll demand, ensuring that I am. Wake up! (hefting me with a foot) Didn't you hear something? Experience should have taught her by now that if there is 'something' in the house, or out there in the dark, to hear, I will hear it, I will sense it instantly and alert her. Experience has taught me, when a warning is called for and acted upon, not to expect gratitude. Oh do shut up, she'll groan, flouncing and thrashing under the duvet, it's only a fox or a badger, it's only the moorhens on the river, lie down for God's sake, stop quivering, we've got three hours left before the alarm goes off, go back to sleep. Her behaviour is histrionic in the extreme.

I am at the mercy of her moods. Prodigal with displays

of affection one minute (she winds her arms round my neck in a stranglehold, she imprisons my head in both hands, she stares searchingly into my eyes, she plants lingering, deliberate kisses on my forehead and cheeks and ears, on my chest and stomach – though never yet, thank heaven, on my lips), she will ignore me the next. Accepting an invitation to join her on the sofa, I'm aware that at any moment I may be turfed off. If I had a say in the matter, I would opt for a mean of kindness and considerateness, for nothing more than consistency in these. As it is, lashed to the pendulum of her emotions, swung from extravagance to parsimony, I suffer and endure.

I try to please her, nevertheless. A hopeless endeavour: she is impossible to please. When visitors arrive, for example. When visitors arrive and I, at the slamming of a car door or voices on the path, gear myself up for a vocifer- ous welcome, run to the front door, greet the visitors indi- vidually as they enter – she accuses me of faithlessness. You're not mine, she says, you're anybody's, that's plain to see. If, on the other hand, and taking account of her jeal- ousy, I decide on a low-profile approach, or rather non- approach, slinking up the stairs as soon as the visitors step into the hall, she calls me down and upbraids me in front of them for lack of manners.

She never asks me to accompany her when she goes out in the evenings. I am her one true friend, she makes a point of telling me, I am her angel, her adored, the love of her life, yet on those evenings when she transforms herself from sloven to prima donna, and glides out of the house, she leaves me behind. So much for love! She knows (I cannot disguise it) how intensely I dislike being left alone, how I fear it. Bolt upright on the bathmat, I sit in the bathroom and watch anxiously as she bathes. Haven't you got any- thing better to do? she taunts. Why don't you make yourself useful and get me a whisky? Don't go all hangdog on me, please. I follow her to our bedroom and lie on the bed as she dresses and twists heated rollers into her hair. Applying her mascara brush with a shaking hand, she'll catch my eye in the dressing-table glass. Don't stare at me like that! she'll accuse, I shan't be out long. Now look what you've made me do!

She is a tease. My interest in the natural world, the field study, in particular, I have made of the *sciurus vulgaris* that inhabits our garden, is for her the source of unending and mischievous sport. Squirrel, she will murmur softly in my ear as I doze. Squirrel! she will exclaim from the bedroom window, surveying the wilderness below, squirrel on the warpath! The excitement in her voice triggers, not surprisingly, my own, sends me helter skelter down the stairs to the front door, where I scream with impatience until she opens up. And when she does? And when I sprint to the hornbeam and the beech – what do I find? Not a tail, not a whisker. Not a whiff. Recently, fearing perhaps that she has cried squirrel once too often, she has taken to employing the word 'polatouche' instead. Polatouche! (an urgent whisper or a yell) Polatouche, beloved! I am not moved by this chicanery. Is it likely that *sciuropterus volans*, small flying native of Northern Asia, could be caught disporting himself on the patch of balding moss she calls a lawn?

I am giving you my version of our life, of course, but then she is always giving hers, to anyone prepared to listen. Take the delicate/indelicate subject of breaking wind. Should I, after dinner, say, when we are holed up together in front of the television set, inadvertently break wind, all hell will break loose. Thrusting me from the sofa, she'll march about the room fanning the air with her newspaper. She'll make a to-do of throwing wide the casements and the French windows. She'll pronounce me a Fart-Pot, a Stink-Weed, the Gas-Works. Even an outside temperature of ten degrees below will not save me from banishment to the garden for half an hour or more. If, however, she should be the one (all mammals are susceptible) to break wind, then there is a marked absence of hullaballoo. No confession, no dramatics with newspapers, no risk of heart attack or hypothermia from a sudden introduction of freezing air, nothing. The silence I have learned to associate with her gassy emissions, that marks them, would be hypocrisy enough, but that's not the end of her perfidy. It's become her custom, after a characteristically soundless and offensive expulsion, and on those rare occasions when we entertain the neighbours, to accuse *me*. To put the blame for it on *me*. Whew! Cor! (pointing to my rump, making great play with pinching or holding her nose) So sorry about her! (bundling me off the sofa and out of the door) She's getting old and smelly, I'm afraid, not really her fault, poor lamb, there's nowt to be done! Out you go then, Stinky!

She is a lazy cook. I eat out of tins, as a rule. Very occasionally my diet is supplemented by a few leftover vegetables, originally green, dark brown through reheating by the time they reach me, of no nutritional value whatsoever.

She has a drink problem. It could be that her poor culinary performance is the result of her habit; certainly she is well tanked up by dinner time, stumbling round the kitchen in search of the tin opener (invariably under her nose), berating me for getting under her feet. All very well for you, she complains, you don't have to get the supper, you don't have to do anything useful at all. I'm just your slave, I'm just a dogsbody in this place! Teetotal myself, I'm alarmed at the power alcohol has over the human personality, how it alters and distorts. Alcohol can make her aggressive or lachrymose. It can make her garrulous and dumb by turn. It can cause her to put songs of Love Lost or Betrayed in the tape deck. 'Can't go on/Everything I had is gone/Stormy weather!' howls Sinatra as she mooches about the living room, stopping now and then at the drinks cupboard to refill her whisky glass. Alcohol causes her to perch on the edge of a chair and rock and hum, it causes her to slump in the chair and stare at nothing, or at me, lying doggo on the sofa. Why do you have to look like that? she'll demand. Why do you have to look so nervous? Is it surprising if I'm nervous? Is it surprising that I dread her tears and her hysterical elation? Of the two, it's the latter that holds more terror for me. The latter means Elvis, full volume, in the tape deck, itching like a man on a fuzzy tree; it means that sooner or later she will force me off the sofa into her arms, heave me over her shoulder, then bear me, unwilling partner, rocking and rolling round the living room. Round and round, up and down, cheek to cheek, all shook up. (My heart beats so, it scares me to death.) Only when the tape stops do we; only then will she stagger to the sofa. Only then will I be resettled – that is to say, dropped, dumped – on the sofa.

She is a writer. According to her, all writers drink. Drinking, so she would have me believe, is what all writers do. It's the common bond, so she says, perhaps the sole bond.

She writes in the morning. In the afternoon we go for a walk. These walks, up hills, along the ridges of hills, in woods, beside the river, which should be our most companionable times, which can be the times I enjoy most, will be ruined if she decides to play a 'game', or if we should meet a person or persons with a dog or dogs. I am afraid of dogs, even small ones; large dogs terrify me. At first sight of a large dog, an Alsatian, say, I stop in my tracks and holler in alarm. I scream and shout. I tremble and shake. At the very last minute, when the monster is almost upon us, I run to her, and she hides my head against her trousered knees and holds me till the danger passes. Sorry about her! she'll call over her shoulder, she's an awful baby, I'm afraid (stroking my head and ears); she always cries before she's hurt, comes of having been beaten and abandoned in childhood – I rescued her from the Home, you see! The result is, she's afraid of men and dogs, she can't be left alone for two seconds, she won't allow her mummy out of her sight! These unsolicited betrayals and boastings, despite the sickly anthropomorphism of their style, are usually understood by the dog-walker (tut-tutting in sympathy, tightening his or her grip on the 'German shepherd') as evidence of her caring. If he or she could only know what happens, often, on our walks! If he or she could witness what she calls a 'game'! About this 'game' of hers: it cannot be played in open country; I am safe on the downs. It is restricted to woods, to lanes trapped by hedges or bushes, to scrubland areas of bramble and bracken and gorse. We will be footing it in such a place, she, happy wanderer, laughing and singing beneath God's clear blue sky, I, crisscrossing the path, nose to the ground, absorbed in studying the routes frequented by *meles vulgaris* and *lepus cuniculus*, while at the same time keeping a weather eye on her movements – when she vanishes. My back has only to be turned for a second – and she's gone. I stand on the path and look and listen: nothing. I lift my head and sniff the badger-scented air: no one. Panic fills my nostrils and my bones. What if some terrible accident has befallen her? What if she never returns to take me home? (I cannot drive, obviously; the car is invariably parked miles back.) If she has gone for ever, what then? I try to remember her exact position on the path moments ago, when I last saw her; I try to recall whether she was ahead of me or behind. Fear sends me lickety-split in the direction we were headed, on round a bend, on on, but the path is empty as far as the eye can see. I stop still and howl. I turn and tear back the way I came, past the spot where, I believe, she vanished, on on on . . . nothing. I stop again. I howl. I repeat this desperate exercise, again and again and again. Eventually, I force myself into a more measured pace, zigzagging the path and the wayside undergrowth, checking out the sloe bushes and the sweet chestnuts, investigating every flattened grassblade, every snapping twig, every battered fern. And then all at once I'm on to her; a stop, a false start, a stop, a new start, a twist, a turn, and there, at last, she is – spreadeagled in the bracken, crouched in the hollow darkness of a yew. Alive; in one piece; unharmed. You took your time, she'll say, casual, not bothering to look at me, picking burrs and grasses off her sleeve. What happened to you? (unhurriedly dusting herself down) Good thing I hadn't broken my leg! You ain't nothin' but a hound dog, you know, cryin' all the time, You ain't never caught a rabbit and you ain't no friend of mine! Noticing suddenly my lolling tongue and rasping breath; aware, for the first time, of my distress, she'll go through the motions of remorse: I'm sorry, Angel, hey, forgive me (arms round my neck, cheek pressed against my racing heart). It's only a game, sweetheart, Hide and Seek is just a *game*. You ought to have learnt that by now, Mastermind! I didn't mean to frighten you. You know I wouldn't frighten you for all the world!

I fear she may be homosexual. This self-styled mummy of mine continually expresses a desire for us to get married – to each other. Even if there weren't already just cause and impediment why we two should not be joined, there would still be the problem of our both being female. She does not see this as a problem. Marry me, she'll beg, down on one knee in front of the sofa (where I'll be trying to have a kip), be mine, beloved! Embarrassed by her play-acting, defeated by the evilness of her breath, I'll bury my head under a cushion. Had we but world enough and time, she'll whisper, lifting the cushion, stroking my nose, kissing my nose, this coyness, lady, were no crime – Hey (tweaking my whiskers), what are these, O beauteous one? Brides aren't allowed to grow face fungus, you know, we shall have to invest in a Philips Ladyshave, O Bride of Lammermoor, my own! More alarming than this nonsense are the announcements she'll make out of the blue, over the washing-up perhaps: Well! (brisk and business-like, drying her hands, glaring down at me) The banns are read, the church is booked, *the press is squared, the Middle Class is quite prepared* – but what about you? Have you got your trousseau together? Have you had a final fitting for your wedding dress? for your bridal gown?

If she is not a sapphist, then she is mad. She may well be both.

I mentioned she's a writer. She's writing a book – of fictions, she calls them. Yesterday at breakfast she told me she's planning one about me. She took my head in her hands when she confided this and rested it on her knee. She stared into my eyes. What sort of person are you, really? she demanded to know. Tell me. Go on, *speak*. Uneasy, I tried to jerk my head away. Don't then, she said, bored, dismissing me. Anyway, she said, I can do anything I want, you realise, I can make you a brainbox or a cretin, I can reinvent you as I choose. If I like, I can (buttering a piece of toast, breaking off an unbuttered crust to give to me) get *you* to tell the tale – T-A-L-E not T-A-I-L, dum dum – thereby hangs a *tail*, she said, grabbing mine. I can make you an unreliable narrator, a lying doggo, so to speak – hey, come back here at once, and stop that noise! So sorry about her (out of the window to our new postman, retreating down the path), she likes to act the guard dog, but don't worry, her bark is a million times worse than her bite. Believe me, she wouldn't hurt a fly!

The Wheelchair
Tennis Match

They are picking blackberries. At the end of the garden, beyond the sycamores and the laurels and a dispirited green-stained fence, lay a piece of waste ground. Poll doesn't know who owned it. It was sandwiched between their garden and the next but belonged to neither. To nobody, they thought. To them. It was used as a lavatory by all the children in the road although to the casual passer-by it must have looked impenetrable because of the bramble bushes. These were enormous: tall, wide, dense, circular. White and sweet-smelling in May; dull and green in July; murderous in September when defending their fruit from raiders. In September, the children's legs and arms bore witness to the frenzy of repeated attack: in embedded thorns, in loud weals, in untidy tears and rusty smears, in precise razor cuts beaded with blood.

They were not deterred. They – Poll and her younger sister Annie and their whole gang of six-year-olds (Julie, Nicko, Peter, Jen, Rosemary, Rachel) ate all day. They ate anything, everything. Stealing from garden to garden – their parents' gardens; the gardens of deaf, blind and infirm neighbours – they descended on vegetable patches and orchards and laid waste. The earth-clogged, the worm-holed, the mouth-drying, the throat-burning, the colicky-unripe, the fizzily fermenting, the gone-to-seed and -to-flower, everything.

But on this particular afternoon, the one Poll remembers, their gang is elsewhere. She and Annie are alone, and their visit to the wasteground official. Like the Flopsy Bunnies, they have been sent by their mother to gather blackberries for a pie. To this end they each carry a small wicker basket, and into these go one blackberry in perhaps a dozen. The rest and best they put into their mouths.

From time to time they stop to compare hauls, shaking the baskets to allow the berries to settle; removing the green, the red, the wizened, the mouldy – plus flecks of bramble leaf and grasses that got in there somehow. Quarrelsome children, for once they are not quarrelling. On this dizzy afternoon the heat and silence and their absorption are condensed – so it seems to Poll now. But it cannot quite be silence. Under their feet crackles the dead bracken that is always to be found in this place, and the air around them hums with the annoyance of their competitors: with lastgasp wasps, and senile-demented bluebottles.

'Want a sausage?'

They don't hear him until he speaks. But when they turn, there he is, between them and the gate to the road, a man with a red face and a pale uniform, standing still, breathing fast.

'Want a sausage?'

(Poll thinks now that if they hadn't eaten so many blackberries they would have said, 'Yes,' and gone up to get one. It would have been the natural and logical sequence for children who ate everything, for whom sausage and mash was a favourite food.)

They stare at the man, and suddenly his hands, hanging innocently at his sides, move to the front of his trousers where they fumble, undo, release, pull out – what? Something that springs up, as a Jack from a box, as a genie from a bottle. And at once the hands catch it and close on it and, fast and furiously, polish it.

'Come 'n' get it, come 'n' get your sausage.' The hands fly away, and up it springs again, double the size now, this dark, thick, curving, waving – sausage?

An alive sausage, then! A sausage with a life of its own! A terrifying life. They must have decided this at the same moment, for at the same moment they run – or rather trip, scramble, fall, leap, fight their way – to the fence. Poll's basket is hooked off her arm by a passing bramble, but Annie hangs on to hers, and the blackberries fly after her in a little black cloud as she goes.

The man doesn't attempt to follow them. (Safety in numbers, their mother said later.) It's his stillness that chases them through the fence, into the smelly ditch beneath the fence, up the bank, over the mossed and plantained lawn, where they hear him call: 'Hey! Don't you want your sausage? You never had your sausage!'

He must have been an American GI, their mother said as she stung iodine into their wounds, or possibly a Canadian. She deduced this from the pale uniform they described, from the accent they couldn't place. Now – this was important – had he touched them? Had he done anything to them? Their mother encircled the two of them with her arms, she crushed them against her, she took their breath away.

But – the soft voice of sympathy was exchanged now for the anger of relief – how many times did she have to tell them they mustn't talk to strangers, mustn't take anything from strangers? Ever ever ever. How many times?

But they didn't! But they hadn't!

Hadn't? Didn't? What was this then?

In Annie's basket, nestling in what was left of the puréed blackberries, lay a packet of biscuits, not a make they know. US Army ration biscuits. How did they get there?

Well, into the dustbin with them, horrible, disgusting, sordid, contaminated biscuits! Ugh!

The following day, feeling peckish, they disinterred the packet, shook off its shroud of tea leaves and apple cores and margarine wrappers, tore it open and bit into the first biscuit in the pile. Waste not, want not, as Granny P, their mother's mother, would say.

The biscuit was warm and stale. It collapsed corruptly on their lips as though it had been dunked in tea. It stuck to their teeth and clung to the roofs of their mouths. It refused to be spat out.

*

The child who was murdered was called Kelly. She was six years old. Blue-eyed. Pale-skinned. Fair, wispy and fine-haired. On her chin, a little scar – an indentation you might call it – the result of coming off her scooter in Meadow-sweet Close. (Her mother maintained she was pushed by one of the Boulter boys, Barry probably.) A bright child, if not obviously academic: since starting school in the autumn she had not learnt to read, although she was perfectly cap-able of reading and knew her alphabet, her teacher said. A pretty child, whose smile was spoilt, according to some, by protruding top teeth.

A popular child? Sociable? Friendly-like? Sergeant Mackie flipped a page of his spiral-bound notebook.

Oh definitely. A merry little soul, always in the thick of it, if you get my meaning.

So. So I'd be right in thinking she'd be one to talk to a stranger then? To go off with a bloke she didn't know?

Oh no, never. Joan were always telling her. We all did. We was always telling the children –

Nevertheless, on the evening she disappeared, Kelly had been sighted licking an ice-cream cone on the corner of Shelston Road, and talking to a man. Two people had seen her – Sue Phillips and Jackie Morris. Jackie Morris said the man was red-haired. Neither of them had thought anything of it at the time. The Shelston Road post office and shop, where all the children in the neighbourhood bought their sweets and ice cream, was only a few yards away. It was broad daylight, five-thirty or thereabouts on a July evening; the turning into Meadowsweet Close – where Kelly lived – was less than a two-minute walk; there were no roads to cross; the sun was shining . . .

Jackie Morris told Sergeant Mackie she wasn't worried because she thought the red-haired man was Kelly's uncle, Dave something from Birmingham way. He'd been over visiting once or twice. She thought it must be him, like as not. Kelly hadn't looked upset and she hadn't thought anything of it. She wished she had now! She wished to God she had now! (Jackie M. put her head in her hands.) She was never going to be able to forgive herself, she told Sergeant Mackie.

The last-known person to speak to Kelly was Alan Prentice, shopkeeper of the Shelston Road shop. She'd wanted an ice cream, Mr Prentice told reporters, but she was a penny short. He'd had to count out the change she had on her and explain. In the end she'd bought some loose sweets – cherry bootlaces was one item, if he recalled correctly. He'd given her a paper bag and she'd collected the sweets herself, as was the custom in his shop. Then they'd reckoned up together on the counter. But she was disappointed, he said, she'd wanted an ice cream. Now he regretted he hadn't let her have one, and to hell with the money. If he could put the clock back, this old phoney said on camera, he'd give her all the ice cream she could eat, and she'd never have to pay a penny for it.

Poll didn't know Kelly and her family. She read the reports in the local paper ('Have you seen this little girl?' the headline said, above a smudged, laughing image that already fixed Kelly as a victim); she saw the coverage on the regional TV news. Interviews with Alan Prentice, with neighbours, school teachers, school children. Interview with Kelly's parents, Joan and Harry Taylor, slumped together on their living-room settee, Kelly's dad's arm around his wife's shoulder, Kelly's mum's eyes swollen and closed, her hands twisting in her lap: 'All I can say is – if you've got Kelly – if you're watching – bring her back – please – bring our baby back.'

Poll didn't know Kelly and her family. She and Ned, who'd been married about a year at this time, lived in another part of the town, just off the centre, in a Victorian terrace Poll – though not Ned – liked to pretend was Georgian. Poll was expecting their first baby, and perhaps because of this, perhaps because of all those increased hormones that play havoc in some pregnancies, triggering off food fads and sickness and heightened sensitivity, Kelly and her fate affected Poll more than they would otherwise have done. Watching the TV reports, reading the *Gazette*, Poll frightened herself into believing that Kelly was an omen, that whatever happened to Kelly might, in time, happen to her own unborn child. Another thing she did, only slightly less morbid, was allow her imagination to suppose that had she and Ned been married long enough to have a child Kelly's age, that child would have been at school with Kelly, her best friend even, aware now of Kelly's absence in the playground, her empty desk in the classroom.

Poll allowed herself to imagine this, but it was nonsense. She and Ned and any child they might have had would never have known Kelly. Kelly lived in Meadowsweet Close, part of a network of Closes and Drives and Ways that made up the Shelston council estate of pebble-dashed Fifties semis and bungalows. Her father was a bus driver, her mother a dinner lady at Shelston Road Primary, the school that Kelly herself had been attending. Poll and Ned were professional people. Ned was an architect, newly qualified. He worked for a firm in the High Street, but had plans to set up his own practice. Poll was an assistant librarian in the new public library. The new library, double the size of the Edwardian building it replaced, had been designed to cater for the influx of Londoners that light industry was about to bring, was already bringing, to the town. The surrounding chalk hills, grazing land for centuries, were being carved and crisscrossed, dug up and cemented down, to make way for the housing estates and trading estates the Londoners would need, for schools and shopping complexes, for a church and a crematorium. Ned's firm had been the architects for the library – a concrete and plate-glass construction with a flat roof and blue laminate panelling let in between the ground and first floors – and sometimes Ned would pop in in his lunch hour and lean on the counter and ask cheerful and confident questions, in front of Poll, of the other librarians. How did they find the shelving? The lighting? What was their, what was the public's reaction to the Reference Section? (A circular area, and on a lower level, to the right of the entrance desk.) Oh fine, the other librarians would say, fine. Which was not true. The steps down into the Reference Section put some people off. They put off young mothers with pushchairs and old people with sticks. Wheelchairs couldn't go down those steps. No handrail put some people off. And none of the librarians liked the lighting, overhead fluorescent strip, bright white and dazzling. The nearest thing to daylight, Ned assured them, but it wasn't. Daylight doesn't give you headaches. No one ever had a headache in the old library. Poll thinks now that the other librarians lied because of her, because she was married to Ned; but also because in those days architects were gods you didn't argue with, and not the overpaid environment wreckers they're considered to be today.

Poll didn't tell Ned what the librarians really thought of his library, but she quizzed him about other recent building, stuff his practice was not responsible for. The council houses on the new estates, for example, that appalled and depressed her – he didn't approve of those, did he? I mean, why did they have to have flat roofs? Why couldn't they have had chimneys? No chimneys gave them a concentration-camp look, surely he must agree?

They didn't have chimneys, Ned explained patiently, as to a small child, because they didn't have open fires, or solid-fuel stoves to cook on. They had central heating and electric or gas cookers. Central heating was not only more effective, it was cleaner, it was labour- and time-saving. Who these days wanted to shovel coal and coke? Not the people on those estates, you could be sure of that. And why should they? When their fathers had spent a lifetime digging coal, when their great-great-grandfathers had, in all probability, spent their childhoods climbing chimneys? To stick a chimney on the side of a fully centrally heated house would be a lie, Ned told her, a sentimental lie, a sort of fake *nostalgie de la boue* if you like. Ned should have been a teacher, Poll sometimes thought. He had the power to open up and expand; he had the authority, when he chose to use it, to shut down and stamp out.

Poll and Ned had an open fire, in fact there were fireplaces in nearly every room of their Victorian terrace house, though they didn't use them all. They were living in one room while they decorated. Or rather undecorated. A spare, comfortless elegance of white walls and polished boards was what they were aiming for. In the evenings, as soon as they were home from work, they'd put on dungarees and get out the sander and the Nitromors and the blowtorch. Poll was always the first to flag: being pregnant made her back ache, and the smell of the blowtorch made her throw up. She was too tired, and felt too sick, to cook what her mother-in-law called 'proper' meals. They'd flop on to the lumpy chaise longue Poll bought in a sale, and eat a bacon-and-egg sandwich and watch television.

'The body of a small child, believed to be that of Kelly Taylor, missing since last Tuesday, was today found buried on wasteland near her home. She had been sexually assaulted and repeatedly stabbed.'

Poll had not forgotten about Kelly when she and Ned saw and heard this on the national TV news. It would have been impossible to forget her in a town like theirs, which, for all the expansion and development going on (the new 'trial' one-way traffic system round the centre was exercising tempers, and legs, that summer), was as yet no more than a market town. She had not forgotten about Kelly, but she had pushed her a little to one side, in the way of these things; 'on hold' she would say now, though the expression was meaningless then. What everyone in the town was consciously, or unconsciously, doing was waiting. For the confirmation of fear. No one in the library, no one Poll had spoken to in the street market and at the ante-natal clinic, believed Kelly would be found alive.

'Why?' Poll asked Ned when the news was over; when they'd seen an Identikit impression of the red-haired man police wished to interview (Kelly's uncle had been eliminated from enquiries: he and his family were away from home on a holiday camp holiday; he and his wife had won an Old Tyme Dance competition the night his niece went missing); after the camera had homed in on a small tent set

up over the body, to allow for essential forensic tests to be
carried out before the removal of the body. 'Why do men
do it?'

'Don't look at me,' Ned said. 'It isn't all men.' He had
no idea, he said, why some men, some sick, mad, men, did
it. Any more than he knew why some women consistently
cuffed their children, and slapped their faces.

Ned said this with feeling. His own mother had been a
cuffer and an ear-boxer, a whacker and a slapper. 'Habits
like those are hard to break in families,' Ned told Poll when
they decided to get engaged, 'they reinforce themselves,
they continue down from generation to generation. But I'm
aware of it, I know the damage violence can do. I shall
never hit my children.' (And he had not.) This bruised
childhood Ned seldom spoke about moved Poll. It was a
cause of her loving him; it was one of the reasons she'd
married him.

'Don't look at me,' Ned said again – because Poll was
looking at him. She was examining his ordinarily handsome, usually gentle, occasionally tense, face. Because the
men who did it, it often came out, were not monsters. Not
everyday monsters. For every loner oddball who kept an
arsenal of sawn-off shotguns in his living room, and whose
crime, when committed, came as no surprise to anyone,
there were all these ordinary men. Family men, solicitous
husbands, caring fathers, thoughtful neighbours. Men who
were liked at work, who were active and respected in the community. Church-goers, team-games players, all-rounders,
men of whom neighbours would be prepared to swear: No.
Not him. He could never have done it. Not him.

Yet he had. Yet they did.

And women did not. Women did not sexually assault,
and torture, and then murder, other women's small
children. Whatever they might do to their own, whatever
else they were capable of, not this. (After the Moors Mur-
ders, Poll had to reconsider her verdict, but came to the
conclusion Myra Hindley was a one-off, and that the essential truth of it still held.)

*

When Poll's children were old enough (Zoë arrived two years after Caro, Nadia five years after Zoë); when they were, in turn, old enough to run outside and play, Poll told them a cut-short and watered-down version of the sausage episode, and she also told them about Kelly. Not to scare them – she managed to contract Kelly's abduction and murder into a sentence – and not to put them off men, though Ned said she was in danger of doing just that, but to make them aware, to make them wary, to protect them, to put them on their guard. Isn't this what all mothers do?

'Kelly lived in this town,' she told Zoë, when Zoë was six or so, 'in this very town.' (This must have been before they moved, five miles out into the country and into the house Ned designed and built, when Nadia was one.)

'Kelly is a rather dreadful name, don't you think?' Zoë enquired innocently. Darkly.

A hundred years later, or so the passage of time since her daughters' babyhood seems to her when it does not seem the mere blink of an eyelid, Poll is waiting for Zoë, her and Ned's second daughter ('middle daughter,' Zoë sometimes says, jokily reproachful, 'middle, unwanted, unloved daughter',) who's coming home for the weekend. An unusual occurrence? No. Zoë comes home regularly at weekends. The need to restock her London larder with food from her parents' larder is one reason for returning; a desire to renew her acquaintance with her mother's washing machine and tumble dryer, is another. This weekend is a special occasion, though. Tomorrow, Saturday, is Zoë's twenty-second birthday. She's driving down from Wandsworth to spend her birthday with her father and her mother, and then on Sunday afternoon she'll drive back again to Wandsworth and celebrate with her friends. Scabby, a stained-glass designer and one of the people Zoë shares a flat with, is organising this celebration. Zoë, who often brings friends and, sometimes, enemies with her at weekends – Poll can remember an occasion Zoë brought eight of these, on the

train, without warning her mother beforehand; though to
be fair this was a long time ago, Zoë wouldn't do that now
– isn't bringing anyone with her this weekend. She said so
this morning, before breakfast, when she telephoned Poll.
She said, Poll thought she said, 'It'll be just me; should be
home about eight. But remember it's Friday, and you know
what the traffic's like on Fridays. Okay, Old Neurotica?'

And for once Poll stopped herself. For once she did not
come out with any or all of the following: Go carefully.
Don't speed. No speeding. Don't give a lift to anyone. Keep
in the inside lane. Don't fall asleep on the motorway. Don't
stop on the motorway. She did not pass on to Zoë the fog
warning she'd heard on the early news, and she did not
sing out to her, in a zany, cartoon-character voice: Take
care-are! Be smarter than the average bear-are!

Poll's children are kind to her on the whole about her
anxiety. Even nicknaming her 'Hypercool' or 'Old Neurotica' is not really unkind, is more a joke, Poll knows, a
way of defusing the problem, though it does annoy them
sometimes. Nadia is the one who gets most annoyed. She
is the youngest, seventeen. When Nadia goes to stay with
her friend Danielle, and Poll rings to see if she got there
safely – Poll doesn't put it that way, naturally; she thinks
of an excuse: something Poll meant to ask her before she
left; something Nadia asked Poll to do while she was away,
and that Poll has forgotten, or is pretending to have forgotten – Nadia is annoyed. And embarrassed. Take last time:

'Why are you ringing me?' Nadia asked, and then, when
Poll had trotted out her excuse – the Doc Martens Nadia
had left on the stairs that did, or did not, need mending:
'You're not ringing about them. You're just checking up if
I got here.' Why d'you do this? You'd soon know if I hadn't.'

'All mothers worry about their little darlings,' Poll said,
light and bright as may be, 'it's natural.'

'No they don't. It isn't. Not when they're big.' She was
sorry, Nadia said, she couldn't talk now, she was tied up
at the moment and had to go – she and Dan and Dan's
boyfriend Martin were in the middle of a Bondage Sex

session in Dan's bedroom. When they'd had enough of that, they'd be mainlining in the lavatory. They'd be using Martin's needle, but it was okay, she told Poll, there was nothing to worry about – Martin had only had one gay relationship. And she'd be back home on Wednesday, always supposing she wasn't raped and murdered on the train. 'Bye-eee!'

(When Nadia returned home after this visit, she told Poll what had really happened. They'd been eating supper when Poll telephoned, and as soon as the phone started ringing, at the very first ring, Dan's mother had said, with a tight little smile, 'That'll be your mother, Nadia, wanting to know if you got here all right.' Everyone present – Dan, Dan's mother, her Auntie Vi, her two brothers, her boyfriend Martin – had laughed. No way was she prepared to go through that sort of humiliation again, Nadia told Poll.)

Nadia always makes jokes about Poll's fears – jokes that have a sharp edge. A serious person in many ways, she refuses to be serious when Poll needs her to be. She refuses to be serious about AIDS, about the danger of contracting HIV. Well, Poll may be neurotic, but all parents fear AIDS, don't they? All caring parents preach safe sex nowadays, surely? To their teenage children. Take Nadia: she looks sexy, she is sexy; she likes boys. Does she sleep with boys? Poll isn't sure, but according to surveys most seventeen-year-olds do. A lot of fifteen-year-olds do. 'You must get yourself properly kitted up,' Poll has told Nadia, 'just in case.' Nadia should carry condoms, wear a Dutch cap. She should never never have sex without double protection – 'You don't know where that boy's been!' Poll's offered to go with Nadia to the Family Planning Clinic; she's offered to make Nadia a private appointment with her own gynae-cologist. 'Give us a break!' is Nadia's usual response to her mother's care and understanding. 'What d'you think I am? An easy lay or something?'

Zoë is kinder than Nadia about Poll's anxiety, and more tolerant. But she is older. Twenty-two tomorrow. On the table of the dining area is a pile of the gift-wrapped consumer semi-durables Zoë asked for and Poll has bought for Zoë: a wok for the stir-fry Zoë and her friends are into at the moment; a stoneware teapot for the herb teas they brew up night and day; an oil lamp so they can see what it is they're eating and drinking. In the larder is the sad cake with twenty-two candles Poll made yesterday.

'What a sad-looking cake!' Ned said last night when he encountered it on a brief fact-finding tour of the larder shelves. 'Who's going to eat it all? Is Zoë bringing someone down this weekend? Lyn, for example?'

Poll was surprised Ned asked this question. The last time Zoë brought Lyn down Ned had, according to Lyn who complained afterwards to Zoë, as good as made a pass at her. Leered, at any rate. Lyn hadn't liked it. To begin with she'd thought it was a joke, and then when she realised it wasn't she'd hated it.

'What balls,' Ned said when Zoë confronted him with Lyn's accusation at supper one evening. (He'd given her the opening, he'd asked: 'What news of your blonde friend, whatsername – Lyn? We haven't seen much of her lately.') 'What balls,' Ned said at supper. 'I was only doing my hostly duty; I was merely being attentive and hospitable to a pretty girl.'

'That's it, that's exactly it,' Zoë said. 'A pretty girl. If she hadn't been, you wouldn't have taken any notice of her. You didn't take any notice of Evie, who, I'd like to remind you, was also here that weekend. But then she isn't blonde, and she hasn't got legs that start under the armpits.'

'Hey pardner – come to my defence.' Ned appealed to Poll, up the other end of the table.

Poll wasn't sure she could. She hadn't liked Ned's attentions to Lyn either: the quick glances, the protracted stares, the eager, flirtatious teasing, the ready laughter (when nothing funny had been said); and then, on Sunday, his seeking out of Lyn in the garden where she was sunbathing, and squatting down beside her naked back, and showing her his designs for the Business Centre. Poll had watched this from the kitchen window as she cooked lunch. She hadn't liked it. But she'd thought: He's only making a fool of himself, boring her, being ridiculous. Poor old Ned.

Then she'd remembered that of the women she knew whose husbands had left home, three had been thrown over for girls young enough to be their daughters.

Poll didn't support Ned that night at supper. Instead, she gave him a search-me, leave-me-out-of-this, could-just-about-be-seen-as-jokey, shrug.

'Your mother gobbles up all the young men you lot bring to this house,' Ned said. 'Boys, I should say, beardless youths. Now that's disgusting, if you like.'

'Not true,' Nadia said. (Poll wished she hadn't.) 'She talks to them. She asks them about themselves. Some of them may fancy her. That's not the same thing.'

'I'm being got at' – Ned returned to his cheese soufflé and stabbed it with his fork – 'by a coven of witches.'

'Didn't know a coven could be three,' said Nadia, pausing to drain a glass that was already empty of wine. 'Dunno why but I had this sort of idea there had to be thirteen to make a coven. A coven of three is news to me – sounds like poetree, hee hee hee hee,' said Nadia, who never knew when to stop.

When Zoë said, 'Should be home by eight,' Poll thought at once: I won't begin to expect her till eight-thirty. After all, she might be late leaving. There might be roadworks, a contraflow system, somewhere on the motorway. There nearly always is. Also, she might have to stop for petrol on the way. Let's make it a quarter to nine then. Poll told herself this, she prepared and protected herself; but here it is, eight-twenty only, and already she's starting to feel twitchy, to smoke more than she normally would, to drink more than she usually does, to get those fears that, without invitation, will fly into her head at such times, and nest there.

How do you know Zoë's on her way down from London

at all? these nesting fears enquire. How can you be sure she
got back to her flat after work in the first place?

Zoë is a painter, her work is painting. She paints portraits
to commission. She goes into people's houses and flats and
offices with her painting kit, plus the camera she uses as an
aide-mémoire, and sets up her easel and paints. The number
of sittings varies, but it's never many – Zoë's good at getting
a likeness. Another thing she paints is murals – muriels she
calls them – on bathroom and lavatory walls, on garage
doors, and she prefers these commissions because they
allow for invention and imagination, they leave room for
the exotic and the erotic, the zany and the bizarre. She's
going to do a mural for her parents when she can find the
time. Poll wants it in the kitchen. Her idea is to take down
all that open shelving Ned designed, and have nothing on
the wall except Zoë's muriel. Where would she put the
saucepans and dishes, etcetera? (It was Nadia who asked
this.) Well, she'd chuck most of them. They didn't need
half the stuff they had; they only used a fraction of the stuff
they owned.

Zoë likes what she does, and she earns enough, most
months, to get by. The disadvantage is, you can't get hold
of her in the daytime, as you could if she, say, worked in
an office or a bank. There's never any knowing where Zoë
might be. She could be anywhere in London, or in the
country. She could be up a track or down the motorway.
In the clutches of a rapist; on the bed of a canal.

When Zoë left art school and, because she did not want
to teach or apply her art to industry, came up with the
portrait-and-murals combo, Ned and Poll were supportive,
although Poll foresaw possible dangers for Zoë in her
chosen lifestyle, and certain anxiety for herself.

'You must never go anywhere without leaving your
address and telephone number with someone,' Poll warned
her, 'and you ought to meet your customers first, preferably
in company, before going to their homes or whatever.' (Poll
was thinking of that young woman, Suzy Lamplugh, the
estate agent from Putney, who – some years ago now –

went to meet a 'Mr Kipper' at a house in Shorrold's Road, and was never seen again.) Zoë should, ideally, keep a book of her appointments by the telephone in her flat. So that if she didn't come home, people would know where to look for her.

'By people, you mean you,' Zoë said.

'Some of your clients will be unknown quantities,' Poll told Zoë, 'who've contacted you through advertisements. They may not all be bona fide. Some of them may have something other than a portrait or mural in mind.'

Most of her customers were women, Zoë told her mother, who wanted portraits of themselves or their children as a present for their husbands. None so far had seemed to want sex with Zoë; none so far had tried to murder her. 'But okay, Hypercool, I'll leave a note of where I'm going.'

Poll doubts that Zoë does this.

Well, did Zoë get back safely from her portrait or mural, or from the studio she shares in Ealing, today? Did she? It's eight-thirty. Poll will phone the flat and find out. No, she'll wait till eight-forty-five. Zoë might ring her before then: sometimes, if she's later than she says she'll be, she rings Poll from the service station on the motorway.

No, Poll will do it now. And put her mind at rest.

Poll lights a new cigarette and goes through to the living area. (She can't make a call without a cigarette; she can't receive a call without one. As soon as the telephone starts ringing, Poll's searching for a pack, a lighter, an ashtray. There've been occasions when the caller has rung off before she's managed to get these items into line.) She pressbuttons Zoë's number. In Zoë's flat the telephone rings twice, then: 'Hi,' says Zoë's voice, 'Jeff, Scabby, Jules and Zoë aren't around at the moment to take your call, but if . . . ' Poll replaces the receiver. She won't leave a message. She doesn't want to hear any more of Zoë's ghost voice.

In the past half-hour the living-area windows have turned navy blue. Late September. Poll dreads the winter. Not the cold, that doesn't bother her, and she prefers naked trees to clothed ones – no, it's the fog and ice she dreads, the invisible roads, the skids, the pile-ups, the Motorway Madness, as the media call it.

But at least today was sunny. It didn't rain. The forecast fog didn't materialise. The roads must be dry. Poll will put the potatoes on now because Zoë could be here at any minute.

On her way to the kitchen Poll stops in the hall and puts her head round her husband Ned's study door. Ned's study has a door, one of the few rooms – areas, as Ned prefers to think of them – in the house, which he wanted to be as open plan as English winters would allow, that has. It's a light and airy – cold, Poll often thinks, beautiful but cold – building, due largely to the vaulted hall and glass roof at its centre. (This glass roof – it's too big to be called a skylight – is a trap for birds' droppings and nesting materials and has proved impossible to clean.) Instead of doors, Ned used archways and varying floor levels to divide his areas. The effect is attractive, but the different floor levels can be hazardous. When Poll's Aunt Lucy comes to stay, Poll has to follow her everywhere with warnings: 'Careful! Two steps down here!' or 'Beware ramp ahead!'

Ned is in his study, not at his drawing board, but at his computer. Playing with it. Feeding it, as though it were a baby in a high chair. The white walls are bluetacked with photographs and drawings. Above the drawing board are photographs of Erno Goldfinger and some of his creations: the Trellick Tower (that Poll hates), Alexander Fleming House and the *Daily Worker* building. Below these is a collage of recent Oxbridge architecture, at the centre of which stands its architect, Richard MacCormac, president of the RIBA and Ned's current hero. (Poll's hero too, as it happens, not so much because she admires his Blue Boar Court at Trinity, Cambridge, and his Sainsbury Building at Worcester, Oxford – although she does admire them – but because she thinks he's a devastatingly attractive man.) Round the walls are Ned's drawings for the proposed Business Centre in their town. He's been invited to submit these, but Poll imagines it's just a courtesy request; she doesn't think he has a hope of getting the job since it was his former practice, after all, that's responsible for the stained and crumbling concrete of the library – the library that the council are, at this very moment, threatening to close and possibly demolish.

Ned doesn't share Poll's pessimism. He's confident. He's a doer and a trier, someone who doesn't give up easily, if at all; someone who goes for it, who – his expression – 'says Yes to life'. (Ned's going to be County Architect when Andrew Pinsett retires – 'just you wait and see'.) Poll respects this attitude when she's not annoyed by it. She wishes she had it herself.

'Hallo there,' Ned says without turning round, 'you've just managed to screw up my jump instruction. Is supper ready?'

'Zoë isn't here yet.' This isn't a moan. This is a bright and breezy statement of fact, the way Poll says it.

'Do we have to wait for her? She probably won't be here till ten. And I want to watch the movie.' There's a Chabrol film on tonight – *La Femme infidèle*, or *Le Boucher* – one of those. They must have seen it at least three times. How on earth can Ned want to sit through it again?

'She said she'd be here by eight. It's twenty to nine now.'

'The traffic's awful on Fridays,' Ned tells his computer, calm and casual. 'Look, if you're going to the kitchen, could you get me another whisky? Just a small one. I'll be through in ten minutes.'

Calm and casual. Calm and comforting. Comforting?

Ned will never discuss Poll's anxiety. He ignores it, he pretends it doesn't exist. Perhaps he thinks it's the best way of helping her, or perhaps he doesn't care. Whichever it is, a part of Poll would like to goad Ned into feeling anxious. To really feel it. To weep with anxiety. To scream with it. She would like him to scream, just once. And isn't it possible that if he were ever anxious, and showed it, she herself would not be?

In the kitchen, Poll scrubs potatoes and puts them on to boil. She places three rainbow trout and some butter and

a piece of fennel in a pan. She washes and drains a lettuce,
she crushes a clove of garlic, she makes a French dressing.
Eight-fifty-five. She takes Ned his whisky. She comes back
to the kitchen and pours herself one – her second. She lights
a cigarette – her fifth since eight o'clock. She walks through
to the living area. Scabby and Jules and Jeff may be home
by now and know if Zoë left on time, or at least where she
is. In the living area, the telephone rings before Poll can
put out her hand.

'Hi there!' Zoë's voice.

'Zoë! Where are you?'

'Zoë? Zo-ie. Thanks a bundle. You're enough to give
anyone an identity crisis. I shall tell my analyst about this.
It's not Zoë. It's one of your other daughters, your daughter
Caro as it happens, calling long distance to talk to her
mother who never calls her.'

'Oh Caro! Oh darling!' (Disappointment can sound like
relief, can sound like joy, if you try hard enough. Poll
believes this.)

Poll's daughter Caro is ringing her from California, which
is where Caro lives. She is married to Joel, a Californian
and a farmer, whom she met in London when Joel was over
on a sightseeing trip. (It was a pick-up, though Poll has
never told her friends that. 'They met socially,' Poll tells
anyone who wants to know how Caro and Joel got
together.) Joel farms grapes and oranges. He and Caro have
twin sons, Denzil and Jan, nearly three years old. Poll last
saw her grandsons when they were eighteen months. On
the table beside the telephone are framed photographs of
the boys taken at Christmas; one is laughing, one serious,
both are curly- and fair-haired, like Joel. Poll thinks it's Jan
who's laughing, she's pretty sure about this. Ned says could
be, but what difference does it make?

When the twins were born and Joel telephoned with the
news, Ned – who up to then had never hinted that he was
anything other than thrilled to have three daughters and no
sons – said, with astonishing bitterness, 'Trust Caro to have
a son, two sons, first go. She always gets what she wants.

Always.' An eruption which made Poll wonder if there were other things, profound and substantial things, in Ned's life or in their lives together, he might be dissembling about.

Poll talks to Caro over the air waves; Caro talks to Poll. Poll tries not to give Caro any sense of her anxiety, any idea that, just at this moment, she wishes Caro were Zoë. And in any case she's been waiting for Caro's call. The last letter Caro wrote was over a month ago. Six weeks is about as long as Poll can manage without news. After that she begins to feel edgy. To wake at three and not to go to sleep again until six-thirty (twenty minutes before the alarm goes off). To accost or avoid the postman, depending on how the superstition of the day dictates. To jump at the phone, and – why not? Caro might have decided to fly over on a surprise visit – the door bell. Even so, even with all this hyper-anxiety going on, Poll won't ring Caro. Not yet. Not till she's desperate. This is in case there's no one in when Poll telephones. This is because Poll once tried to reach Caro in her faery land forlorn for six days and nights without success. Forlorn! the very word is like an unanswered telephone bell. Where could she, where could they all, be? Out shopping – at midnight? At an all-week disco – with the twins? At the bottom of a lake? (There is no lake where they live, but they do have a pool, a small one, for cooling off rather than swimming in, that Joel dug for his family last spring.) Where were they? Oh where?

Two years before, Ned and Poll had spent their annual holiday on Caro and Joel's farm, in their one-storey, wood and plate-glass, ranch-style farmhouse. As Poll, for the umpteenth time, sat in her living room with her ear pressed to the receiver, listening to the forlorn ringing, she pictured Caro's house and Caro's living room. She made a tour of it. She picked up a painted decoy duck she'd admired; she felt the blade of an old Sioux dagger Joel's grandfather had left him; she stared at the rough stone chimney-breast she and Ned, sleepless on a futon in the back bedroom, had agreed was somehow acceptable in California. She made herself examine the ugly yellow piano Joel plays jazz on,

and the bookshelves of unreadable books (on sea-fishing
and canoeing, on jazz trumpet and jazz piano) she'd wondered about on their visit. Then she walked through to the
kitchen, and out again on to the porch. She leaned over the
rail and called them: 'Caro! Joel!'

In front of Caro's porch, a dusty track stretches away to
a group of eucalyptus trees. Each evening of her stay, Poll
had watched the sun go down behind those trees. She examined the trees now, she watched their leaves shiver and
dissolve in the hot wind. She called again. She went back
into the house.

What happened next, what she found in the house, she
told no one, although she imagined telling Ned. In her
imagination she cornered him, and sat him down and told
him, 'I won't describe what I found there. I can't. Reread
Truman Capote's *In Cold Blood* if you want to know. See
the film, if there was a film. I think there was. Watch any
TV chiller documentary. Read the report of any horrific,
random killing any day in any newspaper, if you want to
know what I found in our daughter's ranch-style house.'

Poll got hold of Caro eventually. They'd been away. Of
course! She and Joel had taken the boys to Maine for a
week, to stay with Joel's sister Ellen – a fishing trip, for
Joel. The boys had loved it. And the sharp air, the 'really
green' grass, had made Caro homesick for England. Poll
didn't mention Truman Capote to Caro, or any of it. All
she said was, she and Dad had been a bit worried not
knowing where they were.

Caro's exasperation came across in measured, emphatic
patience: 'Mum, I'm a grown woman. I'm a marr-ied
wo-man. A moth-er. I'm sorr-y I forgot to tell you we were
planning this trip. But. But really! I can't tell you everything
we do! And don't drag Dad into this. He's not an hysteric,
he's cool.'

Poll and Caro have nearly finished their conversation. Caro
has just been telling Poll that Denzil, poor old love, has

been in bed all day with a bad headache and a high temperature, and Poll has resisted making any mention of meningitis. She is about to pass Caro over to Ned, who has tucked up his computer for the night and is standing by her elbow.

'Just before you go, Mum, is Zoë with you? I believe it's her birthday or something.'

Poll tells Caro, yes, Zoë is expected home for her birthday, but she hasn't arrived yet. She says this in as light and casual a way as she can muster because Ned is standing at her elbow.

'Don't worry about Zoë for heaven's sake,' Caro says. 'She'll be fine. She has the most highly developed sense of self-preservation of anyone I know.'

Poll wasn't worrying about Zoë, not until Caro mentioned her. For the ten minutes or so she was talking to Caro, Poll almost forgot Zoë. Now she has to worry again. It's nine-fifteen.

While Ned is talking to his eldest daughter, Poll goes back to the kitchen, the place dictator Nadia insists ought to be a mini-ecosystem – 'in fact the whole house ought to be,' Nadia told her parents. Poll's kitchen was far from being a mini-ecosystem, according to Nadia. Her fridge and freezer were full of CFCs, her cleaning cupboards bursting with phosphate-ridden detergents and cleaning fluids and aerosols, her larder a poison cabinet of E-numbers and additives. Last Wednesday when Nadia came home from school she gave her mother a lesson in environmental awareness. She scoured the kitchen drawers and cupboards and threw out the worst offenders. She removed the plastic rubbish sack – 'unbiodegradable' – and replaced it with four strong recycled paper carriers which she labelled Bottles, Cans, Paper, Veg. All bottles must go to the bottle bank in the town, Nadia instructed Poll, all cans to the recycling depot, ditto. Poll is not unaware, as it happens, she's been meaning to separate refuse in this way for some time, and she's doing her best now with Nadia's strong paper sacks. But they take up a lot of space and they aren't strong enough. Broken glass pierces them; wet potato peelings rot them. And what time has she got for all these trips to bottle banks and recycling depots? Nadia is unfair, also: Poll's been taking her newspapers to the Save the Children Fund collecting point for years.

In her born-again kitchen, Poll drains the potatoes, what's left of them, and turns the fish. (The heat must have been too high, the trout have jumped out of their skins, their eyes are hard and opaque with surprise.) She takes a clean white tablecloth from the dresser and puts it on the table. She lays the table for three. (Is it tempting fate, when you are expecting someone for supper, to lay the table before that someone has arrived?) She takes candlesticks down from a shelf, she fetches a jug of Michaelmas daisies from the sideboard; she smooths ruckles from the altar cloth. (Altar cloth? No, tablecloth.) She tops up her whisky. She lights a cigarette. Why does anyone have children?

It's quite dark now. And no welcoming outside light on for Zoë! Poll walks to the front door to remedy this, then she opens the door and steps outside.

Poll's and Ned's drive is steep and short. Too short to be called a drive. A driveway, then. She walks down the short steep driveway to the road. When they first came here there was a gate at the entrance, an old farm gate Poll liked, it gave a feeling of rurality, it added a sense of history to the neo-Modernist house that Ned built. But the gate was too old and fell to bits, and now only the gateposts remain.

It's a clear, bright night. Stars, no wind. There could be frost later, Poll realises. She walks into the road. After three whiskies – is it three? – she isn't drunk, just light-headed. Just heavy-hearted. Zoë, where are you?

At the end of Poll's residential road, a farm track when they moved here, is the B-road that cuts through the village, that cuts the village in half. This road is a lot busier than it was when Poll and her family moved here. In those days most of the traffic was agricultural: tractors and ploughs and hedgecutters and silage carts and combines – efficient mud-sprayers that kept your windscreen well greased in winter months; bulky and inexorably slow movers that came between you and any chance of catching the London train. Now the traffic's all sorts of – surprisingly speedy – things: tankers and containers and articulated ten-tonners, cars pulling caravans, cars pulling horse trailers, cars pulling boat trailers (the Water Theme Park at Longmere is only a mile away), and, Fridays-thru-Sundays, the big, high-powered estate cars weekenders drive. When Poll moved here, the villagers would ride their bikes along this road; they walked their children and their dogs along it. Poll had done so. Walkers could stop and chat to neighbours over garden hedges in those days.

Poll stands outside her gateposts and watches headlights on the B-road. They sweep down the hill, black out where the new barn conversions block them from her sight, snap on for the cricket field, off again where the church conversion towers above everything – off on off, like neon signs, like programmed Christmas tree lights. A hundred yards from Poll's turning the road bends sharply, and faint-hearted drivers – women – slow here; drivers bound for Poll's turning have to slow here, they have to slow and change down. Poll follows the Christmas tree lights, she listens to the engine notes. Wait! Even now a car is slowing for the bend, changing down, roaring, slowing right down, turning . . . Headlights swing up and over the hedge, graze it with technicolor, isolate a wheelie dustbin, turn their attention on Poll, dazzle her. Zoë!

The car, sleek and city clean, bound for the Thompsons or the Porters or the Blackwoods or the nameless couple who moved into the Old Pigsty six months ago, and whom Poll has still not asked in for a drink, glides by.

Walking back up the driveway, very slowly, head down, hugging herself, Poll sees more lights. Two tiny penlights this time, under a bush. A cat, the cat, Zoë's cat – that her parents look after now Zoë lives in London. He throws himself at her feet and then rolls on to his back, crying piteously, something he does when he wants his stomach rubbed. (Is the appearance of Zoë's cat, now, at this moment – and crying – significant in any way? In any

sinister way?) Poll scoops him up and he clings to her
furiously, stabbing her in the neck and the shoulder.

At supper – for Poll has decided it can't wait any longer
– Ned says, 'Why aren't you eating?' He bones his fish
neatly and delicately, he takes his time squeezing a lemon
quarter, twisting the pepper grinder, licking his fingers.

'I am eating.' (Not long ago, Poll is remembering, Zoë,
driving back to her flat after an evening out, had to stop
at a red traffic light, and a man tried to get into her car.
He managed to open the passenger door, but the lights
changed and Zoë sped away. Saved by a lucky light and a
cool head. 'You must keep your car doors locked,' Poll told
her, 'don't go anywhere without locking your car doors
first.' 'Okay, Neurotica,' Zoë said, 'but what if I'm in an
accident and unconscious and the car's on fire, how's
anyone going to get me out in a hurry?')

'This is rather nice wine' – Ned congratulates the bottle,
tapping it with a finger. 'Really quite drinkable. Where's
Nadia, by the way? Shouldn't she be here? Shouldn't you
be worrying about her?'

'She's still in Newcastle,' Poll reminds Ned. Nadia went
to Newcastle on Wednesday on a school field-trip. They
went by coach, and Poll suffered beforehand envisaging
bald tyres and a drunken or sleepy coach driver, an over-
weight coach driver all set to have a heart attack at the
wheel. The party was due back today but Nadia decided to
stay on an extra night with a student friend in Jesmond and
is coming home tomorrow for Zoë's birthday. (She actually
let her mother know this change of plan.) Poll cannot worry
about Nadia now because she's worrying about Zoë. She's
still thinking about that man at the traffic lights. She's
wondering: Is Zoë always lucky? Is her head always cool?

'Where are you off to now?' Ned asks Poll.

Fear, like love, like the state of being in love, turns bowels
to water. As a cure for constipation, fear is more efficient
than any purgative or enema.

'I don't know how we've managed to bring up our
children so badly,' Ned complains when Poll returns from

the lavatory, 'so that they don't even have the courtesy to
ring when they're going to be late. So that we have to wait
two hours for the privilege of eating a piece of desiccated
fish. Where did you get it, by the way? Trout farm or
supermarket?'

'Trout farm,' Poll says. A lie. At the trout farm you have
to stand there accessory while a brides-in-the-bath maniac,
wearing protective clothing, does his stuff – that is, nets a
swimming, leaping, living creature; electrocutes it in a
basin, disembowels it, weighs it and slides it into a mortuary
bag. At the supermarket the fish are already in the funeral
parlour when you make your identification, decently laid
out on parsley pillows in bright white styrofoam coffins.
Nadia, who is vegetarian, insists that it's a cop-out to buy
fish this way – when they are too dead and too decorated
to accuse. If Poll's going to eat them, then she should at
least have the guts to witness their execution, Nadia says.

'Zoë usually rings me if she's going to be late. She usually
does. And it's her birthday tomorrow,' Poll adds. Irrel-
evantly, pathetically.

'You're not really worried about her, are you?' Ned
pushes his plate away, hacks at a sweating tower block of
cheddar, topples it, slaps a wedge of pre-stressed concrete
on to a biscuit.

'She said eight – or thereabouts. She said she'd be home
for supper. It's now' – Poll looks at the kitchen clock, a
schoolroom clock it used to be, which has stopped (did she
forget to wind it?) and then looks at her wrist – 'after half
past ten.'

(Not long ago, a friend of Poll's, Janet Bowman, had
been waiting in just this way for her son Robin to turn up.
She'd decided not to worry, she told Poll later, she'd given
herself all sorts of plausible reasons for Robin's non-appear-
ance. Then, as the hours passed, she had worried. When a
car finally did arrive, it was a police car. Robin had been
nineteen.

These things happen; tragedy happens. Fear is no
insurance policy, calmness is no protection. Neither Janet's

calm nor her fear had protected Robin from the lorry that crossed the central reservation. The line between everything being all right and everything being all wrong, for ever, is just a hairline. A hairline crack. A thought which reminds Poll that Caro and her family live on top of the San Andreas Fault.)

'What do you want me to do?' Ned asks, refilling Poll's glass, refilling his own, 'ring the police? What exactly do you want me to do? Our children, like all children, I daresay, change their plans; they forget to say. I don't know how often they do this, but you never learn from it. You imagine the worst, every time. Why? It's masochism, it's a sort of sickness. I don't know if I can cope with it much longer. I think you need professional help. I think maybe you should give psychotherapy another try.'

This is better. Ned coming out into the open. But Poll doesn't want to go to a therapist, she'd rather talk to Ned about her worries. She did go to a therapist for a time, for post-natal depression after Caro arrived, but it hadn't helped. The therapist had appeared more depressed than Poll, and Poll hadn't enjoyed talking about herself, which was what he'd expected her to do. In the end, she just stopped going.

Poll puts out her hand across the table and touches Ned's hand, which shrivels back up the tablecloth and curls into a ball like a hedgehog.

'All right then,' Ned says, 'let's examine the problem. Let's go through it. What exactly is it you fear? Is it another update of the Kelly syndrome? Tell me.'

Poll tries to examine the problem, she tries to pinpoint her fear. Her conclusion is: I fear everything for those I love. But that will not do for Ned, so she says, 'Well, there's the motorway, and Zoë tired and, you know, not concentrating. Driving too fast, falling asleep. There's that . . . ' Poll nearly tells Ned, but decides not to, her other motorway fear, which is that Zoë's fourth-hand Renault will break down and Zoë have to pull on to the hard shoulder – a death trap at the best of times – and make a call from an emergency phone and then, like that poor tragic Marie Wilkes, wife and mother and expectant mother, be stabbed in the neck from behind while talking to the police from the phone.

'You can't go through the driving bit every time,' Ned tells Poll, 'it makes the children's lives, it makes our lives, a misery. Roads are dangerous! Life is dangerous!'

'Zoë's written off two old bangers already,' Poll reminds him, 'but you didn't let me finish. What I was going to say was, we don't even know if she got back from work all right, do we? The message on the answering machine could have been an old one, they often don't bother to change it.'

'Try the flat again,' Ned says. 'See if one of the others is there.' (Ned has not taken on board the names of Zoë's flatmates. He can never remember that they're Jeff, Scabby and Jules.)

'It's the weekend. They decamp at weekends.'

'Don't be negative,' Ned says. 'Try it,' Ned says, positive and firm.

Poll lights a cigarette, her third in the past half-hour, before leaving the kitchen.

In Zoë's flat the telephone rings four times. Last time Poll tried, the ansaphone cut in after only the second ring, so Poll hangs on, and eventually, 'Yes?' Scabby's voice, breathless from running down all those never-swept stairs to the hall.

'Scabby, it's me, Poll, Zoë's mum. Sorry to bother you. Do you happen to know where Zoë might be?'

Silence. The silence of disappointment? Scabby has an un-reliable boyfriend, Zoë once told Poll, someone who plays waiting games, who blows hot and cold and lukewarm.

'Thought she was with you. Thought she said she was goin' home this weekend.'

'When did you last speak to her?'

'Let's see – must a bin yesterday mornin'. She wasn't here last night.'

'What do you mean?'

'Well, this guy whose bathroom she's decoratin' lives miles out, Kent or Sussex or somewhere. She said, I think she said, she'd stay the night if she was tired or somethin'. She musta done.'

'Have you got an address or number for her there?'

'Sorry?' Scabby sounds amazed. 'Look, I'm sure she'll be fine. She probably worked late, wanted to start early this mornin' so she could get done by the weekend. If she turns up here first, I'll get her to phone you, shall I?'

'Yes. Yes if you could. Yes please.'

'But why didn't she tell me she wasn't at the flat when she rang this morning?' Back in the kitchen Poll asks Ned, 'Why didn't she tell me where she was?'

'Why should she? She probably thought you'd panic, which is what you *are* doing. I wouldn't tell you anything if I was her. She's a grown-up woman. She's twenty-two, for Christ's sake!' And Ned hits the table, and pushes it, and gets up, and picks up Poll's nearly empty cigarette packet and chucks it at her. 'Smoking eighteen of these since I got home is dangerous if you like, and for me, too, the poor abused passive smoker.' (Ned and Poll prove all those surveys which say that more women than men are smoking now; that men, even when they're hardened smokers, can give up, whereas women can't.)

'D'you want milk in yours?' Ned is saying from the work top and the electric kettle. Poll nods. She's trying not to notice his jaw, which is working – tightening and contracting – the way it does when he's angry; the way it does when he wants to keep his anger under control. Some lines of a poem have just flown into her head and are nesting there:

> Because I love her
> The sky is dark above her,
> Because I think her fair
> There is menace in the very air,
> A single leaf on the tree
> Is not more frail than she . . .

This poem, or part of a poem, is what Ned quoted to Poll in the first love letter he ever wrote her. The poem – he couldn't remember its author – expressed, he wrote to Poll, exactly what he felt: that merely by loving her he had, in some inexplicable way, put her in danger. Of course reason told him she'd been perfectly all right, was quite capable of looking after herself, before he'd met her, but now the fact of his love, plus the fear he had of losing Poll, put her at risk. Made her vulnerable. 'By loving you I tempt fate,' he wrote. Poll remembers being touched by this letter which she'd kept in her bag and read and reread until it fell apart – and she'd liked the poem. She'd understood the poem.

She also remembers, later on and in another mood, thinking there was something egotistical and paternalistic and patronising about Ned's sentiments – and the poem's. Other poems, to do with love and loss and the fear of loss, had followed it; all had stopped after they were married. After they were married, the poems vanished, to be taken up, presumably, by other young men in love, until dropped by them. (Poll once read an article in *The Library* which said that, in England at least, only the very young and the very old and the so-called in love read poetry from choice.)

'Don't just sit there – say something,' Ned says. 'Drink your wine, drink your coffee, tell me your fears, let them all hang out.'

Is Ned drunk?

'I'm worried that Zoë might have got herself into some-thing, is with someone, she can't handle – ' Poll stops. She's just remembered that this morning, while she was talking to Zoë on the telephone, she'd seen a magpie from her bedroom window. A solitary magpie parading its sorrow under the beech tree on the lawn. Throughout her conver-sation with Zoë she'd kept her sights on this magpie, hoping against hope that its better half would join it; that Sorrow would, as it were, be surprised by Joy. It hadn't been. The magpie was still mooching under the beech tree when Poll replaced her receiver; it was still unvisited ten minutes later, when it flew up into the tree.

'Forget about yourself for a moment,' Ned says, 'forget about your own hangups and think, if you can, about Zoë. I'm going to open another bottle,' Ned says, and does so. 'Think about our daughter. What sort of person is she?'

'Zoë is . . . ' What? Frail. As a single leaf on a tree.

'A creative person, naturally. But not arty-farty. Not wet. She's got her feet on the ground, she's tough in lots of ways. She can be tough with men.' Ned pauses. 'Remember how she got rid of those two wimps? Derrick, was it? And Kit.'

'Nat.' (But they weren't wimps. Nat wasn't a wimp. And Zoë hadn't got rid of him, he'd got rid of her. Another thing Poll knows about Nat: he beat Zoë up once, when he discovered she'd gone out with someone else. Zoë hadn't come home for a month afterwards. She didn't want her father to see the bruises, she'd told Poll; she thought the sight of them might send him bananas, that he'd go after Nat with a shotgun or something.)

'You're not listening,' Ned says, 'you're not thinking.' He refills Poll's glass; he drains his own. 'You don't want to see reason. You don't want to be comforted.'

'I do. I really do.' Poll reaches for her wine glass, and in so doing knocks over her coffee cup, still full. She sits there while Ned mops up round her, the way she used to mop round their children when they knocked their milk beakers over at tea time.

'I'm sorry,' Poll says, 'I can't concentrate because I'm listening for a car. I just want Zoë home. That's all I want,' Poll says.

'You probably shouldn't have had children,' Ned says seriously and thoughtfully. Drunkenly? 'I see that now. Having children — and I don't mean giving birth to them, I know all about that — takes guts. The guts to nurture and protect, and then let go. To withdraw. The guts to keep calm in a crisis.'

How true! How very true!

'And this isn't even a crisis. It's either a misunderstanding on your part, or thoughtlessness on Zoë's. Or a bit of both. The truth is, you don't always listen to what people say, you're too busy worrying about something else, anticipating some new disaster, to listen.'

Ned has the ability to put his finger on aspects of Poll's character, on truths about it, that can make her blush. The truth is, she doesn't always listen. When she gets lost on a car journey, for example; when she winds down the passenger window and leans across the empty seat and hails a passer-by. If by some stroke of fortune the passer-by is not a non-English-speaking stranger to these parts, he or she is usually keen to set Poll on the right track. People like having a sense of importance thrust upon them; they enjoy doing their good deed for the day. 'Go to the end of the road,' the passer-by tells Poll, 'turn left at the second set of traffic lights, take the third, no, fourth turning left, and then at the roundabout . . . ' While the passer-by is talking, Poll will be concentrating hard – on the passer-by's dentures; on a tulip-red front door behind the passer-by; on a tortoiseshell cat washing itself on the step; on a small boy with a football who might be about to chase it into the road. The passer-by comes to the end of the instructions and repeats them. 'All clear then? Got it now?' And Poll will say, 'Yes! Yes, and thank you so much for your help. Yes, I've really got it now.' The passer-by nods and smiles, and Poll will get into gear and pull away – to where? For she won't have taken in a word. It won't even be that she wasn't listening. It will be that she chose not to listen. A positive decision. Why?

'I don't want to be unkind,' Ned says, 'but there's something distasteful about your anxiety, you know. Something unlikeable, and fake. You have three healthy daughters. You have a part-time job you've told me you enjoy. You have, if I may say so, a more than decent roof over your head. You've had no real worries – so far. What do you know about fear? What do you know about pain?'

Ned points to the pinboard on the wall, the wall where Zoë's muriel should be. Will be. On the pinboard is a lot of – mostly out of date – stuff: invitations and bills and memos, a felt-pen speaking likeness of the Queen that Nadia drew when she was five; and also (what Ned's pointing at) an assortment of curling, yellowing cuttings from newspapers and colour supplements. Vietnamese boat people, massacred students in Tiananmen Square, leukaemia victims of Chernobyl, Kurdish refugees burying their dead in mud, a skeletal, flyblown child clutching a hopeless bowl, accuse Poll from this pinboard. Dictator Nadia pinned them there. 'To remind you you're lucky, Neurotica,' Dictator Nadia said as she fixed a new enormity to the board.

What impertinence! What cheek! What intolerable and mistaken cheek! These images have never made Poll feel lucky. Sad is what they make her feel. Appalled. Fearful. Angry. Uncomfortable. Hopeless and helpless. Guilty. Not lucky at all.

'No one can be coerced into feeling lucky,' Poll told Nadia. 'The lucky feeling is one which, like joy, arrives unbidden and then bathes and blinds you in a sort of – '

'Bathes and blinds you, eh? Wow,' Nadia said. 'Is that a poetry quote? Wowee.'

'You shut up and listen to me,' Poll told Nadia. 'I was being serious. I was about to give you an example of what I mean. I was about to tell you something that happened to me.'

'Okay then, I'm listening.' Nadia sat down at the kitchen table. She folded her arms, in a resigned way, on the table.

Poll told Nadia how once, on her way to work at the library – they were still living in the town then – she'd taken the longer route, the one she didn't often take, via the park. It was a hot day and the tennis courts were full. On one of the courts – Poll hadn't noticed until she was right in front of it – a wheelchair doubles match was being played. Four young men (late teens? early twenties?) playing tennis from wheelchairs. 'Not knocking up,' Poll explained to Nadia, 'not playing patball, playing a hard competitive game, a match.' Poll had stayed to watch for a bit. She was amazed that the wheelchairs could cover the court so fast, and that the boys dared to lean so far out of their seats to hit the ball, 'though they were strapped in, of course, and I think the chairs must have been specially designed – they had tiny seats and backs, they were all wheels really, chariots more than chairs' – Poll looked at Nadia to see if she was listening, and she was – 'and then after a while I noticed that they allowed the ball to bounce twice before hitting it – well, they'd have had to, wouldn't they? Even in those fast chairs. Still, I asked them about it. "Do you have a two-bounce rule?" I called to the boy serving my end of the court. "Yeah we do," he said, "yeah we do." The point of this story,' Poll told her captive audience, who had picked up an empty yoghurt pot from the table and was examining it intently, 'is that while they were playing I suddenly felt wonderfully, extraordinarily happy – and lucky. Lucky to be alive. Lucky to be watching this game. You couldn't feel sorry for the wheelchair players, you see, because they weren't sorry for themselves. You couldn't patronise them. They were saying Yes to life, as your father would put it, and in any case they were playing much better tennis than the ordinary people, the fit people, on the next-door court. I went off to the library soon afterwards, but this excitement, an almost revelatory excitement, lasted all day. Even now, when I'm down, I can draw on that tennis match. Are you embarrassed by this?' Poll asked Nadia. 'Do you find it embarrassing?'

'No,' Nadia said, 'no, it's interesting.'

'What I do know,' Poll said, 'is that if anyone had led me to that court and said, "Come and watch a wheelchair tennis match, it'll do you good, it'll make you realise how lucky you are," it wouldn't have worked. It was the chance nature of it all that did it, that and, paradoxically, the sense of fate I had, the feeling that there was a purpose behind my being there.' 'I can see that,' Nadia said, peering at her yoghurt pot, twisting it round, inspecting its outside and then its inside, 'but – if you'll forgive my saying so – it, the match, the fact of the match, didn't really change anything for you, did it? I mean, not permanently? Not, what's the word, fundamentally. It wasn't a turning point. It didn't stop you feeling anxious, did it? It hasn't altered your out-look on life in any way.'

Poll felt deflated. She got up suddenly and left the room. She wished she hadn't told Nadia about the wheelchair tennis match. Telling her was a mistake. Nadia hadn't understood it at all.

'I do feel fear for those I love, I do feel pain,' Poll's head is in her hands, her eyes are on her plate, 'I may not have a right to, but I do.'

'Let's go back to Zoë,' Ned tries again. 'She's cool and competent, sure, but at the same time quite a cautious person, wouldn't you say? Not really a risk-taker, not like Nadia. She's like you in that way. She takes after you in that.' Ned looks pleased with this insight. He drains his glass and refills it. He tops up Poll's glass. 'You don't need that cigarette,' he tells her, but not crossly this time, quite benignly and matter-of-factly.

'I do,' says Poll, who by automatic reflex while Ned was talking had glanced at her watch. Five to midnight, the watch said. Five to midnight. And where is Zoë? Zoë, where are you? Poll's hands are trembling. Her legs are shaking. Had she been alone she'd be pacing up and down by now, prowling; drinking not wine but whisky, swig after swig, glass after glass; smoking fag after fag, pack after pack. Ned's calm is keeping her from this necessary ritual; his presence is holding her prisoner in the kitchen, at the table.

'You're not an easy person, you know,' Ned says. 'It's not easy being married to a woman who's in love with her children. We've been sitting here God knows how many hours and you still haven't asked me – you haven't asked me once – how I got on at the doctor's today.'

'Oh Ned. Oh my God.' Ned's had a problem with his eyes lately, with his eyesight. A focusing problem. Also, and more peculiar, a reading and writing difficulty. It was hard to explain exactly, he told Poll a month ago when he first noticed it. It was just that he'd found himself reading words wrong, in newspaper articles and so on, and having to go back and reread them, to check. He'd been typing things wrong too and at first he'd thought there must be a gremlin in the word processor. Did he have headaches? Poll dreaded to know (the words 'brain' and 'tumour' had flown into her head and nested there), but Ned said not that he'd noticed, no more than usual. 'You must go to the doctor anyway,' Poll told him, 'we must get this sorted out.' He knew what the doctor would do – ban the booze, Ned told her gloomily. Then all of a sudden it had got better, gone away, vanished, just like that. And the same week Poll read a piece in the paper about eye stress and the contribution computer screens and VDUs make to this. She showed the article to Ned. 'That must be it then,' Ned said. He sounded relieved, but disappointed too. 'My job's supposed to be creating fashion, not following it,' he told Poll.

Then last week the problem returned. An intermittent fault, Ned concluded. He didn't sound too worried about it. 'Perhaps I need new specs.' Poll said nothing. She just went to the telephone and rang the surgery and made an appointment.

'Tell me, quick,' Poll says. (How could she have forgotten Ned's appointment, after all those sleepless nights worrying over it? What sort of monster is she? Why didn't Ned remind her at breakfast that he was going to the doctor today?) 'Tell me what he said. Tell me what he did.'

'There's no hurry about that, there's very little to tell you, we'll talk about it in a moment,' Ned says. 'I haven't done with Zoë. I was saying she isn't one to court danger any more than you are. Isn't that true?'

Well.

Well no, as it happens. Not true. Not true of Poll.

Because once, a long time ago, after a day up in London seeing a friend and Christmas shopping, Poll had picked up, or allowed herself to be picked up by, a man, an American, on the train; had got off the train with the man (this was at the stop before her own station), had got into his car and driven with him out of the town; and then, in the entrance to a field, made love to him and let him make love to her in his car.

Done it with him. Gone the whole way. Had sex with a stranger in a remote place in a car.

Want a sausage? Want an ice-cream cornet?
Yes.

Still, it was a long time ago. Young people do do mad things sometimes, dangerous things, things they later wonder about and regret.

It was not a long time ago – not long enough. Poll had been a woman, not a girl, at the time. A wife, at the time. A mother of three.

Poll has never told Ned about this. If he ever found out, he'd leave. If Ned knew, it would confirm his belief that the victims of rape are seldom entirely innocent; that there is always some measure of provocativeness, albeit unconscious, on the victim's part, and therefore of provocation.

An outrageous belief. Six-year-old Kelly, those teenage girls pulled from bicycles and assaulted in ditches, those octogenarians raped at knife point in their own beds by midnight intruders – provocative?

'I did court danger once.' It's Poll's voice, a drunk version of it, saying this. 'I did, you know.'

'Well, you can tell me about it in a minute,' Ned says, 'because I think I heard the telephone.' (Poll can hear it too, now.) 'Shall I answer it? Or do you want to?'

'You.' Poll hasn't the strength to talk to detective sergeants or brain surgeons at the moment. She can't manage a conversation with a life-support-machine monitor. No. She will sit here and wait. She will sit at the table, numb and dumb and deaf, and wait for Ned to return and tell her the worst. Whatever it is.

But after Ned has left the kitchen, she gets up and glides, a zombie or a sleepwalker, into Ned's vaulted and galleried hall and through the archway to the foot of the iron staircase – from which position it is not difficult to overhear what is being said by a speaker on the living area telephone.

'Thank God for that,' Ned is saying. 'No, of course I

wasn't watching the movie. What happened to you? Where are you now?'

Silence from the living area, silence in the hall, while Ned is told the answers to these questions; while Poll releases a long, exhausted, wonderful breath.

'Oh I seeee,' Ned says at last. 'Well, I wish you'd tried again. It wasn't off the hook, it was Caro. What? I can't hear you. Oh I see. I told your mother she must have got it wrong. She'd got it into her head you were coming home for supper, so . . . No, I am not drunk!

'I'm sure you did if you say so,' Ned says.

'Well I was a bit worried, if you want to know. Just a bit – it's catching.

'Oh yeah, of course she was. Oh absolutely, a nightmare evening. Complete panic stations. She had you dead and buried, dead anyway.

'Yes. Yes I did. Thank you for asking . . . I can't go into all that now, we'll talk about it when I see you . . . No – look Zoë not now, it's late. No, no, no, she doesn't. No. Do you want to talk to her? She's in the kitchen. Okay, I'll tell her. Yup. Oh, by the way, happy birthday! What time shall I tell Mum we can expect the birthday girl tomorrow, give or take an hour or six?'

Laughter from Ned. Laughter from Zoë too, probably.

Time, Poll thinks, for her to leave the hall. Time for her to speed back to the kitchen and turn on the hot tap and get stuck into the washing-up. Then, when Ned reappears, the table will be cleared, the plates and glasses stacked, and there she'll be, brisk and sensible in the sink. Getting on with life, saying Yes to it.

'Zoë's all right.' She says this aloud. Not on the motorway embankment with her throat cut, not gagged and tortured in a rapist's lair; alive. Alive, and laughing and joking on the phone to Ned.

Poll stands swaying at the sink, and hot water, a balm, flows over her hands and her wrists. She is free to think lucky thoughts now; she can conjure up a wheelchair tennis match if she wants to; or she can remember Zoë's birth,

twenty-two years ago today; she can picture Ned, a con-
stant among the masked and gowned comers and goers in
the delivery room, squeezing her hand, giving her gas and
air and courage. And she can listen to him, hear him – as
Zoë arrived – shouting: 'It's a boy! Oh no, whoops, sorry,
it's a girl.' (This is Zoë's favourite story about herself. On
the one hand it illustrates her subtlety and ambiguity, on
the other it proves her 'poor, unloved, unwanted, middle
daughter' theory.)

Poll is free to say 'Thank you' now. She can thank heaven
and her lucky stars and God.

Thank you God.

Thank you God – except. No. No, she will not allow
herself to dwell on negative things. The fact that Zoë isn't
here yet, for instance; the knowledge that Nadia (who also
has to get home tomorrow, on dangerous British Rail track,
on a dangerous British Rail train) is taking her driving test
next Wednesday and with Nadia's luck – and Poll's – will
pass it. Nadia's plan to fill her year off between school and
university crossing Africa by Land Rover and alone is not
a fit subject for contemplation at this lucky minute. And if
Caro and her family choose to live on top of the San
Andreas Fault, well, good luck to them! So do millions of
other intelligent people. There are a lot worse places to live
than Southern California, for heaven's sake!

But there's something else, isn't there, not listed in Poll's
catalogue of anxieties? Around the edge, below the surface,
at the back of the mind, on the tip of the tongue, unfinished,
threatening something. She's trying to focus on it at this
moment, she's trying to worry it out of its hiding place and
into the open, so she can examine it and deal with it.

She's still doing this when Ned comes back to the kitchen
and stands in the doorway and leans there, his eyes shut,
his arms tightly crossed, hugging himself. Hugging a secret,
it occurs to Poll. Hugging a dark secret, biding his time.

High Teas

It was over tea that Mrs Peverill had her weekly skirmishes with the vicar. Unsatisfactory skirmishes, where no ground, it seemed to her, was ever gained. The teas, the skirmishes, had come about this way: a year before, at her daughter Imogen's insistence, Mrs Peverill, in her late seventies, long widowed but only recently infirm, had moved from a big old house in the North-East to a little new house in the South-West. The village, five miles from the market town where Imogen and her family lived, had been chosen because it was large enough to support a Church of England church and a High Street of shops that between them purveyed meat, groceries, wine and tapestry wools. There was even a miniature Lloyds Bank.

More than anything else, it was the shortness of the walk to church that appealed to Mrs Peverill. She had been uprooted. She had left behind in Yorkshire all that survived of a lifetime's friends and enemies and acquaintances. She was in need of spiritual solace.

What she could not know was that the church notice-board by the lych gate, whose comforting promises, in black and gold, of Morning Service, Holy Communion and Evensong she could (if she leaned out a little way into the almond tree) see from her bedroom window, was a relic merely. By the time Mrs Peverill arrived in Upton Solmore, the service that prevailed at St Werburgh's was one entitled Family Eucharist.

That first Sunday when, in good faith and in good time and carrying her father's prayer book and *Hymns Ancient & Modern*, Mrs Peverill stepped into the porch, she was

handed ('They were forced upon me,' she told Imogen later)
a small, red, laminated notebook and a revised *New English
Hymnal*.

Mrs Peverill had known, of course, of the existence of
the new services, but they had never been a threat to her.
At home in Yorkshire, the rector had said he was too old
to learn new tricks, and his Parochial Church Council had
been determined not to. The trial offers of *Series 2* and *3*,
and later, of *Rites A* and *B*, had been speeded back whence
they came. (A few years earlier the *New English Bible* had
met with a different fate – relegated, within six months of
its introduction, to a shelf in the vestry broom-cupboard,
where Mrs Peverill had encountered it each time her name
came up on the cleaning rota.)

In her pew at the back of the church, Mrs Peverill opened
the red notebook and turned its pages in dismay and disbelief. They were printed in alternate blue and black type.
The service was to be conducted by someone called the
President. The prayers and responses, when not new and
unfamiliar, had been chopped and changed almost beyond
recognition and appeared to be in the wrong order. God
was addressed throughout as 'you'. The Nicene Creed
began 'We believe . . . '

When the service was over, Mrs Peverill stumbled out of
the porch close to tears, and did not hear the vicar's words
of welcome or notice his proffered hand; but later in the
week, on Friday, at tea time, he came to call. He followed
her into the kitchen and stood jingling his pockets while
the kettle boiled, and then he carried the tea tray into the
sitting room.

'You've managed to make this room most attractive
already, I must say!' the vicar said. 'It was rather sombre
when old Jerry Cartwright lived here.'

'Thank you,' Mrs Peverill said. She wasn't at all sure she
liked the idea of the vicar having an earlier knowledge of
her house and her sitting room.

'This cake is really something!' The vicar beamed. 'Did
you make it yourself?'

'In Yorkshire,' Mrs Peverill said, 'which is my home, I was used to making a fruit cake on Fridays, in case I had visitors at the weekend.'

'Old habits die hard!' the vicar said. He munched his cake with enthusiasm. Mrs Peverill sipped her tea.

'Pardon me for intruding' – the vicar put his plate on the tray and brushed crumbs from his trousers – 'but you seemed distressed after the Eucharist last Sunday. And then you rushed away before . . . ' He abandoned this sentence and tried out another: 'Have you some troubles you feel you might like to tell me about? A bereavement perhaps? A loss of some kind?'

'Yes,' Mrs Peverill said. 'Yes, I have.'

The vicar leaned forward, his hands on his knees. They were square hands. He was a stocky young man, whose upper arms bulged in the sleeves of his blouson jacket. A muscular Christian, Mrs Peverill decided. He peered at her expectantly. His eyes were very blue and round.

'I have suffered a loss,' she said, 'the loss of the *Book of Common Prayer*, the King James Bible and *Hymns Ancient & Modern*. This happened to me in church, in your church, last Sunday.'

'Oh dear, oh dear,' the vicar said. 'Oh dear, oh dear, oh dear, oh dear.'

'I had never been to a service of Rite A until then,' Mrs Peverill spoke very slowly, 'and I could not follow it. I did not understand it. Nothing, well, very little, was familiar. They have even altered the Creed, you know, and mucked about with the Lord's Prayer.'

The vicar smiled; he started to say something, but Mrs Peverill put up a hand. 'I felt, I feel – how shall I explain this? – robbed and cheated. Robbed of comfort. Cheated of drama and mystery. Of poetry.'

'Poetry?' the vicar said – as though, Mrs Peverill thought afterwards, she'd said something blasphemous ('as though I'd said something blasphemous,' she told Imogen on the telephone).

'Poetry,' Mrs Peverill said, and after that she was silent.

For the vicar, having got over his shock, was laughing. Not in a scornful way, but in a hearty and appreciative way, as at a good joke. From now on, Mrs Peverill vowed, she would keep her emotions to herself, and fight him on the facts.

'You left out the Comfortable Words on Sunday,' she said, 'though there was some sort of version of them in the notebooks.'

'Optional,' the vicar said. 'Optional.' He tried to drain his cup, but it was already empty. 'I do say them sometimes.'

Mrs Peverill felt obliged to offer him another cup of tea, and more cake. He accepted both.

'I think I understand how you feel,' he said presently. 'Some people, usually senior citizens like yourself, tend to have a bit of difficulty at first. But they get used to it, and when they do, they prefer it. Hopefully, you'll come to see Rite A as a refresher course to your faith, one that adds a new dimension of participation and corporate worship. The laity have far more to do nowadays. No chance of falling asleep while the minister does all the work for you!' He laughed. His teeth were very white, his gums very red. 'Anyway, the 1662 Prayer Book, that you set such store by, is a distortion, a *travesty*, of the 1549 original. The spirit of the new liturgy – one of celebration rather than sacrifice – is far closer, you know, to what Cranmer had in mind.'

Mrs Peverill did not know, and did not believe it.

'In what way, Vicar?'

'Tony, please,' the vicar said. 'We won't go into it now,' he continued heartily, rising to his feet, 'but I'll call again if I may, so that we can continue with our chat and, hopefully, iron out some of your problems. By the way,' he said at the door, 'we won't have to make do with those rather naff little pamphlets much longer. Our ASBs – Alternative Service Books – should be here any day now.'

At home in Yorkshire, Mrs Peverill remembered, watching the vicar jog down the path, the rector had once, over a post-PCC-meeting glass of sherry, asked the members for their interpretation of the initials ASB. '*A Serious Blunder*,

I imagine' – Miss Hawkley, the secretary, had drained her glass and reached for her coat – 'unless *A Synod Botch*.'

Mrs Peverill did not grow to like Rite A, let alone prefer it. A year later, she had, however – and this frightened her – grown used to it, in the same way that she'd become inured to, while not approving of frozen vegetables and decimal coinage. She kept her grief and anger alive by repeating, in church, the true, the only, Lord's Prayer and the Creed; and by responding 'And with Thy Spirit' when the rest of the congregation chanted 'And also with you'. She kept her grief and anger alive by thinking up, during arthritically wakeful nights, questions on doctrine and liturgy to tax the vicar with, and by devising traps for him to fall into. He had got into the habit of calling in, on his way home from weekly visits to the hospice, on Friday afternoons, at tea time.

'Tell me, Vicar,' she said invitingly, having waited until his mouth was full of cake, 'do you believe in the responsibility of the individual?'

The vicar nodded, being unable to speak.

'The new Rite does not seem to,' Mrs Peverill said. 'I refer to the Creed and this "We believe" business.'

The vicar swallowed. ' "We believe" is consistent with the new spirit of unity and sharing,' he said, ' "though we are many, we are one body" – you see.'

'No, not really. No, I can't say I do.' Mrs Peverill took her time and sipped her tea. 'How can I know what anyone else believes? I can only speak for myself. In any case, Creed comes from *credo*, not *credimus*.' In the night, when she'd planned the assault, the vicar had turned pale at this point, and run his fingers distractedly through his hair. In her sitting room, he remained rosy and unruffled and finished his cake without urgency. Afterwards he took a large and not especially clean handkerchief from his trouser pocket and wiped his hands and repocketed it. Then he beamed at her.

'You're a tease, Mrs Peverill. But I don't think this sort of – how shall I put it? – nitpicking, pedantry, over one small word is really helpful, do you?'

It was not pedantry, Mrs Peverill knew, it was passion; and the following Friday she renewed her attack.

'This Gradual nonsense,' she began as, having finished tea, they walked down the garden to inspect the herbaceous border she had recently planted. 'Every Sunday you announce: "The hymn for the Gradual is . . . " You can't have a hymn *for* the Gradual, you know. A Gradual *is*. What it is is an antiphon, sung between the Epistle and the Gospel, from the altar steps. You don't, we don't, sing it from the altar steps. Last week you stuck it in between the Gospel and the sermon. Moreover, there's no mention of it in Rite A – nor in the Prayer Book. It belongs, properly, in the Roman Catholic Mass.'

I've got him now, she thought, I've got him now. Confronted with this evidence, he will have to admit defeat. He will have to –

The vicar continued his progress along the path. 'The new Rite,' he said in equable tones, 'has been designed with a wider and deeper ecumenicism in view, and it allows, at certain stages of the service, for the personal discretion and preferences of the President. There's no room any more for a separatist approach. We live in a secular age. The Church is under siege. We must appeal, we must be seen to appeal, to all our brethren of no matter what denomination, to all who fight under Christ's banner. You're very brave,' he said as they reached the end of the garden, 'to plant perennials – all that splitting and staking. We go for annuals at the vicarage. The minimum of work, I always say, for the maximum of colour.'

Mrs Peverill could not always contain herself until Fridays to bombard the enemy. Sometimes she accosted him in God's house, or rather in His porch.

'No Prayer of Humble Access today, I notice,' she said tartly, shaking out her umbrella and then snapping it open. 'Your version of it, that is. Or is that optional too?'

'We were running a bit late.' The vicar smiled a benign smile. 'But yes, since you ask, it is up to me whether or not I include it. If you look at your service book you'll see that the words "all may say" precede it. "May", not "must". On the credit side, I trust you noticed that the Epistle this morning was taken from the Authorised Version – especially for you! You didn't receive the Eucharist today – I hope the old leg isn't playing you up?'

'I was not in a state of grace.' Mrs Peverill gave him a sharp look from under her umbrella, before braving the rain. 'I did not feel in love and charity with my neighbour.'

'I can never make out whether he's High or Low,' Mrs Peverill said on the telephone to her daughter Imogen. 'He says minister, not priest, but the bell rings before Communion and his vestments are all colours of the rainbow. High, I suppose. And Low. A bit of both.'

'I don't know why you go on with all this, Ma,' Imogen said. 'It isn't getting you anywhere. You won't get the Prayer Book back, or King James. You won't change anything.'

Mrs Peverill said nothing.

'You know I do get a bit bored sometimes with this litany of complaint,' Imogen continued, 'and it's not exactly Christian, is it? Baiting the vicar. He probably means well. No offence meant, Ma.'

Mrs Peverill said nothing.

'If I were a believer,' Imogen said, 'and if it were me, I'd be quizzing your Tony on the issues of the day – his stand on women priests, for example, his views on evangelicalism and homosexual clergy. Things that matter. There isn't a *Mrs* Vicar, by the way, is there?' she added darkly.

'History matters,' Mrs Peverill said coldly, 'language matters. A prayer book is a book of prayer. A service book, on the other hand, is the maintenance bumph one keeps in one's glove compartment –'

' "Kept" in your case,' Imogen said. 'You haven't got a car any more,' she reminded her mother.

'I bet you didn't know they've mucked about with the hymns as well,' Mrs Peverill said. 'You used to be fond of hymns as a child. I bet you didn't know that.'

'Did they have to alter the hymns too?' she asked the vicar over tea.

The vicar put his hands to his head, as if to ward off blows. 'Not substantial alterations, surely?'

'Last week we had "Lead us Heavenly Father", and while I was singing "Lone and dreary, faint and weary, Through the desert Thou didst go", you were all singing about Jesus being self-denying and death-defying and going to Calvary. Odd, isn't it, that we continue to address God and Jesus as "Thou" in hymns? They must get rather confused, I imagine.'

'Perhaps "dreary" is not the right adverb to describe Our Lord?' the vicar suggested, stretching a hand for a third piece of cake.

Mrs Peverill took the last silver-paper angel from the box at her feet and hung it on the lowest branch of the St Werburgh's Christmas tree.

'Angels from the realms of glory,' the vicar sang tunelessly in her ear, 'wing your-or flight o'er all the earth . . .' He was hovering at her elbow, waiting for her to finish her decorating so that he could test the fairy lights. These, a collection of alternate red and yellow bulbs strung along a chewed flex, were more giant than fairy, and too clumsy for the branches. They quite ruined, Mrs Peverill opined, the delicate effect she was wanting to create. She sighed.

'At home in Yorkshire,' she remarked, in the tone of someone determined to extol, to a present, unsatisfactory employer, the virtues of a past one, 'we had real wax candles on the tree. Candle flame sheds a holy light.'

'So you mentioned last year,' the vicar said, 'and I can only repeat: the fire risk is too dodgy.'

'Is it too dodgy to ask, Vicar, if we could have 1662 for Midnight Communion this Christmas? I am, after all, seventy-nine. It could well be my last . . . '

'I doubt that very much, Mrs P.' The vicar laughed. 'But it will certainly be my last Christmas – in Upton Solmore. I couldn't tell you before because I hadn't informed the churchwardens, but the fact is, I'm off to fresh fields and pastures new. I've seen the bishop. Merseyside will present a very different sort of challenge, of course, but hopefully one . . . '

Mrs Peverill did not hear the vicar's next words. She was in a state of shock. It was not his misquoting Milton – hardly a surprise from one who did not know an adjective from an adverb – that upset her, but the implication of his news. What would she do with herself in future on Friday afternoons? How would she endure her wakeful, painful nights? How would she fill her life at all?

'I shall miss your teas, I must say,' the vicar was saying when she'd found herself a pillar and enlisted its support, 'and our chats. But – who knows? – if the PCC deems fit, the new minister may reinstate a form of service that's more up your aisle.'

Mrs Peverill said nothing. The next incumbent would not restore the Prayer Book to St Werburgh's: the ASBs were already in the pews. Far more likely he'd be a rock guitarist *manqué*, and invite his congregation to sing *Lord of the Dance* for the Gradual. The devil she knew was, at least, unmusical.

The devil she knew moved the stepladder away from the Christmas tree.

'That looks great, Mrs P. Now for our Regent Street happening! If you'd like to turn off the overhead lights, I'll switch on the tree.'

Mrs Peverill reached up for her switch; the vicar bent to his. And in the second before the ancient Bakelite plug burst (setting fire to the flex and dispatching Tony to pastures newer, and more challenging, even, than Merseyside), the dark tree bloomed with a thousand candles; while on every branch – Mrs Peverill would later swear – angels from the realms of glory stood poised to wing their flight.

The Dying Room

I think I left my wireless in the drawing room, his mother said. Could you get it? I'd be grateful.

His mother and he were in the kitchen. He took a big breath. He said, You can't use that word any more, I'm sorry, we've decided.

What word are you talking about? his mother said. She took a tray of cheese tartlets from the oven and put them on the table. His mother is a cook. She cooks for her family when they're at home and she cooks professionally: for other women's freezers and other women's lunch and dinner parties. She also supplies, on a regular basis, her local delicatessen with pâtés and terrines and tarts and quiches. Blast, these look a bit burnt to me, his mother said. Do they look burnt to you? What word can't I use?

'Drawing room', he said. It's an anachronism, it's irrelevant. It's snobbish. It has associations with mindless West End theatre. It's embarrassing.

His mother said nothing for a minute. She looked thoughtful; she looked thoughtfully at her feet. Then she said, Who are 'we'? 'We' who have decided?

My sisters and I, he told her. Your children. All of them.

I see, his mother said. First I've heard of this, I have to say.

The point is, he said, our friends, the ones we bring here, find it offensive – or a joke. And so do we. It is offensive, and ridiculous, to continue to use a word that means nothing to ninety-nine per cent of the population, that ninety-nine per cent of the population does not use.

Hang on a minute, his mother said, I just want to get

this straight. You're at university, and most of the people you bring here, from whatever background, are students too. Are you saying that this doesn't make you an elite of some kind? Are you telling me that the words you use in your essays are the words ninety-nine per cent of the population uses? Don't look at me like that, his mother said. If you want to know, I don't feel that strongly about 'drawing room'; it's what your father called it, it's the habit of a lifetime, but you can break habits. I have wondered about it. The room in question is rather small for a drawing room. What word would you like me to use instead? 'Lounge'?

There were other words, he told his mother.

Are there? his mother said. What's wrong with 'lounge'? I bet 'lounge' is what ninety-nine per cent of the population uses. But if you don't like it, if its airport and hotel connotations bother you, how about 'front room'? Will that do?

The room his mother calls the 'drawing room' is at the back of the house and looks on to the back garden. It looks on to a square of lawn with three apple trees on it, two mixed borders either side and, beyond the lawn and divided from it by a box hedge, the vegetable garden: peasticks and bean poles and a rusty fruit cage and a potting shed. A cottage garden, his mother has always described it as.

I can't call it the 'morning room', his mother murmured, more to herself than to him, because we tend to use it mostly in the evenings. I can't call it the 'music room' because none of us plays an instrument, and because all those gramophones – those CD and tape-deck affairs – are in your bedrooms. To call it the 'smoking room', though when you're at home accurate, would be tantamount to encouraging a health-wrecking practice I deplore.

His mother was mocking him. She was, as usual, refusing to address the issue, a serious and important one. She was declining to engage with the argument. He said so.

Address the issue? Engage with the argument? His mother turned the phrases over and weighed them in invisible scales. Engage with the argument. Is that an expression

ninety-nine per cent of the pop . . . ? Well, no matter. Where
was I? I know, in the 'parlour'. I like 'parlour', I rather go
for 'parlour'. It's an old word. It conjures up monks in
monasteries having a chinwag, it conjures up people in ruffs
having a tête-à-tête. Then there's the ice-cream side of it,
of course – oh, and massage, and nail buffing and leg
waxing . . . Which reminds me . . .

Oh for God's sake, he said.

I like 'parlour', his mother said. I think I like 'parlour'
best. But on the other hand – *parlare, parlatorium* – a bit
too elitist, don't you think? On the whole?

Look, he said, there are other names for rooms, ordinary
ones, not jokey or archaic or patronising, that you haven't
mentioned yet, that you seem to be deliberately avoiding.

If you mean 'sitting room', his mother said, I did think
of it, it did occur to me, and then I thought, No, too safe,
a compromise choice, with a whiff of amontillado about it.

It's less offensive than 'drawing room'. And it's more
exact – people do tend to sit in rooms.

Probably it is for you, his mother said. You and your
siblings and friends are great sitters. Great loungers and
withdrawers too, I might say. But I don't have that much
time for sitting. In the room that for the moment shall be
nameless I tend to stand.

His mother was standing as she said this. She was standing by the stove, lifting the lid from the saucepan, giving
the soup a stir. He was sitting on a chair at the table,
lounging perhaps. He sat up. He stood up.

You haven't got an ashtray, his mother said, here, use
this. By the way, his mother said, did I ever tell you about
the misprint your father found in the local paper once? In an
estate agent's advertisement? 'Five bed, two bath, kitchen,
dining room, shitting room'? Or perhaps it wasn't a misprint, who can say? This soup doesn't taste of anything
much, his mother said, come and try it. Come and tell me
what you think it needs.

He took the spoon from his mother's hand and tasted
her soup. It's okay, he said, it's fine, could do with more

salt. The name you're avoiding, he said, the name we use, as you must have noticed, that we want you to use, is 'living room'. A room for living in. The room where people live. Graham Greene wrote a play about it. No, he said (for he could see his mother was about to interrupt him), there are no jokes to be made. I defy you to be satirical about this one. 'Living room' is accurate. And it's classless, it embraces all. The pathetic thing is (and he banged his fist on the table) it'd be impossible to have this argument anywhere else but here! It'd be meaningless anywhere but in Little England. Christ, what a shower!

Nineteen fifty-three, was it? his mother said, or nineteen fifty-four? The year I saw *The Living Room*. Dorothy Tutin was made a star overnight – don't think that sort of thing happens any more, does it? I'd seen her in *Much Ado* at the Phoenix, but . . . Look, it's accuracy I want to quiz you about, his mother said. Pass me that colander, would you. No not that one, the red one. Think for a moment – where are we having this conversation? If we can be said to live anywhere, it's the kitchen – except for your grandfather, poor man, who lives in the lavatory. No, we live in the kitchen and we make occasional forays – withdraw, if you like – into –

You're so clever, he said, you think everything can be reduced to a clever, silly, word game.

No, his mother said, no I don't, I just want to understand your motives, which I suspect are suspect.

Our motives, our motive, is clear, he said. There's nothing eccentric about it. We're egalitarians and we want to live in an egalitarian world. Drawing rooms – withdrawing rooms, as no doubt you'd prefer – have no place in that world. They have nothing to do with the real world as it is now. They have to do with privilege and power. They have to do with tribalism in the worst sense.

His mother took a bunch of parsley from a jam jar on the windowsill. Do come and see what these sparrows are up to! she said. Damn, you're too late, she said. She put the parsley on a chopping board. Then she took five soup bowls off the dresser and put them in the bottom oven. She straightened up.

He said, Look, doesn't it embarrass you when you say 'drawing room' to Mrs Todd, for example? Doesn't it make you feel uncomfortable? Doesn't it? It does us, I can tell you.

His mother looked astonished. She said, You astonish me. Why ever should it? It doesn't embarrass her. I'll tell you how it works. I say to her, Oh Mrs Todd, the children were down at the weekend, and you know what that means, so I think the drawing room could do with some special attention . . . or she'll say to me, Thought I might do the lounge through today, Mrs Symonds – kids home Sunday, were they? Point is, we have our own language, a language we feel comfortable in, and we stick to it. Both of us. Not just me. Don't think it's just me. But we understand each other. We do. And – though you may not believe this – we're fond of each other. We've got a lot in common. We're both working women, we're both widows. We've been seeing each other twice a week now for what? – fifteen years. I know a lot about her life, I know all about our Malcolm and our Cheryl and our Diane and our Diane's baby Gary – who's teething at the moment incidentally – and she knows even more about my life. I remember her birthday, and she – unlike some I could mention – always remembers mine. I went to see her when she was in hospital, and she came to see me when I was. She came on the bus the day after my op, and then later in the week she got Malcolm to drive her over after work. Malcolm's pick-up is very unreliable, you know. He spends all his Sundays working on it, but even so it invariably fails its MOT. If it isn't the gear box it's the brakes, and if it isn't the brakes it's the exhaust . . . I'm very much afraid Malcolm was sold a pup.

If you're such good friends, he said, if you know everything there is to know about Mrs Todd's life, how come you don't call her by her first name? How come she doesn't call you by your first name?

Ah, you can't catch me there, his mother said. The answer

is because she doesn't want it. I asked her once. She'd been here about a year, and I said, Mrs Todd, don't you think we've known each other long enough to call each other by our Christian names? Mine's Elizabeth, as I expect you know. And she said, Think I'd rather leave things the way they are, if it's all the same to you, Mrs Symonds. So we did. I did feel crushed at the time, I did feel a bit snubbed, but I don't think she meant to snub me. I really don't think she did.

About 'living room', he said.

Oh that, his mother said. If that's what you're set on, I'll give it a try. But if you want to bring Mrs Todd into line, I fear you've got problems – she's a 'lounge' person, definitely. 'Definitely' is another of her words. She says 'definitely' very often when I'd say 'yes'. Do you find your microwave has made life easier, Mrs Todd? I'll ask her, and she'll say, Oh definitely, definitely. It definitely do, definitely. Mrs Todd is a very definite person. If you think you can get her to turn her lounge into a living room, well, good luck.

I never said I wanted her to alter anything, he said. You're putting words into my mouth. I never said that. Of course she can keep her lounge. We want you to get rid of your drawing room, which is quite different. He hesitated. He said, We won't bring our friends here unless you do.

Can I have that in writing? his mother said. Joke, she said, when she saw his frown. Could you pass me that baking tray please. Actually, Kit, I don't like your tone. Dictatorship and blackmail seem to be the names of your game. Why? Couldn't you wait for evolution to do the job? You won't have to wait long. 'Nurseries' – in houses large enough to have a nursery – are mostly 'playrooms' now. 'Studies' have turned themselves into 'telly rooms'. 'Drawing rooms' are dying even as we speak. By the time my generation is under the sod, the only 'drawing rooms' left will be in palaces and stately homes. Truly, you won't have to wait long.

If you want to make yourself useful, you could lay the table, his mother said.

What I don't understand, his mother said, is why you have to be so heavy about all this. If your friends don't like the vocabulary I use, couldn't you make a joke of it? Couldn't you just tell them your mother is an eccentric old bat? That sort of confession would improve your street cred no end, I should've thought.

There isn't any point in going on with this, he said. There isn't any point in trying to have a serious discussion with you. You're the personification of the English disease, the English upper class disease, of superciliousness. Everything you've said this morning, and the way you've said it, is offensive, but you can't even see it, you can't even hear it. If you knew the way you sound to ordinary people! 'Our Malcolm' and 'our Joanne' – mocking and superior, that's how you sound.

Diane, his mother said, Diane, not Joanne. I wasn't mocking, I assure you, I was borrowing. I was repeating. And who's calling who ordinary? No one's that ordinary. In my experience most people, when you get to know them, are extraordinary. Look, if you're not going to lay the table, d'you think you could stop hovering and sit down?

I didn't mean 'ordinary', he said, I meant 'other'. Other people. You mentioned palaces and stately homes a minute ago, he said. What you don't seem to understand is that this place is a palace to some of the friends I bring here. In fact that's exactly what Julie said the first time she came down. She walked in the door and said, God, it's a palace! You never told me your mother lived in a fucking palace, Kit.

I don't get this, his mother said. First it's 'drawing room', then it's the way I talk, now it's this house. You keep moving the goal posts. Are you saying people shouldn't be allowed to live in five-bedroomed houses, in five-and-a-half-– if you count the box room – bedroomed houses in case other people, who live in two-bedroomed houses or flats, might think of them as palaces? Is that what you're saying?

I happen to know that Julie liked this house. She came down early one morning that first visit – you were still in bed – and had breakfast with me. She said, I really love this place, Elizabeth – it's magic. I'm going to live in a place like this one day. We went round the garden and she knew the names of everything. Monkshood! she said, my dad won't have monkshood in the garden . . . I was fond of Julie. She was a very nice girl. I was sorry when you gave her the push.

Martin found you frightening, he said. D'you remember Martin?

That's okay, I found Martin frightening, his mother said.

When I say 'frightening' I mean 'posh', he said. I met Martin in the pub the other night and he seemed a bit down and fed up with life – well, with his job really – and I asked him if he'd like to get away to the country this weekend. He wanted to know if you were going to be there. I said probably you would, it was your house. And he said, Well, think I'll give it a miss then. No offence, but your mother and her 'drawing rooms' and 'wirelesses' and 'gramophones' are a bit posh for me. He pronounced it 'poshe'.

Well that hurts certainly. Yes it does, his mother said. Could you come here a minute, I can't read this without my specs, does it say two ounces or four?

Martin spent a lot of his childhood in care, you know, he said. Four ounces, he said. He was shunted from council home to council home. From the age of seven, that is. Before that he lived in a one-room flat with his parents. They ate in it and slept in it and his parents screwed in it. A lot of pain went on in that living room. His father beat his mother up in it – night after night after night. Dreadful, bloody beatings. If Martin tried to stop him he got beaten up too.

That is very dreadful, his mother said. Poor child. Poor Martin. I didn't know that. I am very sorry indeed about that.

So you can probably see why 'drawing rooms' and such would put him off, he said. Piss him off. I mean, what the fuck have they got to do with his life, or with anything he knows about? Like fucking nothing.

Yes I do see, his mother said. I understand now why he's on the defensive. What I don't understand is, why, if you're so fond of him, you didn't warn me about all this before he came down here. It would have saved me asking him all sorts of tactless questions about his life and family, and him having to skate round them – which is what he did do.

How patronising can you be! he said. Martin doesn't need explaining, or explaining away, by me or anyone. He is himself, he is a valuable human being.

His mother took her mixing bowl and egg whisk to the sink and ran the tap over them. She turned the tap off, twisting it hard. Remind me to get something done about this washer, she said. She said, Why do I get the feeling that, for you, only one sort of person, from one sort of background, is a valuable human being? Why do I get the impression that, in your view, a person has to have been brought up in an obviously deprived environment to know anything about pain?

I haven't said that, he said.

So much so that I feel I've failed you, that you'd have preferred to have had Martin's childhood, that kind of misery being the only passport – as you would see it – to full membership of the human race.

You're silent, his mother said. She tapped him on the shoulder. Hey, look at me.

He looked out of the window.

Let me remind you of your father's childhood, his mother said. It was a very comfortable, green-belt childhood. There was a cook, Inez I think, and a maid. Two maids. There was a nanny until your father went away to school. There was a big garden with a shrubbery one end to play in – though he had to play by himself most of the time, of course, being an only child. There was all that. There were also your grandparents who hated each other. They slept at different ends of the house, but in the evenings when your grandfather came home from his office they sat together in the drawing room in their own special chairs and tormented each other. Your grandmother had the edge, she was the cleverer. She was frustrated. Nowadays, I suppose, she'd have been a career woman, and perhaps not married. From all the evidence she despised men. While this ritual was going on, while they goaded and persecuted each other, your father was made to sit in a corner and play with his Meccano or read a book. He was not allowed to interrupt and he was not allowed to leave the room. At six-forty-five on the dot your grandmother would take a key from the bunch on the thin leather belt she always wore and unlock the drinks cupboard, and the serious whisky drinking – and the serious torturing – would begin.

I know about that, he said, you've told me about that.

There was no blood, his mother said, there were no visible bruises, just –

I've got the point, he said, you've made your point.

When your father was dying I thought about the nightmare he'd had to endure while he was growing up. I wondered if it might have been responsible in some way for his illness, if the stress of it had made him vulnerable, damaged his immune system. D'you think that's possible?

Could be, he said. Could be. I don't know.

I wish you'd known him, his mother said. That's the worst of it, your never knowing him, or rather being too young to remember him. That photograph on my dressing table, the one of you aged eighteen months or so with Daddy. You're looking up at him and you're hugging his knees. Now I remember that occasion – I took the photograph. I remember the way you ran, well, staggered up the garden – you were a very late walker, you know, very slow to get yourself off your bottom – and threw yourself at him. You nearly toppled him. And then I pressed the button. I remember that afternoon very well. I remember your father telling me there was no point in taking any photographs, the light was too poor . . . well, I remember it all. I remember how tired your father was. He was already ill but we didn't know. I remember that you had a tantrum about ten minutes before I took the photograph. You lay on the grass and kicked and screamed. But you don't remember. You don't remember him, and you don't remember you – or any of it. It's just a photograph to you.

Cass and Anna remember him, he said, they say they do. They've told me things.

He did his dying in the drawing room – as it was then called – his mother said. He wanted to be downstairs so he could see into the garden – walk into it to begin with. When he was given his death sentence, at Christmas, he set himself some targets. The start of the cricket season – on telly – was one. The peonies and irises out was another. We had wonderful irises in those days, the proper rhizomatous sort, the tall bearded ones, a huge bed of them your father made. He was passionate about his irises, quite boring about them. Irises are tricky things, they like being by themselves, they don't like being moved, they have to have full sun, you're supposed to divide them every three years immediately after flowering – it's quite a performance. It takes patience to grow good irises, and your father was not a patient man. He was a quick-tempered man. I was quite jealous of his irises and all the patient attention they got. Every weekend spent in the garden – or the bloody potting shed. Graham Greene has got a lot to answer for, if you ask me.

He had not known about the irises. He said, Did he see them? Were they out in time?

Some of them were out, the ordinary white flags, and the blue ones. The red peonies were out, the *officinalis*, but the pale ones weren't – you know, the Chinese ones. The ones he liked best weren't.

I don't think I knew he died in the living room, he said. I don't think you ever told me that.

He didn't die in it, his mother said. About three weeks before he died we moved him upstairs. It had become impossible to look after him properly downstairs, and it was too noisy. Small children – you were only two and obstreperous – kept bursting in. When they carried him upstairs, which was difficult because he was in agony, I waited at the top, on the landing; and when he saw me he said, Next time I go down these stairs, folks, it'll be feet first. He said it to make me laugh, to make the doctor and the nurse – who'd made a sort of chair for him out of their hands – laugh. It was brave to make that joke, but it was cruel too, because three weeks later when he did go down the stairs, in his coffin, I kept remembering him coming up, I kept hearing him say, Feet first.

If I don't talk about it much, his mother said, it's because I don't like thinking about it. I prefer to remember your father before he got that bloody disease. He was a different person before he got it. I don't mean just because he looked different – obviously if someone loses six stone in a short time he's going to seem different, he's going to feel unfamiliar – I suppose because we tend to think of a person's shape as being part of their personality, of being them – but that wasn't the real problem. The real problem I discovered was the gap there is between the living and the dying. An enormous, unbridgeable gap.

We're all dying though, aren't we, he said. From the moment we're born you could say we're dying.

Don't give me that, his mother said, don't give me that claptrap. Could you move your elbow please, I'm trying to lay the table. I want to give you a knife and fork.

Sit down, he said, stop working and sit down and talk to me. Just for five minutes. You never sit down and talk. You never tell me anything. You never tell me anything about you.

It's lunch time, his mother said, we can't talk now. Grandpa will be starving. Could you go and tell him it's ready and give him a hand down the stairs. I fear we're going to have to have a lift put in, you know, or –

What is lunch? he said. What are we having? Fish fingers and peas? he said hopefully, beefburgers and beans, sausage and chips?

I wish you hadn't mentioned sausages, his mother said, why did you have to mention sausages? Okay, I'll tell you, his mother said (as though he'd asked her to, which he hadn't, he hadn't said a word), why not? I'll tell you. When your father was dying, before he got to the point of not wanting anything to eat at all, the only thing he wanted was sausages. I'd put my head round the door and ask him, What d'you fancy for lunch today, darling? and he'd say, Bangers and mash. Then I'd go away and cook him something quite other – something I thought would be nourishing and easy to digest, that would slip down. I'd bring in the tray – he'd be sitting with his back to me, shoulders stooped, head supported by a hand, looking out at the garden – and he'd say, without turning his head because turning and twisting were very painful for him, Doesn't smell like bangers. And I'd say, You just wait and see. I'd put the tray down on a chair, and tuck a napkin under his chin and adjust the invalid table and wheel it up over his knees, and put the plate on it and whip the cover off and say, There! Doesn't that look delicious? And he'd stare down at the plate. I asked for bangers, he'd say eventually. I was expecting bangers.

I don't think I let him have bangers more than twice in the whole of that five months, the whole time he was dying, his mother said. I don't know why I didn't give him what he asked for. I've tried to work out why I didn't.

He said nothing for a minute. Then he said, You thought they'd be hard for him to digest, you thought they'd make him uncomfortable.

Did I? his mother said. What would a bit of discomfort have mattered? He was dying, for God's sake! He wanted bangers.

Say something! his mother said. I've shocked you, haven't I? I can tell.

No. No, you haven't, he said. Look, I'd better go and get Grandpa, I'd better go and find the girls.

Could you bring me my wireless at the same time? his mother said, I want to hear the news. I'm not sure where I left it, downstairs I think, in the – in some room or other.

Spoilt

❦

As soon as Nita and Krystal were strapped in the car, he ran back into the house and dialled Sylvie's number.

'She's gone.'

'You sure? You sure she won't be back for something?'

'Yeh. Sure. She left an hour ago. She's on the train.' He waited a moment. 'I love you. Correction – I fancy you.'

'Yes.'

'You are coming round tonight, aren't you, after the kid's in bed?'

'Well. If it's okay to. If you really think it's safe.'

'What are you wearing?' He always asked this question. Her answer, whatever it happened to be, always excited him. Tortured him.

'I'm not dressed yet.'

'I want you. I want you now.'

'I want you.' But, because she never volunteered any desire, merely repeated back to him, without urgency, his own, he was never convinced that she did want him. Except when they were in bed.

'Sylvie – ?'

'Stew, I got to go. I'm not dressed, I told you, I'll be late for work. See you this evening, 'bout ten, hopefully. You going down the Job Centre later?'

'Might do.' He felt like adding, What the hell business is it of yours? You're not my wife – but stopped himself.

'I only ask because if you are coming into town, pop in and see me.'

*

This business with Sylvie had started three months ago, not long after Milsom's Motors, where he'd been head salesman for five years, had gone bust. (Expansion just before the recession really bit had been the cause of that: Milsom paying over the odds for the plot next door for additional parking, while not having paid off the bank loan for the new showroom.) He'd been in the Job Centre, casting a hopeless eye over the Miscellaneous board, when she'd materialised beside him: a slight, blunt-nosed girl in a pink shell-suit and pink and green trainers, and with what he thought of – despite evidence everywhere that it was women nowadays who wore it – as a young lad's haircut: quiff in front, razored back and sides. What little there was of her hair was a reddish blonde. She'd taken her eye off the noticeboard for a second and given him a sideways, con-spiratorial look, at the same time sucking her teeth in a way that clearly said 'sod this lot, for starters'; and he'd cheered up suddenly. (Her eyes were grey-green, heavy-lidded, sleepy-looking; and later that morning, sinking his third pint in the regulars' bar at the Crown, he would think about her eyes, the colour of them, the lazy way she opened and shut them.) 'Here's one should fit you to a T,' he'd said, feeling pretty damn sure no offence would be taken, ' "Experienced boner required for local poultry factory, hun'red and twenty pound a week, Mon to Fri, 8 am to 5 pm. Will consider person with butchery experience." ' 'Perfect,' she'd said at once, closing her eyes slowly, opening them half-way, 'just the ticket for a vegetarian. I need look no further then, need I?'

That was as far as it had gone then, but not long after-wards, when he was again in the Centre (Employment Ser-vice, they were now calling theirselves), sitting across a table from a bitch who was taking down particulars of his educational qualifications and work experience, who was reassuring him that while it was an undeniable fact that car sales opportunities were, in the current economic climate, on the downturn, she was nonetheless optimistic that a person with his proven work record and selling potential would not be out of the marketplace for long, he'd seen a backview of pink shell-suit over by the Sits Vacant. On his way out she'd accosted him. 'Got one for you – look. "Pollution Control Officer. Degree- or diploma-qualified, with several years' related experience. To develop control procedures and compliance monitoring." Okay?' 'A doddle,' he'd said, 'straight up, Guv, no lie, job's good as mine. Cause for celebration' – he rubbed his hands. 'Care to join us for a coffee at Molly's, over yonder?' To his amazement she'd said yes. (She'd said, 'Yeah, okay then,' and 'Why not?')

When Milsom's Motors collapsed and he had to break the news, Jackie, his wife, who in another role was head stylist at Jason James Hair Studios in the High Street, had been sympathetic. She'd put her arms round him and held him. She'd printed a Max Factor kiss on his forehead. 'It'll be all right, love, you'll see. We can manage for a bit. Listen' (gripping his shoulders), 'you'll be okay. You can sell anything. As I said to Jason only yesterday, "He could sell a cycle to a paraplegic, that one could." So stop fussing. You've got what it takes – unlike some as I could mention,' – 'some' being the layabout first husband she'd traded in for him.

Jackie's sympathy, which after that first evening had manifested itself in practical ways – she'd cut and restyled his letters of job application, she'd given a new look to his CV ('Make that Maths CSE an O-level, Stew, they're never going to check it'), and typed these up – had lasted only a month. When the month was over, leaving no prospect of an interview, let alone a job, she'd turned into someone else, someone who sighed and flounced and found fault, someone who snapped about the place like a dog snapping at flies, the martinet he'd witnessed at Jason James, running a critical finger round the back wash-basins, chivvying the juniors with a broom.

'You're never going to get yourself a job at this rate, not

if you don't buck your ideas up, you won't. You're not even any use as a house husband; couch potato's what you're fast turning into. Look at you' – Jackie, smart as a new paint job, poised for the wonderful world of work, for the great hairdressing salon of life, glared at him from the front door.

'Fine time you've picked to take up cigarettes again. I can't pay off this mortgage on me own, y'know. No way. Turn round, Anita' – brushing some imaginary dust from her small daughter's shoulders, tucking the child's shirt collar inside the collar of her blazer. 'Don't imagine I'm going to fund that filthy habit. Well, we're away now, Stewart. Shopping list's on the worktop, and for Pete's sake, control yourself – I expect to see some change from that twenty pound. Do what you can with the washing machine, it might only be the plug wants looking at. Janet's off, so I'll be working till seven tonight. Can you be sure to fetch Anita from Jean's by four-thirty at the latest, and give her her tea . . . ' The front door slammed behind them, the porch shook, a hanging basket of plastic geraniums, immediately inside the door, dithered for a second before deciding to spin. House husband and couch potato made his way to the kitchen in search of his cigarettes, a can of Hofmeister and the *Express*, transported these consolations to the lounge, settled himself on the settee, lit up, opened his paper, ring-pulled the can of beer – and was caught by Anita, staring and mouthing at him through the patio doors. Small fingers drummed silently on the double glazing. Cursing, he stubbed out his fag, pushed himself out of his Dralon refuge and slid back the doors. 'Well?' 'Stew, can you mend my bike today please? You promised. You said you'd do it last week, you – ' 'Okay, okay. If I have a minute.' (Was it his imagination, or did his step-daughter give him a pitying look?) 'Off you go now, don't keep your mother waiting, you'll be late for school.'

It was later that morning, when, every page of the paper read and double-read, three empty beer cans interred in the dustbin and most of the cigarettes smoked, he'd taken the piece of paper containing Sylvie's phone number out of his trouser pocket and unfolded it. ('I'm stopping up my auntie's at present, Haydn Close – you know, off Hollybush Road,' she'd told him over coffee at Molly's, in answer to a casual enquiry as to what sort of journey she had to get home. 'She's a supervisor at Safeway's. She leaves for work at half-seven. I'm usually in till one. If you want, give us a call. Or don't. I'm not bothered either way.') After picking up the receiver and then ramming it back – he did this twice – he had given Sylvie a call.

No job. No wheels (his car had, naturally, been a company car – well, demo model, Sales for the use of). No dosh. No self-respect. No respect. The butt, increasingly, of jibes from the milkman and the postman, even from Terry, the barman at the Crown. ('Another pint, was it? What are we using for cash, old son, dare I enquire?') And now Anita, for whom he'd been hero number one, despised him. Around the time he and Jackie were thinking about getting hitched, and talking about it, most of his mates had tried to put him off. 'What d'you want to go and land yourself with another bloke's kid for?' But he had wanted to. He and Anita had hit it off from the word go. So much so that at breakfast on the second morning of his honeymoon, sipping a fermenting pineapple juice – he'd ordered grapefruit – looking out of the hushed dining room at clouds massing above a gun-metal sea, he'd interrupted a silence with 'Wonder how Nita's getting on at Jean's.' 'It's me daughter you're in love with, Stewart Harrison, I've always known it, I've always known you only wanted to marry me because of her.' Jackie had laughed, and then said, 'Many a true word spoken in jest.' And laughed again. An elderly backview at the next table had turned round and glared.

Anita was a great kid, quiet and good-natured, no trouble at all. She was on the skinny side, but pretty in a pale and blue-eyed way. Her hair, which was naturally wavy, was so fair it was almost white. She had a Danish look, he thought, Danish or Swedish, one of those. He discovered early on that he liked it when people who weren't in the know assumed she was his daughter: 'Does your little girl want an ice cream?' 'What pretty hair your little girl has!' He never told them she wasn't his, and though he always feared Anita would betray him with an indignant, 'He's not my dad,' or, worse, 'My daddy's left home, he doesn't love us any more,' with accompanying waterworks, she didn't.

'Nita ought by rights to have a brother or sister,' he'd told Jackie at the start of their year-long engagement. 'Being an only's no good for a kid.'

'I'm an only, I'd remind you, and it's been good for me. Don't call her Nita, there's a love, I didn't give her a pretty name like that for you to go and mangle it.'

The question of another child, his and hers, had come up more than once because he'd always wanted kids, or thought he had. He hadn't been able to budge her. No way was she going to jeopardise her career and the mortgage – and Anita's future, 'my priority, as well you know' – by having another. She'd never said otherwise, she'd been quite straight with him. If he was serious about wanting a kid then that was that, they'd better pack it in now. Pity, wasn't it, he hadn't said all this prior to their engagement, before spending a small fortune – correction, large fortune – on that engagement party?

Not long after, in mellower mood, in bed, she'd brought the subject up herself: 'You don't really want a kid, do you, Stew? Not when we've got so much going for us' (combing a manicured finger lingeringly through his chest hair), 'not when you've already got two girls, not when you've got me and Anita to spoil?'

He did spoil Anita. Correction: he had spoiled Anita. When he'd been in work. Little presents and surprises from time to time, things he knew she hankered after: a matching 'sapphire' necklace and bracelet from Woolies, a watch with a Mickey Mouse face, a Sunday visit to Alton Towers, the latest Cindy Doll outfit. She was always appreciative. She'd make him bend down so she could get her arms round his neck, and then she'd hang there, feet way off the ground, throttling him, refusing to let go. Sometimes, Jean, the neighbour-friend of Jackie's who did the afternoon collecting from school of their two daughters, would drop Anita off at Milsom's on her way home; and Anita would make herself useful in the showroom, dusting his desk and the chrome rims of ashtrays, rinsing coffee cups. (Cona coffee, served in white and gold cups, had been on offer to all his customers.) If, when she arrived, he was busy, arranging finance at his desk with a client, she would stand quietly beside him while he pen-pushed and form-filled and chatted up, a skinny angel in a navy and white uniform. If there was no one in the showroom, he'd walk and talk her through the cars parked on the royal blue, industrial-weight, carpet. He'd give her the whole sales routine. He'd open doors, explain dashboards, demonstrate kiddie-locks and electronic windows and sunroofs, sound off about fuel injection and power-steering, compare the price and advantages of this or that model. 'Which one are you going to go for then?' When, after a bit of female shilly-shallying, she'd made her choice (her decision based more on appearance – she favoured sports models, blue or silver, even red if a metallic finish – than on his info), he'd allow her into the car. Pushing herself forward, sliding on the cellophane protector to the edge of the driving seat, she'd usually just about manage to get her small hands on the steering wheel. Br-r-m br-r-m!

He had spoiled Anita, if you like, but then she was easy to spoil. And spoiling her hadn't spoilt her.

He had wanted to spoil Jackie, but it was impossible. 'Oh Stew, I've had my eye on these for ages' (lifting whatever it was from the tissue paper, holding it against herself). 'Pity it's peach though. Had me heart set on apricot – you won't mind will you if I . . . '

And now, when there was someone else in his life he really wanted, needed, to spoil, he was thwarted.

'I want to give you everything, Sylvie. Anything at all you fancy. I'd like to buy you the whole effing world.'

'Oh yeah – I've noticed. The moment you walked in the joint I could tell you were a man of distinction. A real big spender.' She was always teasing him. Torturing him. Her eyes, challenging, secretive, indifferent, lazily opening and closing, daily destroyed him. He propped himself on an elbow and examined her eyes, the sulky, pale lids, the not quite believable (but they were real) lashes.

'Don't stare at me, Stew. S'only a small pimple, nothing a dab of OXY 10 won't cure. It'll be gone tomorrow. Come here.' Pulling his head down.

Her eyes. Her breath, perfumed with lager and cigarettes. (As must be his own, he suddenly realised.) Her mouth. He kissed it, hard, and then invaded it. Coming up for air, he kissed everything his mouth encountered on that smooth face: eyelids, nose, ears, forehead, spiky hair, a pimple that didn't exist. 'I'm mad for you, Sylvie' – removing a reddish-blonde strand from his tongue – 'it's killing me. I want you all the time. I'm a desperate man.'

'Prove it then.'

She didn't like it when he got serious. She didn't want a heavy scene. 'Keep it light, boy' – as though it was her, not him, had done those eleven extra years on the planet – was her response to his declarations of love. 'Don' spoil it.' Don't spoil it? How could loving a person spoil anything? He'd asked her this and been even more hurt by her reply: 'Listen, I like you very much. You've got a great body. You're a good screw – yeah, you are. You even smell nice – lotsa guys don't. But why should I get involved? What's in it for me? Don' tell me you'd exchange Jackie and that palace of yours for an unemployed twenty-year-old and a flat up Barham.' (Barham was the oldest and roughest of the four council estates in the town, the one people avoided landing up on when they were allowed any choice. Sylvie had lived on it till she was fifteen, till her dad got work in a sausage factory in Trowbridge and moved his family there.) 'Don't tell me you'd be prepared to give up precious little Anita. Be honest. We're havin' a bit of fun, for as long as it suits – till either or both of us gets a job – and let's keep it that way. There's gotta be some compensations for being on the dole.'

No love then. His reward, most weekday lunch times and early afternoons, for his bus and foot slog across town to Sylvie's auntie's place, was sex. Sylvie, when in the mood, was generous and inventive and energetic in bed. (On the bed. Across it. On the bedroom floor. In the bath. In an orange, stretch-covered armchair. Upright, against the vestibule wall.) 'Tell me what you'd like, don't be shy, tell me' – unzipping him like a banana – 'otherwise I shall have to take the matter into me own hands – so to speak – shan't I?' Something that had shocked him at first, that had taken a bit of getting used to, but that once he had got used to it, he couldn't get enough of, was the way Sylvie talked while they were making love – correction, having sex. Jackie, like most of the women he'd ever been with, was pretty much silent on the job. Sylvie talked. What she went in for wasn't chatter. It was encouragement. Encouragement and invitation and suggestion. Rallying and prompting. Very often she'd give him a running commentary on their match – on what she was doing to him and what he was doing to her and what they were about to do to each other.

Drinking a post-coital cup of Safeway's Blend in Sylvie's auntie's kitchen, watching Sylvie – a heartbreaking sixteen in her T-shirt and jeans and trainers – snap off a piece of her gipsy cream and hold it up, giggling, just beyond reach of Tarzan, her auntie's foulmouthed boxer, he found it impossible to connect her with the sorceress on the bed who, minutes earlier, had done those things to him. Who'd done those things, who'd whispered those words. Those dirty, exciting, mindblowing, words.

'I'm at my wits' end, Stewart. You knew perfectly well Anita had to have her blazer back for today. You aren't asked to do much. The little you are asked to do, you don't do. You better get yourself down to Bollom's as soon as they open, and then take the blazer up to school. Give it to Mrs Castle, in the office.'

'Okay. Sorry.' He'd forgotten about the blazer, which Jean had dropped off at the cleaners on her way back from school, to be ready for him to collect at five. All this panic because today was School Photograph day, and Jackie wanted Anita looking her best. It was nonsense anyway because most of the kids didn't even own blazers, which were optional. What the majority had was anoraks – 'any colour, so long as it's navy blue,' as the note from the headmaster, reminding parents of the minimum requirements as regards uniform ('some, who shall be nameless, appear to have forgotten') had – ha ha ha – put it.

'Look, Stew' – Jackie's face and voice softened. She stretched a hand across the breakfast table and touched his hand. 'This situation isn't easy for any of us. But you're not helping us, or yourself, by taking this attitude. Being sorry for yourself's not going to solve anything. It definitely won't pay the mortgage, and let me remind you we're two months in arrears. Finished, pet?' – turning to Anita, who sat, eyes cast down, fiddling with a piece of unwanted toast. 'Go and brush your teeth then.'

When Anita had left the room, Jackie leant towards him. 'Look at me, Stewart.' He had no desire to look at her. The Warm Peach pancake cheeks, the Frosted Turquoise eyelids and Ultramarine Long-Lash lashes, the Wild Tango (Hi-Gloss) lips, all of which had been part of her allure, which at the beginning had made him proud to be seen with her, now disgusted him. A suffocating blast of Estée Lauder knocked him backwards in his chair. 'I said, "Look at me." ' He looked at her. 'Do you have any idea what you're doing to that child upstairs? You're breaking her heart, you know. You are. You never talk to her, you never play with her, she might as well not be in the house for all the notice you take of her. As she sees it, she's lost her daddy, the only one she's got. How you can do this to her, how you can behave like this to a small kiddie, beats me. She's always thought the world of you, you know.'

'I'm sorry.' He was sorry. Somewhere, at some level. He hadn't wanted to hurt Anita. He hadn't known that he had. Or had he?

'She's given over asking you to mend her bicycle. Pathetic, isn't it? Well, I promised her bedtime you'd do it today without fail, so you'd better. We can't go on like this, Stew. I can't. It'd be different if you could make yourself useful at home till you find work. You said you'd do out the bedroom, remember. You have all day, every day, to do it in. The paint and the paper's been sat on the landing over a month now.'

'Okay OKAY OKAY OKAY.' Gordon Bennett.

'I've been wondering whether you shouldn't go down Doctor Taylor's for a check-up. You're always so tired when I get in, and what you've got to be tired about – '

'I said I was sorry, didn't I?'

'Stewart, it's our marriage on the line. That includes the bedroom, and I'm not talking about decorating. It wasn't a brother I was looking for when I married you.'

'Mu-um!' – Anita, mournfully, from the porch.

'Coming, love. Stewart, I need to know that you're going to get your act together – in every department. It's Birmingham next week. I want to feel easy in my mind that while I'm away you'll be coping, and Anita properly looked after. She could stop over at Jean's, but – '

'No.' He suddenly felt very strongly about this. 'She stays here with me.'

'Mum!'

After he'd delivered Anita's blazer to Mrs Castle in the office ('Well, we'll hardly be needing that, I'm glad to say. Proper shirts and blouses weather this is, for a change'), he made his way to Sylvie's place. The residential part of the town had grown up around the sides of a series of steep hills, the northernmost of which had, until the mid-Seventies, been grazing land for sheep. Haydn Close, the last spec-built mini-estate to go up before the building trade went down, had been set in the middle of this, in a cleft between Mozart Crescent – two half-moons of detached, chalet-style homes – and Beethoven Row – a line of reconstituted stone bungalows overlooking the main road. Haydn Close consisted of a series of split-level three-bedroom, maroon brick terraces, four houses to each terrace. Stewart, on his first visit to Sylvie, had sensed something familiar about the layout, and had then remembered delivering a car to the close while it was still being built, to a couple who had just moved in to the one completed terrace. The husband had made him stand in mud and builders' rubble and admire the special features of his home: traditional farmhouse roof in pale orange pantile, curve-topped window frames in natural wood, pantiled porch, solid wood front door (if quick off the mark, the man told Stewart, buyers had been allowed a choice of oak, mahogany, or pine finish) with bottle-glass fanlight. The new Ford XR3i, buffed into hard gloss magnificence by one of Milsom's school-leaver apprentices before departing the showroom, had sat in the road ignored.

Haydn Close, unremembered by him before Sylvie came on the scene, had, since Sylvie, become a magic place, the place he was happy in, the only place he wanted to be. When he wasn't in it, he thought about it, could conjure at whim the landscaped grass frontages, strimmed to within an inch of their lives and planted out with For Sale boards plus the occasional shrub or ornamental tree; the two rows of discreetly sited lock-up, up-and-over garages, facing each other across a pink-paved divide; the tortoiseshell cat which, having taken a liking to him, would often abandon her wheelie-bin look-out to escort him on the last nerve-racking stage of his journey – up the winding, crazily paved path to number 25. Where Sylvie lived. Where Sylvie, and her auntie Shirley she was fond of, and her uncle Raymond she wasn't and seldom made reference to, and Tarzan the foulmouthed boxer, lived. Diamond-paned leaded lights to

the windows (some of the houses had plain glass casements). Brass furniture on the front door (some of the doors
had iron). Oak finish.

He stood in front of this door now and tugged the fancy
brass lever that activated the chimes. 'Ding dong. Ding
dong ding dong. Ding.' Music to his ears.

She waited until after they'd tried, successfully, two or three
variations of the thing they always did, and were having a
fag break, lying on their backs in the not large enough bed,
watching the smoke from their cigarettes come together and
entwine and eventually disperse along the ceiling, before
delivering her blow.

'Stew, I've got a job. Boots.'

'Kinky boots?' Her last job had been sales assistant at
Tandem shoe shop in the High Street.

'Boots the Chemists. Dirty pics department – well, photographic counter. I start Monday.'

He'd sat up then, and stared at her. 'You can't!'

'I gotta work, Stew. I gotta pay my way. My uncle put
me on final warning last week. "Either you get off your
backside and find a job or you go back home to your
mother's." No way am I going back to Mother's.'

He said nothing for a minute. Then, furiously: 'You can
lie there all calm and tell me that. Knowing it's over, you
and me is over, that my life is ov – '

'Stew.' She put a finger on his lips. 'Don't.' He jerked his
head away.

'Look, it's not been getting any easier up my end.
Remarks have been passed about the "regular visitors –
naming no names, mind – certain people entertain".
Another thing, I've left the sheets out on the line once too
often. My auntie thinks I've got what she likes to call a
"cleanliness fetish". At least that's what she's calling it for
the minute – but she's not stupid, I might tell you.'

'I've seen your auntie.' He hadn't been going to tell her
this.

'Oh yeh? How'd you know it was her?'

'She had her name on her uniform.'

'Sounds possible. Light us another fag, Stew.'

It was possible. (He lit her a fag.) It had been. Like this: Safeway's, 11 am or thereabouts, last Thursday. Him in the checkout queue with a trolley-load of consumer perishables: Bold Ultra all in one, as seen on telly, Typhoo tea bags, ditto, own brand cereal masquerading as Weetabix, own brand jam and coffee and lo-sugar beans . . . and the check-out girl saying to the woman in front of him, 'If you can just hang on a couple of ticks, I'll call a supervisor to attend to your query' . . . He'd been standing there, shifting his feet, boring a hole in the supervisor, willing the old bat to get on with it, p.d.q., when he'd noticed the identity badge on her bosom. Mrs Shirley Jackson. *Mrs Shirley Jackson.* Who's she when she's at home? Sylvie's auntie, that's who! He'd found himself grinning in a daft way. Staring at her (mannish hands, fleshy nose, Princess Di hairdo, late for-ties), he'd told her, silently but quite plainly: I screw your niece. She screws me. We do it every day. We do it in your house. We do it in your orange chair. You've got Spanish dolls in the alcove in your lounge. You've got an avocado bath and basin and toilet. I've pissed in your toilet.

In the car park afterwards, trying to push a trolley, whose wheels were bent on going the opposite way, in the direction of Jackie's Fiesta (she usually lent him her car for the big weekly shop), he'd thought: I'm wicked. I'm a monster. I'm going to hell. And grinned to himself. And done a little dance with his wayward trolley.

'What's this about my auntie, then?'

'Nothing, I just saw her once, that's all.' He buried his face in the paradise that was her neck. If he could just die here. Now.

'Stew, we can still see each other, you know. It's not exactly slave labour at Boots, I do get the odd half-day.' Then, after a pause, she said, 'Didn't you say something about having to fix a bike this afternoon? Without fail?'

Standing inside her front door, trying to leave, not

bearing to, knowing she wanted him to, his hand on the latch, having promised himself he wouldn't mention the subject, he reminded her about Birmingham.

'You haven't forgotten about Birmingham?' Jason James were sending Jackie and Helen, the senior stylists, on a two-day cutting course and competition. (£200 cash prize, plus weekend for two in Minorca, plus a year's free supply of Medusa Hair-Care products to the winning salon.) Jackie was determined to win the competition, which was to be judged by a London big-wig. She and Helen were leaving first thing Thursday, coming back midday Saturday. They had decided to let the train take the strain, which meant Stewart having the use of Jackie's car. Not for joy-riding though. If he thought that (he had, for all of two seconds), he had another think coming. No, he could make himself really useful for once – 'and give Jean the break she deserves' – and do the school runs. Morning and afternoon. All four of them.

(Jackie hadn't mentioned the evenings though, those two long evenings, Thursday and Friday, she wouldn't be home. When Sylvie would be there. 'Well, I s'ppose I could come down and keep you company for a couple of hours while you're babysitting – no harm in that, is there?' – Sylvie's reply, when he'd first put it to her.)

Now she said, 'I haven't forgotten, but – '

'You are going to come?' – as casually as he could manage.

'If you want me to. If you think it's, well, safe to.'

Which was not the right answer.

On the way home he made a detour via Manfreds in Silver Street, and bought a bicycle chain and some nuts and a puncture kit. Afterwards he called in at the Job Centre where he learned he could, if he had a mind, be a part-time bar person, £3.50 an hour, at High Post Hotel; or, if he was fully trained and state-registered and had had experience in caring for the elderly, a general nurse at Sutton Nevey Nursing Home. (29 beds. Wage: to be discussed.)

*

He and Jackie were up with the birds on Thursday morning.
He made them both a cup of tea while Jackie ran from
airer to ironing board to suitcase, and made lists and fired
instructions. 'I'm putting the money for the milkman here.
Okay? Anita's to be in bed by half past eight – nine at the
very latest – she's not staying up watching TV all hours
with you. And you're to keep an eye on her if she goes
outside to play; she either stops here in the garden, or she
can go down Jean's after tea. Nowhere else, and nowhere
on her own.'

An hour later, he and Jackie and Anita stood in the
porch, waiting for the taxi that would take Jackie and
Helen to the station. He'd offered to drive them, but as
Jackie pointed out, it was the wrong direction for school
and too early anyway for Anita who 'had to get a proper
breakfast inside her and leave time for a visit to the toilet'.
The taxi was late and Jackie kept looking at her watch.
She was all keyed up and nervous about her appearance,
smoothing the skirt of her lime two-piece, inspecting an
imaginary ladder, tweaking her shoulder pads into position.
'You look great,' he said, suddenly deciding that heartiness
might be the best mode to get them through the waiting,
'doesn't she, Nita? Doesn't your mum look triffick?' Anita
nodded. 'Well,' he continued, rubbing his hands, 'Nita and
I have certainly got our work cut out while the boss is
away! There's the little matter of a certain young lady's
bicycle to repair.' (The chain he'd bought yesterday had
turned out to be the wrong size, would you credit it.) 'Then
there's the master bedroom to decorate, and when we've
got that lot sorted m'partner here's going to help us weed
the front bed and give the back lawn a trim and brush up
– ain't that so?' – winking at the partner, who did not wink
back.

The taxi, one of four two-tone (cream'n'green), suspen-
sion-free crates belonging to Courtesy Cabs, with Helen on
board, jolted to a stop at the gate. 'Good luck, love, you'll
win the comp – no prob, it's a cert.' And shutting his eyes

tight he braved the Max Factor health hazard zone to press his lips to hers.

Inside the cab, Jackie wound down the window. 'You be good, you two, and behave yourselves. I might try and phone tonight, but there's a reception for candidates some-when this evening and I may not be able. You've got my number, should anything crop up.' Anita stood on the pave-ment, quiet and solemn, one hand doing the stiff little sideways wave that royalty give till her mother was out of sight.

'Hop in, then.' Anita and Krystal, Jean's daughter, were standing by the Fiesta, dressed and ready for school. He had made Marmite and lettuce sandwiches for Anita's lunchbox, and put in a strawberry yoghurt with a plastic spoon, and an orange drink in a carton with a drinking straw, as per instructions. As per instructions, he'd checked out the contents of his step-daughter's satchel, and added a clean handkerchief when he found there wasn't one. After he'd settled the two girls in the back seat and done up their seat belts, he said, 'Just remembered something – sit tight, shan't be a minute' – and went back into the house. And phoned Sylvie.

Mid-morning, having stowed the vacuum cleaner in the cleaning cupboard under the stairs, he made himself a mug of instant and took it and his fags out into the sunshine of the back garden, and sat in a white plastic patio chair, special offer from the local filling station, and shut his ears to the accusatory stutter of a senior citizen's lawnmower, and daydreamed until he slept.

It was two o'clock. The kids didn't have to be fetched until three-thirty. But before that there was a bicycle chain to exchange, and a few bits and pieces of grocery shopping to do. He pocketed the twenty-pound note Jackie had put out for him on the worktop, and wrote himself a shopping list. Jogging down the front path, he threw Jackie's car keys in the air and caught them, and as he did so caught sight of Audrey from across the road hurrying to the bus, a toddler in one hand and a cigarette in the other. The longest legs out, he used to think in the days when he'd fancied her. The longest legs out in jeans, the smallest waist, the sexiest bum, the biggest tits.

Sylvie was standing behind the Photographic counter, sideways on, talking to a dark girl on Cosmetics and Fragrance. She was wearing uniform, well of course she would be – white blouse, with short sleeves, navy piping on the cuffs. (Her lower half presumably clad in the pencil skirt, kick pleat, he could see on the assistant with a wire basket wandering the Babyfood aisle.) In her ear-lobes, in place of the tiers of jagged foundry waste, or the shiny chrome hubcaps, that usually weighted them, were demure gold studs; and pinned to her blouse, just above the right breast, was a badge. As he approached the counter he could read BOOTS, the familiar logo-script, in a diagonal across the corner, and alongside it her name: Sylvia Martin. Sylvia, eh? Who's she when she's at home?

'Customer.' Debbie Durnford, Beauty Adviser, gave Sylvie a warning nudge. He was caught in the full green beam of Sylvie's headlights as she turned to face him.

'Can I help you?'

'Sir.' More aggressively than he meant.

'Pardon?'

'Shouldn't you say, "Can I help you, *sir*?" '

'No one's said.' She sounded put out. 'They told me courtesy and efficiency are the keys to customer satisfaction. Nothing about "sir". What would "sir" like then?'

If you're not careful, sir will tell you what sir would bloody well like.

Above her head hung a cardboard oval that had a night sky with a yellow crescent moon and two white stars on it, and the words 'Overnight film processing' underneath.

'I've got this film wants processing.'

She waited courteously with her hand held out while he went through the pretence of searching his pockets.

'Black and white film takes longer. Regrettably, we do not have the facilities on the premises to process black and white film overnight.' She was talking like a recorded message. 'So if your film – '

'Sylvie. For God's sake. Be nice.' He couldn't cope with this, any of it. The hard glass counter that separated them, the unblinking stares of a thousand Canon Sureshots on the display shelf, the cheerful boxes of Kodak Gold 200, the romantic night sky above her head. Her eyes. Her mouth. (She seldom wore make-up and was not wearing it today – unless on her mouth, which bore a faint smear of red, as though she'd been eating strawberries.)

'I am nice. Hey!' – turning to Debbie, who, ears pinned back no doubt, was replenishing a counter showcase with jars of Ultramoist cream make-up – 'I am nice, aren't I? Wouldn't you say I was nice?'

'Very nice.' Smirking and examining her nails.

He was aware of a queue forming behind him, of exasperated sighs and impatient feet. 'Well, I'll be off then.'

'Your film will be ready later, if you'd care to collect it.' A long, steady look. Then, dipping her headlights, engine note a whisper: ''Bout ten o'clock, okay?'

Outside the school he sat in blazing sunshine in a blazing car, and smoked two fags, and felt stupidly happy, and watched the world go by.

They were hardly away from the school gates before a small voice from the back seat said, 'I feel sick.'

Gordon Bennett! 'I expect it's the heat.' He tried to sound sympathetic. 'Put your head out of the window. Take some big big breaths.'

After a minute or two, the small voice said, 'I feel very sick.'

'She felt sick in geography. Mrs Bailey said her head felt

hot. She didn't eat her sandwiches dinner time neither.'
Krystal was evidently enjoying her role of know-all and
doom merchant.

'D'you want me to stop?' – in a bark, braking.

'Yes. No. Yes.'

He pulled in to the kerb; he leapt out of the car; he
pushed the driver's seat forward; he grabbed Anita. Too
late.

Anita lay on the settee, eyes shut, a damp face flannel on
her forehead, a plastic bowl at her elbow. Jean sat beside
her, stroking her hand. Krystal, still in her school clothes,
knelt on the floor and pressbuttoned the TV remote control,
channel-hopping without the sound on. He stood in the
doorway.

'Well, doc, what's the diagnosis?' – with a heart like lead.

'Not sure. She's very hot.' Jean bent her head over
Anita's. 'How are you feeling now, sweetheart?'

'Feel sick. My head hurts.'

'Could be a bug,' Jean said, 'could be something she's
ate. Is there a sickness bug doing the rounds at school,
d'you know, Krystal? Krystal!'

Krystal, momentarily engrossed in the *All-New Popeye
Show*, did not turn round. 'No. Dunno.'

'Bed's the best place for you, my love. Pop your arms
round m'neck, and up we'll go.'

He followed them upstairs with the bowl, scowling,
hating the whole world. And another thing – if it was
anybody's job to carry Anita, it was his.

As she and Krystal were leaving, standing outside on the
path, Jean said, 'Remember, just keep her quiet and see she
has plenty of water to drink. She's had two tablets now, so
providing she manages to keep them down, she could have
another two at' – she looked at her watch – 'half-eight. If
her head still hurts her. With any luck she'll be asleep in a
minute, poor mite.'

Did Jean reckon he ought to phone Jackie and tell her?

'Oh no, Stewart, I don't think that's necessary. No point in worrying Jack, is there? Between you and I, kiddies are always getting these upsets, running high temperatures. Anita'll probably be right as rain in the morning. She hasn't vomited since the car, has she?'

But what if Jackie phoned him? What if she phoned at Nita's bedtime and wanted a word? What then?

'You can tell her Anita was tired and went to bed early. That's hardly a fib, is it?'

He stood on the step and watched them go down the path, Krystal skipping ahead, Jean puffing behind. The back of Jean's turquoise silk-knit was all grooves and hummocks where a too-tight bra fastening, and too-tight bra straps, had dug in.

'You got to try and go to sleep, you know. You'll feel a whole load better if you do.' This was his third visit to the sickroom in half an hour, and he was running out of comforting things to say. At the front of his mind was the question: What do I do if I can't get her to sleep before Sylvie tips up?

'I can't. My head hurts.'

'I know, darlin'.' He picked up the tumbler by her bed. 'How's about another sip of champagne?'

'Yes.'

He sat on a chair and propped her head with one hand while he steered the tumbler with the other. A couple of drops of water made it into her mouth; a gallon ran down her chin and soaked the front of her nightie.

'Sorry, angel.'

Her head fell back on the pillow as soon as he released it. 'Stew, can't I have another Disprol? Pleeease' – in a groan.

He looked at his watch. Two and a half hours to go before Sylvie was due. How was he going to hang on that long? 'Not quite yet. Soon. How's the old tum-tum? You still feeling sick?'

'I don't know. My head hurts.'

He wanted to escape (and tidy the lounge, and get the drinks and the eats together, and think about Sylvie), but she wasn't ready to be left. His eye travelled from the Snoopy poster on the back of the door to Tiny Tears in a bassinet under the window, to the row of books, mostly paperbacks, on a shelf he'd put up last Christmas. There weren't many because Jackie didn't believe in clutter. (All books, and most toys, Jackie considered Nita was too old for found their way to the OXFAM shop, pronto.) 'Would you like me to read you a story?' Once upon a time he'd always read her a story at bedtime. He'd read to her or else he'd got her to read to him. One or t'other. They hadn't shared a reading session for weeks, he realised. Months.

'No. Thank you.'

Before he left the room he turned her pillow over, and planted a kiss on her scorching forehead, and told her he'd pop back soon – 'You better be asleep my girl when I do' – and pretended he couldn't hear the 'I want my mummy', muffled, to the wall.

'You should've told me about this when I phoned,' Sylvie said, 'I'd never have come over if I'd known. I could tell there was something up anyway, you sounded so strange.'

Sylvie had phoned him from a call-box ten minutes ago, 'just to check you haven't got surprise visitors'. When the phone rang, he'd leapt at it, certain it was Jackie. Hoping it was Jackie. (After his last plod up the stairs to Nita, he'd decided that if Jackie rang, he'd tell her. He wouldn't phone her, but if she phoned him, he'd tell her.)

'I wanted you to come.' He took Sylvie's hand across the kitchen table. 'I was lonely. I needed you.'

'It's not right. Not with the kid being so poorly. Being asleep's one thing, being – '

'She is asleep.' (She'd better be. She ought to be. At half past eight, her whole body a radiator, her headache still bad, he'd given her four Junior Disprol, dissolved in water.

He'd consulted the packet first. '6–12 years = 2–4 tablets every 4 hours.' So he'd given her four. Which an hour later hadn't done the trick. Which should have done the trick by now.) 'S'all right, Sylvie, I promise you. She's fast asleep. She's had four aspirin. She'll be okay in the morning.' He beamed at her. 'How's the little wage-earner then?'

'Okay. Not too dusty.' She tossed her head, pleased with herself. 'Stew, this is a gin and a half. You won the pools?' She dipped a finger in her glass and chased among the ice cubes for the slice of lemon he'd been careful to put in. She kept her eyes on him as she sucked it. 'What are you trying to do' – she lowered her eyelids slowly and raised them again – 'seduce me or something?'

'What say you we relocate to the lounge?' His heart was thumping so hard he was sure she could hear it. 'It's more comfortable on the settee.'

They were on the floor, having rolled there from the settee, when Anita started to scream.

'Why didn't you telephone earlier?'

It wasn't Doctor Taylor, it was one of his partners at the Health Centre, a Doctor Kettle (with a big nose and a poncy voice) he didn't know. The medic on duty.

'She slept for a bit, so I thought she was okay. Children are always getting these upsets, running high temperatures, aren't they?' – defending himself, parroting Jean.

'Am I right in thinking you're the child's step-father, not her father?'

'Yes.'

'Where's her mother?'

Where indeed? When Nita had started that terrible screaming, and gone on and on until he'd got his arms round her and held her, he'd known that he had to phone Jackie. Nita was a brave child, never one to make a fuss. German measles, mumps, chickenpox, scarlet fever, she'd weathered all these with scarcely a moan. A little angel, he'd described her to Jackie. And Jackie had said, 'You ought to take a leaf out of your angel's book, Stew. You make more fuss over a common cold than she does with the mumps. Men!' And here was his angel screaming. And then, when she'd stopped screaming, whimpering. Begging: 'Take the pain away, take the pain away.' And wanting no one but 'Mummy, Mummy, Mummy!' – 'I'll get her, I'll get your mummy.' So help me. But when he searched the pinboard in the kitchen, and the notepad by the phone, Jackie's number wasn't there. He'd thought back, he'd tried to remember what she'd said. He'd tried to remember the name of her hotel. And suddenly he'd had a picture of himself leaving the house that afternoon, tearing the top page (which had something written on it?) from the note-pad, scribbling a shopping list in a space (or on the back?): 'Bike chain. Oil can. Half bottle gin. Tonic. Lemon. Pea-nuts. Crisps.' He'd gone through his pockets, desperate. And as he'd done so had had another picture of himself, coming out of Safeway's with his carrier bag, crumpling the defunct shopping list, dropping it in one of those newly erected, black and gold litter bins the council had thought fit to waste his poll tax on . . . Next, he'd phoned Jean – and got her husband Vernon: 'Jean went round her dad's this evening, she's not back.' Clunk. Bloody hell! 'Calm down, Stew. It's the doctor you ought to be phoning, that's who' – Sylvie, pale and serious, her hair still damp from their exercise, zipping up her jacket in the hall.

'Her mother's at a hairdressers' conference in Birming-ham. I've been trying to get hold of her.'

Doctor Kettle didn't answer. He was busy with his stetho-scope, and then with his fingers, knocking them on Nita's chest and back. Knock knock knock, tap tap. He drew her nightdress down again over her stomach. He lowered her gently on to the pillow. He placed his hands either side of her neck, pressing. 'Does this hurt? Or this? Here? Or here?'

Everything hurt. Everything did, everywhere he pressed, hurt Nita.

'Now I want you, if you can, to lift your head off the

pillow. I'm not going to help you. There's a girl. Take your time.'

Nita couldn't do this. She tried. Tears rolled out of her eyes. 'Take the pain away! Mummy!'

Poor baby. Poor angel. Her looks all spoilt. Black circles under swollen lids; blotched, swollen face; hair dark and matted. Soaked . . .

'I think we should have her in hospital and do some tests. If I could use your telephone?' – rising to his feet. 'Perhaps you could put some night things and wash things into a bag? You've got a car, I take it?'

When Doctor Kettle came back he said, 'They're expecting her. Coulsdon Ward, second floor. Just let the porter know you're there, or tell the reception desk, and they'll send someone with a stretcher.' Before leaving the house, he said, 'Keep trying your wife, won't you? There'll be a payphone on the ward.' And then, as an afterthought, 'I take it you are fit to drive?'

Up on Coulsdon, Anita was put in a side ward. A single room, pink, shiny walls, green curtains. Dazzling overhead lights. 'Next of kin?' – 'Well . . . ' – 'Sign here, please.' He did so. It was after midnight, but in Nita's side ward it might have been midday. A nurse sped past him with a drip, and fixed it up – 'Just hold your hand still a minute, sweetheart. That's it. That's the way. What a pretty bracelet! Did your boyfriend buy you that? Let's have these lights down a bit, shall we?' – whipped the thermometer from Nita's armpit, looked at it, twice, shook it, stuck it in a plastic tumbler, sped out. Sped in again with an electric fan, plugged it in. 'We've got to get her temperature down, okay?' – to him.

And now a male face, and white-coated shoulders, round the door: 'Is this the lumbar puncture patient? Right, Staff, shan't be a minute. – Oh, are you the child's father? Could I have a word?'

Stewart went out into the corridor.

'Look, we're pretty certain that what we've got here is meningitis. What we don't know yet is what sort. In order to discover that we have to do a lumbar puncture and see what her white cells are up to. When we know more about that we'll know what treatment to give.'

'What – ?' He wasn't sure what question he was asking.

'Well, basically there are two sorts of meningitis – bacterial and viral. If it's viral, it'll largely be a question of bringing her temperature down – tepid sponging, fan, etcetera, and giving her something for the pain – and we'd expect to be beginning to feel better tomorrow. If it's bacterial – well, it's, shall we say, trickier, and we treat it with antibiotics.'

Ridgemont. It had suddenly come to him. The Ridgemont Hotel. 'D'you think I could phone my wife – Anita's mother?'

'Use the one in Sister's office. Third door on the left.'

When he came back from phoning Jackie (who had been asleep, who when she'd understood what he was telling her, had been fearfully awake), Nita was being wheeled out. 'Me and my friend here are just going to take a little ride to the Treatment Room,' the nurse said, hooking up the drip. 'Your daddy will be here waiting for you when we get back – won't you, Daddy?'

'Course I will.' He tried to smile. 'Mummy may be here by then too.' (From Birmingham? In the middle of the night?) 'Mummy's coming.' He touched Nita's burning hand.

'Mummy,' Nita moaned. 'Mummy. Take the pain away. Mummy.'

The nurse called over her shoulder, 'We can probably fix you up some sort of bed in the day room if you like. See if there's a nurse on the desk . . . '

An hour later, pacing the corridor outside the Treatment Room, bowels water, checking his watch every two minutes, he made a bargain with the God he didn't believe in. 'If Nita gets through this, if she's okay, I'll give Sylvie up. I'll never see her again. I'll' – a sudden picture of the broken bicycle in the garage wounded like a punch in the gut – 'I'll be a good husband and father. I'll get a job.' And tried to blot out the memory of Sylvie's look, holding his look, across the kitchen table. And tried not to listen to the voice from somewhere that told him if Nita was okay, if she did get better, he could always adjust the bargain.